NO  OF
SEA ARY

BRIDE of the SEA

Copyright © 2021 Eman Quotah

All rights reserved. No part of this book may be used or reproduced in any manner whatsoever without written permission from the publisher except in the case of brief quotations embodied in critical articles or reviews. For information, contact: Tin House, 2617 NW Thurman St., Portland, OR 97210.

Published by Tin House, Portland, Oregon

Distributed by W. W. Norton and Company

Library of Congress Cataloging-in-Publication Data

Names: Quotah, Eman, author.
Title: Bride of the sea : a novel / Eman Quotah.
Description: Portland, Oregon : Tin House, [2021]
Identifiers: LCCN 2020034682 | ISBN 9781951142452 (paperback) | ISBN 9781951142469 (ebook)
Classification: LCC PS3617.U68 B75 2021 | DDC 813/.6--dc23
LC record available at https://lccn.loc.gov/2020034682

First US Edition 2021
Printed in the USA
Interior design by Diane Chonette
www.tinhouse.com

BRIDE
OF
THE SEA

A NOVEL

EMAN QUOTAH

 TIN HOUSE / Portland, Oregon

To Mom and Baba

And to Andrew

"We do tell you the best of stories . . . When Joseph said to his father, 'O father, I have dreamt eleven stars and the sun and the moon; I saw them prostrating to me' / [His father] said, 'O my son, do not tell the story of your dream to your brothers . . .'"

—The Qur'an, SURAT YUSUF (JOSEPH)

BASMALAH

2018

Hannah dreams the family buries her mother, a woman they haven't seen in more than forty years. Hannah herself hasn't seen her mom in twenty years. The family buries Sadie in view of the Red Sea, a few miles from Jidda, where she was born. The water is a perfect, unending slab of turquoise.

Hannah focuses on the horizon. The Arabian Peninsula and everything on it disappear—the land behind her, beneath her, beside her. Hannah stands on firm ground. Ahead of her: miles and miles and miles of sea.

Before the burial and the sea, Hannah is in a small room with low cushions. Her mother's body lies in the middle of the floor on a sheet spread over a silk rug. Women in mourning white hunch over the body, the sleeves of their long dresses rolled to the elbows. Though she can't see their faces, Hannah knows—the way you sometimes know in dreams—who is touching her mother's lifeless

skin. Hannah's grandmother, Aunties Randah and Riham, a handful of female cousins.

They wash the hands and face three times, the arms, the feet,
as though preparing the body for prayer. As though the dead could
pray. They slide the washcloth down the body's right side and its
left side, press the stomach with their flat palms to force a bowel
movement. After they wash the body, they expertly swaddle it in
white cotton, as though readying a baby for sleep. All that shows is
a pale face, cheeks like crumpled sheets of unbleached paper.

The women burn sandalwood incense. In real life, someone
would be howling with grief, calling her mother's given name:
"Saeedah!" They would call Hannah's name, too, her other name:
"Oh, Hanadi! God have mercy on your mother! God forgive her
and protect her!"

In this dream: watery silence, as though they are at the bottom
of the sea. Her mother looks harmless. Quiet and still. An object.

The sea becomes a great, brown, expansive lake. A sea again. A lake.
Hannah turns from the water. Men in white thawbs, brown mishlahs, and white headdresses carry the body, the bundle that is her
mother, down a beach that shines like a coin.

The body is veiled, disguised. It could be anyone. Maybe it is not
her mother. Maybe bodies have been switched.

Soon the men, these uncles and cousins, both close and distant, are digging and digging, their thawbs hiked up around their
waists and tucked into their boxer briefs, their mishlahs and headdresses thrown into a big pile on the sand. Behind the men are
waves, and there is sound: a *whoosh* and *crash* and someone cussing, and though Hannah doesn't understand the Arabic words,

she recognizes the tone of frustration, like someone stubbing a toe or jolting an elbow.

Meanwhile, the men dig and dig and the sand won't stop filling in, and the cussing continues, and the waves crash.

One of the men realizes they forgot to say God's name before they started. That part Hannah understands—a miracle of dream-translation.

The men put down their shovels. Together, their voices singsong and thrumming, they say,

Bismillah-ir-rahman-ir-raheem.

In the name of God, the Merciful, the Compassionate.

OUT OF THE LAKE

1970

BUQJAH

In weekly letters to his family in Jidda, Muneer will not write about coming back to the Cleveland Heights rental house after his journalism class and driving up the dark, half-shoveled driveway, his headlights illuminating Saeedah in a bank of snow up to her knees. She wears jeans and a turtleneck stretched tight across her belly, which is as round and hard as if she'd tucked a football under her top. No coat. Her lips are darkened with cold, her hair bright and glistening with flakes. She holds a metal shovel above her head, as though she wants to thwack someone.

He won't write that he's surprised she's home. She never tells him how she spends her time or who she's with, or asks him to drop her off or says she needs the car, or answers with more than "class" or "study group" or "the library" when he asks where she's going with the classmates who come to pick her up.

She is nineteen. He is twenty-three. They have been married for a year and a half and their first child will be born soon. And the word *divorce* is whispering in his ear, a secret no one else knows.

Muneer does not want to hear it. "God forgive me," he says, yanking up the parking brake and leaping out of the car without cutting the engine. "For God's sake, what are you doing?" he yells, his voice harsh against the night's snowy hush. He grabs Saeedah's arm, and she wrenches it back.

"Come inside," he whispers. "It's too cold."

"I'm sweating." She leans on the shovel. "Leave me alone."

"Let me finish the shoveling," he says. "It's better for the baby."

"I can do it."

Icicles hang like legs of lamb from the eaves of their rental house, and six-foot-high, coal-black snow piles obscure the sidewalks. Standing outside this short time he finds himself shivering despite his long johns, wool socks, fur-lined boots, a turtleneck under a sweatshirt under a down coat. His toes feel like marbles. His breath leaves his body like a storm cloud.

He leaves her shoveling. His fingers stick to the ice-cold doorknob as he opens the unlocked front door. She says it's the heat of shoveling that made her shed her outerwear, but every day she forgets her hat and gloves, her scarf. This is not the first time she's ventured into the northeast Ohio winter with no coat.

"Jinn take her," he mumbles as he shoves his way inside and slams the door.

The foyer's warmth soothes him, until he sees her gloves like shriveled leaves on the floor. Her scarf winds its serpentine way to the door, as though she took the time to spell her first initial with it as she left. Her stiff knit hat is propped beside the gloves.

He drapes her coat over his arm, turns the porch light on, and again steps outside. Bundled in snow and night, the world looks smaller and snugger than usual.

Saeedah has moved to the driveway—but when he gets nearer, he fears her shovel, the way it slices through the snow, the way she seems to be keeping him at a distance with the purposefulness of her shoveling. With a deep sense of futility, he holds the coat open while she digs the driveway clean, the sound of her scraping ice echoing along the dark street. Someone else is shoveling somewhere, too. When she gets to the car, she opens the door, reaches in to turn it off, and removes his keys. He comes down the steps. She gives him the keys. He keeps the coat. She goes back to shoveling.

Back in the house, he folds and stacks Saeedah's things and sits in the lawn chair she has placed by the door to take off his boots. He tells himself he has stopped being angry that Saeedah won't take care of herself, or let him take care of her. She'll do what she does, no matter the consequence. His mother told him so, before he and Saeedah were engaged.

He doesn't know what to do.

He tugs his first boot so hard he nearly falls off the chair.

Jinn take her.

He heats leftover lentil soup over the stove, ladles it into a bowl, squeezes a little lime into it, leaves it on the table for Saeedah, and goes to bed without eating. He's not hungry.

Every day lately, including these seconds before sleep, is as tension-filled as a final exam. Tonight, as usual, he's wide awake for an hour, listening for her, hearing nothing, not even the door slamming shut—*did she ever come in?*

Her body jostles him awake at two in the morning. They lie under the electric blanket, back to back, an inch of hot, staticky air between them like an unbridgeable river.

He says in English, "You have to bundle up before you go outside." Bundle. Is there an equivalent verb in Arabic? There is a noun: *buqjah.*

She fidgets against him, her feet still ice cold. He shifts his legs up toward his chest and tries again, in Arabic: "We're not in Jidda."

"You've said that before. We're not in Jidda. I say, I'm not a child." Her voice is as icy as her feet. "Maybe you think I should go home to my mother. Maybe I will."

She's threatened to go home before. He knows better than to believe her. He knows how she feels about her mother.

He yearns to feel what they share, to reach around her and touch her belly. The child growing. Something stops him, a lack of courage, as though he were eight years old and staring at a villa's wall. Wanting to climb it, knowing he can get up but not get down. He was that kind of child, one who stopped himself from doing things, who would rather observe. She was the kind of girl who scrambled up and didn't think twice. No risk seemed to scare her; nothing changed her mind.

Who will the baby take after? He prays for an answer. He prays to strike the hidden word *divorce* from his head.

GECKOS AND JAM JARS

First cousins by their mothers, Muneer and Saeedah grew up together. When he was six or seven and she was a toddler with springy hair, gazelle's eyes, and teeny fingernails like colorless pomegranate seeds, she went missing in her family's three-story villa, in the middle of an evening gathering. Aunt Faizah, Saeedah's mother, had invited her six sisters and their families for dinner. Before the meal, the children played in the courtyard. When they were called inside, someone noticed that Saeedah had gone missing. For half an hour, they scoured the house. The aroma of roasted lamb followed them everywhere, and Muneer became so overcome with hunger he could barely remember why they were tromping up and down the stairs. Unable to find the girl, the aunties herded the children back outside. The women stood in the walled courtyard and whistled, as though they could call a little girl like a falcon.

Muneer's mother narrowed her eyes till they were the tiniest bit ajar, like the eyes of the sleepy alley cats they'd passed on their walk to Aunt Faizah's villa. "Clearly, the girl's not out here."

"She's not inside," Aunt Faizah said. She held her little twins, one in the crook of each arm, like two melons. Her features were stretched with worry, her gaze tethered to the gate.

"How does a little girl get out the gate? And if she did, she'd never go very far," Muneer's mother said.

"Maybe her father left it open. He's always doing things like that."

"Say a prayer for the Prophet and go back inside. She's not outside."

"How do you know?"

Muneer sidled to the stairs and started to climb, dragging his arm along the wooden balustrade. No one followed him or seemed to notice. Upstairs, a series of narrow green hallways led past spacious, dark rooms with ceiling fans whirring. He stepped into the rooms one after the other and let the cool air ruffle his hair, until he found himself in a rose-colored room on the top floor. A gecko the size of his pinky basked in a single line of sunlight that slashed the wall. The lizard's stringy tail flicked nervously; its pinpoint eyes were dreamy. Over the fan's humming he faintly heard a girlish voice singing: "*Wazaghah, wazaghah, wazaghah.*"

There she was, in a built-in cupboard with a dark green slatted door, her fingertips poking through. He couldn't possibly have seen her face through the wood and the shadows, but in his memory, he glimpses her gap-toothed smile, and he knows that she is calling, "Gecko, gecko, gecko."

He thinks of that day in the morning when he finds Saeedah already in the kitchen eating saltines. She's left the cupboard door wide open and the soup bowl empty in the sink. He can't tell for sure if she ate the soup or dumped it, but hopefulness tugs at him.

"Let's go to the beach," he says.

The suggestion is surprising to him, and last-ditch, he admits. But why not? They spent the best day of last summer at the beach, after they learned she was pregnant. She had been sullen for weeks, ever since they'd decided they couldn't afford to go home for the summer. Her father would have paid for it, but Muneer wouldn't accept his offer. One day, he would work at his father-in-law's newspaper, and he wanted it not to be a matter of wastah—connections—but rather of professional integrity.

But the news of the baby had made her smile, and the mood lasted for days. He was giddy, too. They hadn't told their families in Saudi or their friends here, and they held hands in the car as he drove through the low-rise suburbs toward Lake Erie, down the greenway, alongside the salt factory, the giant mural of the Morton salt girl in her rain boots. Saeedah loved the beach, though the water was fresh and brown and smelled like algae, not salty and blue and fishy like the sea they grew up with. They tugged off their sneakers and socks, rolled their jeans up to their knees, walked to the lighthouse and climbed on the rocks. They gazed across the vastness of Lake Erie, no shore in sight, as though they were gazing into the future. The wind whispered around them, lifting Saeedah's nearly waist-length hair like black wings.

Muneer and Saeedah had never seen a lake before. They didn't know that most lakes don't stretch to the horizon like the sea. The sky was as blue as the Red Sea, and they fell on their backs looking up at it, letting the sun warm their faces. Ahead of them lay the baby's birth, Muneer's graduation in the spring, his yearlong internship in the States before going back to be a reporter for her father.

The waves lapping against the shore sounded like a prayer whispered over and over. The sand felt like a net, holding them. He would like to go back to the beach and recapture the feeling. But Saeedah waves her arm at the window, the porridge-gray sky, and the wiry trees. She smiles a wide, taut smile and rolls her eyes.

"Wouldn't you say it's too cold for the beach?"

Last winter—her first—wasn't like this. She wore her hat and gloves and wound the itchy blue scarf around her neck, and together they complained about the weather. They'd watched the year's first snowfall, the flakes like thousands of tiny miracles. They'd held out their hands and the snow landing on their skin felt like nothing. "Mashallah," they'd said together, standing in the driveway. Their tongues stuck out involuntarily to catch the little bits of moisture, and their words came out garbled: "Mathallah, mathallah."

Neither of them knew how to cook, so they'd spent a month's rent on phone calls to their mothers. To measure the rice, they'd need a jam jar, his mother had said. He and Saeedah hadn't hesitated, emptying a whole jar of raspberry jam into the garbage disposal. Saeedah bent her ear to the phone, pulling the cord across the living room so she could relay their mothers' recipes to Muneer in their kitchen, which was not much bigger than a bathroom. The Bukhari rice came out too moist, stewed with cinnamon sticks and cardamom pods that lay bloated and spent alongside the chunks of lamb. Later, they tried chicken and rice poached in milk. Saleeg was meant to be soggy, Muneer joked, so of course they mastered it easily.

Back home, each of these rice dishes was served on large round aluminum platters to dozens of guests. In Ohio, Muneer and Saeedah ate their Bukhari rice and saleeg straight from the pot. They discussed inviting friends over to share the food they cooked, but there wasn't room, and truthfully, he didn't want to share her.

Her laughter, like the wind chimes tinkling on their neighbor's porch. The sound of her voice reciting ingredients to him. The way her lip and eyebrow jutted up to the right as she concentrated on chopping onions and cilantro for hot sauce.

What he and Saeedah need, he decides, moving quickly from the beach idea, is people around them. People to eat their food. Muneer invites his best friend Jameel to come over Saturday evening after their shift at the pizza parlor, where they both earn a little extra to send home to their families while they live on student stipends from the Saudi government. He and Saeedah have Muneer's small stipend. They have to stretch it further than a single guy like Jameel.

Jameel is studying to be a dentist. He drinks beer, smokes menthol Lucky Strikes, and dates American girls. His teeth are whitened and as startlingly bright as his patent leather loafers, while Muneer's teeth are stained yellow from too much fluoride in the drinking water growing up in Jidda. The two of them went to the same public high school, and their fathers had neighboring dress shops in the Old City. Jameel's father had the greater business acumen, opening stores in new parts of the city with the help of his other sons.

On Saturday morning, Muneer drives to Aladdin's on Carnegie to stock up on ingredients for the feast. Saeedah has already left for a study group or the library—as usual, he doesn't know where she's gone.

He returns with rice, lamb, cilantro, pita, plastic packets of cinnamon and cloves, dried orange and fresh oranges, carrots, tomatoes, and two hot peppers the size and shape of his thumbs. Saeedah sits in the wicker rocking chair reading an Arabic translation of *Gone with the Wind*. He notices signs that prove his point about bundling up: Her hands have cracked and bled along the knuckles. Her lips are so chapped they look perpetually rouged. Her hair flickers with electricity. He wants to offer her petroleum jelly and ChapStick.

Instead he says, "Didn't I tell you Jameel is coming?"

She turns a page. "Welcome to him."

"Do you want to help?"

"Welcome to you."

It bothers him that she won't say a straightforward "No." Alone in the kitchen, he preps the lamb and rice. He grates orange peel into the pot, and the scent adheres to his hands. He goes into the living room to ask Saeedah a question, but she's disappeared. The empty chair rocks.

He calls into the bedroom, "How much hot pepper in the salad?" His words drown in her silence. Is she in the house?

The doorbell rings, and Jameel arrives with Diane, a woman he's been dating since last year. She's an elementary school teacher with long, straight, hennaed hair and a silver cross at her neck the length and width of a pinky nail. Once, when Muneer picked Jameel up at her place, her German shepherd, Jack, scared the shit out of him. This is the story Jameel chooses to tell when Saeedah comes out of the bedroom.

She greets them in Arabic, kisses them on both cheeks, and lets Diane touch her belly and *ooh* and *ahh* over her. Everything seems so normal. Muneer can't believe he thought things were strange between him and Saeedah.

"And Jack licked him on the eye and he had to wash his face seven times!" Jameel says.

"I don't understand why," Diane says. "They were kisses."

"Dogs are dirty," Saeedah says.

Muneer agrees, yet the way she says it, and the way Diane freezes with her mouth open, as though she is about to disagree loudly, make him jump in quickly.

"He's a nice dog. I was taken off guard." He wipes his face, as though the dog has licked him again. "Let's eat, OK?"

Diane asks if she can help set the table.

"Shouldn't we sit Saudi-style?" Jameel says.

Muneer doesn't care, but Jameel seems to want to turn this into some sort of cultural display. They spread a plastic cloth on the floor and eat with their knees bent beneath them. Diane sits cross-legged.

Saeedah takes a mouthful of rice. "You shouldn't cross your legs," she says. "It's not etiquette."

Diane's eyes, light-colored like marbles, roll up. She tries to cut a piece of lamb with a spoon. "Let's sit at the table. Wouldn't you be more comfortable that way?"

"Can I get you a knife?" Muneer says, feeling sorry for her.

"No, I'm fine."

Jameel rummages in the kitchen and comes back with a butter knife.

"That's no help," Diane says.

Jameel hacks at the meat on Diane's plate, gives up, tears it with his fingers, and offers it to her. Meanwhile, Saeedah puts on her sneakers. With the door open, she stands outside and lets the below-zero air blow in.

"It's pretty cold out there," Diane calls to Saeedah. "Don't you want a coat?"

Muneer's growing annoyance with everyone in the room is like water on its way to boiling, minuscule bubbles in his chest popping, then larger ones, bursting pockets of anger. On the soap opera he watches most weekdays to improve his English, there is a psychologist whose three children are addicts, and it has dawned on him that he, Muneer, is a journalism student unable to uncover the truth of whatever is wrong with his wife and his life. Last week, he took the small reporter's notebook out of his knapsack and stood at the bathroom mirror, interviewing himself.

"When did your wife begin behaving this way? How did she react when you didn't have enough money to go home over the summer? Is there anything you could do to make things better?"

"I don't know," he told the mirror. "No comment."

In his socked feet and sweatshirt, he joins his wife on the front porch, hugging himself for warmth while flakes of snow turn her hair white as an old lady's. His teeth clack; it's that cold. He has never felt so out of place.

"What's going on?" he says.

She turns to him, looking lost. Like she doesn't know what to tell him.

She steps off the porch. Muneer watches her leave a trail of footprints leading to the car. She revs the engine. He returns to his friends and his nearly finished meal.

"That was strange," Jameel says.

"The rice is delicious," Diane says to Muneer. "Is there orange peel in here?"

Jameel scoops spicy duqus onto his rice.

"No problem," Muneer says. "She'll be back soon."

AIRMAIL

There is a gap in Muneer's memory of Saeedah five or six or seven years wide. She was a dirt-faced, plait-haired little girl in the courtyard one minute, and the next, mashallah, a beautiful woman glimpsed from behind a screen.

At a late-night family gathering at Aunt Faizah's house, he'd left the men's salon to go to the bathroom and glimpsed her. The latticework screen between them turned her face into a beautiful jigsaw puzzle, challenging him to piece it together. She had little gold earrings like berries and her palms and fingernails were henna stained, rust red. When she moved her hands, it was like a flash of plumage from behind a bush. He thought of her as a bird, never still except in the pause before it flew from a branch.

Someone saw him, and the girls and women squawked and covered their heads and faces.

"God forgive you, go back to the salon," Aunt Faizah said.

Before they whisked her off, Saeedah smirked at him, like she was having the last wordless word. She mouthed something: *Cigarette?* He didn't smoke, but he slipped outside into the courtyard and waited. The dark sky was swirled with clouds, like foam on Turkish coffee. Servants had set out lengths of plastic cloth, little bowls of cucumbers and tomatoes, chopped cilantro with lime. Soon they would bring out the trays of lamb and rice, spiced with cardamom and cloves. He could already smell the food.

"What are you daydreaming about?" she said.

"God, you're like a jinni, appearing out of nowhere."

She wore a black dress with the neckline cut straight across from shoulder to shoulder and the hem at her knee, and a black leather headband. He had never noticed the mole exactly in the middle of her cheekbone before.

"You got cigarettes?"

He covered his mouth with his fingers and nodded toward the gateman and the cook, an Egyptian husband and wife, who were descending the steps burdened by an enormous tray of rice and lamb. It wouldn't be proper for them to catch him and Saeedah flirting. She curtsied like a queen in a movie and disappeared into the house, leaving him to wish they'd had more time. The rest of the night was other men talking at him.

Muneer and Saeedah's worlds were separated, but her face lived in his mind. He thought of her often in the weeks to come.

At first, he didn't think of marrying her. His plans were nearly set: he had applied for a government scholarship to go to the States to study. His brother Bandar had gone to Germany and Belgium and Canada, staying long enough in each place to decide he wanted to study somewhere else. He'd come back from Toronto a few months before with a big, bushy head of hair that their father threatened to cut whenever he saw it. Midsentence while serving a customer he'd say, "Can you believe that's my son? I'm going to cut his hair in the middle of the night." Bandar scowled. Muneer marveled at his brother's disrespect.

From Canada, Bandar had smuggled a dozen little bottles of alcohol, hiding them in a pair of tube socks stuffed in his shoes. Muneer half admired his brother's gumption and half considered him an enormous fool. If the customs agents had caught Bandar, they would have thrown him in jail. To drink the gulp-size quantities of rum and schnapps, Bandar, Muneer, Jameel, and two of Bandar's buddies had driven to the desert outside the city after the last prayer of the day. They veered off-road and drove for five minutes into the desert, keeping the glare of the streetlights in their rearview so they wouldn't lose their way. The sky was so stacked with stars Muneer felt sure he could count the seven heavens. They spread a blanket on the ground in the beam of the headlights, kicked their shoes off, and swigged two bottles each. It was enough to coat his tongue and warm his cheeks, not enough to get drunk on. Bandar claimed the last two bottles, and at the end of the evening seemed the tipsiest. He'd brought a shisha to mask the smell of alcohol. They smoked for nearly an hour and took turns breathing in one another's faces to test how well the ruse was working. The smoke tickled their faces. By the end of the night laughter gurgled in their bellies like the water bubbling in the shisha.

It was the only time Muneer ever drank alcohol, the only time he was ever tempted.

A few nights later, Muneer and Bandar were hanging out with Jameel at their father's dress shop downtown in the Balad. Bandar talked about America as though he'd been there before, as though he were an expert on New York and Chicago and Los Angeles.

"Come with me," he said.

Muneer looked up from the newsmagazine he was reading. Bandar swiped it and hid it behind his back when Muneer reached for it.

"We'll study together," Bandar said. His eyebrows lifted on the word *study*, as if to say, "We will do nothing of the sort."

Muneer grabbed the newspaper his father had left on a stool by the door. He shared his father's obsession with other countries' politics and war, but in the two years since he'd graduated high school, working in his father's shop, he'd started to yearn for more than talking about the news. He didn't want to read the newspapers or listen to BBC Arabic anymore. He wanted to hold a microphone to Gamal Abdel Nasser's face. He wanted to be banging on a typewriter.

"America," said Jameel. He ate watermelon seeds out of a small metal bowl. In front of the shop, their dads sat on overturned buckets passing the nozzle of a shisha back and forth.

"You can both come," Bandar said.

They applied. Muneer waited for news of his university applications and went to the shop daily. He thought about Saeedah, writing her name over and over in his mind. Envisioning the smudged kohl under her eyes. He started to regret applying to American universities. What if God meant something else for him? It so happened that Saeedah's father had run a newspaper called *al-Sharqiyah* for more than a decade. Muneer could work for him, couldn't he?

The more he thought about it, the less he wanted to go. One evening while he was drinking tea with his parents, Saeedah's name fell out of his mouth.

"My sister's daughter?" his mother said.

Muneer's father looked up from behind the pink screen of his newspaper.

"It's not a good idea to marry a relative so close."

The sentiment was something of a newfangled idea, and Muneer watched for his mother's reaction. She measured out seven spoons of sugar for Muneer's father and poured Lipton tea into the small jars they used as their everyday tea glasses. The fat crystals danced in Baba's glass as she stirred.

She handed the tea to Muneer's father. "Why shouldn't he marry my sister's daughter?" she said. She was a woman who would never raise her voice at her husband, but would not always agree with him.

"Go to America," Muneer's father said. "When you come back, think about marriage. Why drag a wife along?"

"You trust young men over there by themselves?" Muneer's mother asked, and when it became clear from her husband's face that trust had nothing to do with anything, she turned to her son and said, "It will be lonely there. You don't believe me, but it will be."

Soon the letters came from America, battered and stained from crossing the ocean. Muneer and Jameel had gotten into programs in Cleveland. Bandar's envelopes contained single pages telling him he had not been accepted.

"I won't go without my brother," Muneer said.

"By God you'll go," his father said. "If you don't, people will think neither of you was smart enough to go to America."

In the end, Bandar went to Dhahran to study petroleum engineering. Muneer and Jameel found an apartment in Cleveland through the uncle of a friend of a friend. They arrived in August. The muggy weather, though ten degrees Celsius cooler than at home, nonetheless felt familiar and welcoming. But soon chill crept into the air, the green of the grass and trees vanished like a mirage, and the sky was the dull gray of his mother's old pots and pans. Everything felt strange. Not necessarily bad, but strange. The cold that burrowed into him, the houses with their aluminum siding and sloped roofs, the lawns, the deciduous trees reaching up to the sky with bare-naked limbs.

He wrote his father letters, and the responses arrived weekly on tissue-thin airmail paper that crackled between his fingers.

I thank God you are learning everything you can, his father wrote. *If I were a young man, I would want to be in your place.*

In December, no letters arrived. Muneer didn't dwell on the absence. With exams pressing on his brain, he hadn't had time to write his father, and so his father had had nothing to respond to. On December 24, Muneer flew home for winter break, his suitcases full of Fruit of the Loom T-shirts for his brothers and Chanel No. 5 for his mother and sisters. When he landed at the Jidda airport and climbed down the jet's rickety stairs to the desert scrub of the landing pad, Bandar was waiting for him, the ends of his red-and-white shimagh folded over his head casually, as though everything were the same. When they hugged and kissed on both cheeks, the cloth of Bandar's headdress grazed Muneer's skin.

"Why are you home?" Muneer said. Bandar's midyear break fell in January, and Muneer hadn't expected to see him for more than a few days.

"Baba passed away," Bandar said in Muneer's ear. "God have mercy on him."

The words made no sense. Bandar's hot breath tickled and smelled of frankincense gum. Muneer couldn't suppress a giggle. His brother pinched him, hard, on the forearm. It hurt like hell.

"He had a stroke," Bandar said. "Two weeks ago."

"Don't lie."

But it was true. Muneer's father was dead and the past two weeks of Muneer's life had been the lie. The meals Muneer had eaten, the TV shows he'd watched, the thoughts he'd had—wrong, wrong, wrong. Every small happiness he'd experienced—a free pizza his boss had given him, an A he'd gotten on a quiz—was a deception. He'd been wrong to look forward to going home and seeing his father, kissing his father's round cheeks; watching his bent, turbaned head as he cleaned his fingernails, one by one, with the cap of a ballpoint pen; listening to him talk about the young Arab generals and the new unity and how their country should be part of that, not leave it to Egypt and Iraq.

Instead, Muneer should have been rubbing his fists into his eyes to stop crying. He should have been helping wash his father, wrap him, and bury him. He should have been looking at his father's face one last time.

At night, lying on a thin mattress next to his brother with the book-hard pillows he wasn't used to anymore, Muneer wanted to put his hand into his chest and pull his whole heart out. He tried. He placed his fingers against his sternum and pressed harder and harder until it hurt and his fingers seized up and he had to go outside to stretch them out and moan with pain and grief because he might wake up his brother if he stayed inside.

Oh, but that was a lie, to let the family think he wasn't angry that they had not told him and sent for him immediately.

Muneer's mother wore mourning white and never left the house, as was the custom for four months and ten days after a husband's death. She kept her hair covered, though only her children and sisters surrounded her. Until his last week at home, Muneer never saw her alone. One evening he found her sitting in the formal salon, pouring tea.

"Sit with me," she said.

"I'm not going back to America."

She mixed his tea with sugar, the way she would have mixed his father's tea. Muneer winced at the sweetness of it.

"God keep you for me and protect you," she said.

The next day she told his brothers he had decided to stay in Jidda.

They had come to their father's formal sitting room, where they sat on low cushions around the perimeter, to decide how they could best care for their mother. There were also two sisters to marry off. It would not be hard to find families willing to marry them. And there was Lujayn, the littlest, to take care of.

"You have to go back to America," they told Muneer. "For Baba and for Mama. She needs us to support her, so you need a good degree from over there."

"And let you lie to me again when someone else dies?"

"God forbid," said Salem, the oldest.

"God knows what will happen, and we'll do what's best, with His guidance," said Sameer.

Bandar came up with the idea that Muneer take a semester off and help out in his father's store. If he had not stayed those extra months, he might not have married Saeedah.

'UQBALAK

The engagement happened more because of God's will—and Muneer's mother's—than his own. On a warm May night, a few months before he was to return to the States, he took his mother to Saeedah's sister's wedding. In Aunt Faizah's courtyard, strands of lights were strung from the top of a pole to the edges of the wall. His mother went inside, complaining about the climb she would have to make to the roof where the women were sitting. In the courtyard, servants had unrolled threadbare woolen rugs from edge to edge and laid out cushions. Some of the men, the early arrivals, sat with their thawbs stretched like trays across their laps and the tops of their socks revealed. Shisha smoke hovered above their heads. Aunt Faizah's husband, Fareed, jumped up when he saw Muneer. Of Uncle Fareed's children, Saeedah looked most like him. Muneer could not look at this man without thinking of the daughter. The way their eyebrows were set high above their eyes, so they looked skeptical or like they were laughing at a joke no one else understood. The dark purple of their lips. The square set of their shoulders, like a doorframe or a gate. Like they stood between him and something mysterious. Were they protecting him from forces that threatened him? Or keeping him from something he wanted? He couldn't be sure, and at the time, the uncertainty intrigued him.

Uncle Fareed kissed Muneer on both cheeks.

"'Uqbalak," he said.

May you be next. Muneer never quite knew how to respond. The sentiment was especially awkward coming from Saeedah's father.

"God willing, Uncle." He hoped he didn't sound eager. Then, an invisible thread drew Muneer's chin upward, as though a fisherman had hooked him. Saeedah's face popped out over the ledge of a second-floor window, and her hennaed hand waved. Perhaps someone was calling her, because she disappeared, thank God, as Uncle Fareed looked up to see what had caught Muneer's attention.

Uncle Fareed seemed to guess it had been *someone.* "Young man, keep your gaze down, like the Prophet says." He chucked Muneer under the chin, as though he were greeting a little boy, and noticed the folded-up newspaper Muneer carried under one arm.

"Is that my paper?" He grabbed it and pretended to read the headline. Uncle Fareed had studied in Cairo and apprenticed at its famous newspapers.

It was not his paper and Muneer felt a bit embarrassed by that.

Uncle Fareed tapped Muneer's arm with the rolled-up newspaper and handed it back. "How are your studies?"

Muneer kept his eyes on his hands to avoid seeking a glimpse of Saeedah. He imagined himself inside the house, following her from duty to duty as she wrapped ribbons around the candles for the zaffah, curled her sisters' hair, and brushed her face with powder.

"I should have gone to Egypt. English is too much for me."

"You're blessed to learn anything you can. You should have written for me while you were here—why didn't I think of it?"

Muneer knew his mother never would have let him go off and write stories while there was so much to do after his father's death.

"In the future, God willing," he said, and left it at that.

There were no other young men in the courtyard—it was a bunch of uncles gossiping. Muneer wandered back to the gate and read the paper.

When the door to the villa swung open to reveal Saeedah, bare-headed and smiling, he knew he would have been disappointed if she hadn't come down. She was framed in the entryway in a calf-length, pleated opal-white dress that was cinched at the waist like an Egyptian film star's dress. Her face was round as a moon, the kind of face poets loved, well-fed with honey-colored eyes. Her hair was flipped from her shoulders to her ears, teased up in the back. Her lips shone with rouge. Almost as tall as he was, she stared straight into his face.

He pulled the ends of his shimagh under his chin and turned his eyes down. He was being disingenuous, and she knew it. "Go round the back," she said.

As though she had nothing to fear.

If her father found out, Muneer's chances of an apprenticeship might evaporate. But he couldn't say no. He left the gate intending to go home and leave her disappointed. But his feet were connected to his heart more directly than his head, and they did as she said. He leaned against the villa's back wall and had nearly reached the paper's back cover when she appeared.

He never learned how she slipped from the villa, around the back of the yard, and out the back gate. But there she was, swooshing her skirts with her hands, seeming pleased that his eyes stayed on her. He folded the paper three times again and tried to stuff it in his pocket, but it was too big, so he tossed it into the street—what other option did he have?—the whole time studying her.

"Anyone famous die today?"

"That's not why a person reads the paper. It's not a film magazine."

She swished the hem of her dress dramatically. "Do you want to kiss me, like in an Egyptian film?"

"Wow," he said, the American word feeling like carbonation in his mouth. "You've never seen an Egyptian film."

A laugh gurgled in her throat and her fingers fluttered mothlike to his cheek. "Yes, I have. Last summer, in Cairo. And once at the American compound here."

He shrank from her, eyes on his sandals, blood pumping.

She kissed his cheek, her lips cool despite the heat around them. His torso twisted and his knees buckled. When she moved away, he straightened and touched his cheek despite himself.

She punched his arm, an almost sisterly gesture, as though she were trying to erase what had happened. Or maybe not. Maybe she was underlining the kiss, claiming him a second way.

"Want to go for a ride?" he said. He leaned against the wall to appear steady.

She walked to the car, which he'd parked at the curb, opened the passenger door for herself, and hopped in.

They drove north, sea to the left of them. He leaned on the open window. Between them, the bench seat was as wide as the Red Sea.

"Where shall we go?" he asked.

"Drive." She unrolled her tinted window.

"Someone might see you." He motioned as though he were rolling the window back up. "You're not wearing a scarf."

"I'm not?" She patted herself on the head. "Oh, I'm not!"

She was funny, but also infuriating. He rotated his hand until she rolled her window up, but not without complaint. "You're the one who let me into your car."

He regretted displeasing her, but he wasn't sure how to reverse things, to please her. He took off his shimagh and handed it to her. "Wear this and roll the window back down if you want."

She let the cloth fall in her lap. "I love the sea," she said. "I don't know if I could live without it."

"In Ohio, there's a lake," he said, immediately wanting to take the words back because they implied he wanted her to go to Ohio with him.

She must have felt a little less annoyed with him, because she opened the window and draped the cloth over her head. She looked like a boy.

"Is Ohio like California?" She wrapped the shimagh across her mouth, like a Bedouin or a bandit. The answer was easily no, but she didn't give him a chance to respond. "I'd rather go to Cairo," she said through the cloth.

He lay his arm along the back of the seat, his fingers just shy of her head. Time stretched out like an expanse of shoreline. She reached over and tapped his fingers. He squeezed her fingers and let go.

They parked at a small, empty park near the edge of the sea. She leaned an arm on her open window. The minutes since they left seemed like a beautiful eternity.

"We'd better head back," Saeedah said. "The wedding."

He sighed, long and low like the sea. "May you be next," he said in a falsetto meant to mimic an annoying auntie or uncle.

"Do you want me to marry next?" She pulled the shimagh from her lips, leaned in, and kissed him. He tasted sweetness, like candied almonds. "God forgive you," she said. Her sly smile a crescent moon.

"God forgive me."

He steered the car back toward her house. The sea was on her side, and he felt as though the night had wrapped itself around them.

Without thinking, he drove to the front of the house. Guests were arriving in sedan after sedan. The cars dropped off the women, whose sequined hems peeked out from under their black abayahs. The men, in their formal camel's wool mishlahs with gold borders, parked and headed for the courtyard.

Beside him, she'd hidden below the dashboard, the top of her head close to his thigh.

"What are you doing?" she said. "Drive around the back."

He licked his upper lip; it tasted like sweat. She widened her eyes: *What are you waiting for?* He let his hand float to the top of her head, and with one hand on the steering wheel, returned the car to their meeting place. Leaving his shimagh behind on the passenger seat, she got out of the car and stepped up onto the high sidewalk. She looked at him once before slipping through the back gate, and his heart flew out to her.

He saw none of what happened after she left him. But later, when they were married, she told him somehow she had convinced herself she was home free, and as she skipped upstairs, she hummed the sweet chorus of an Abdel Halim song. Already, he can't remember which one. She opened the door to her parents' room without knocking. Her aunts had taken the room over for the bridal preparations. Her older sister Randah, the bride, sat on the bed, a floor-length prayer scarf wrapped around her.

"You missed Isha prayer," Randah had said.

"I prayed alone."

"Big liar."

"Bitch."

"Riham saw you. Getting into a car with a boy," her sister said. "She told all of us."

When Saeedah told him what had happened next, he swallowed hard and tried to imagine it: she'd slapped her sister straight across the face. Randah hadn't fought back because there was their mother, a man's thick black iqal in her hand like a weapon. Behind her, Muneer's mother, united with her sister.

"Give her what she wants," his mother had said. "And she won't be your problem anymore. She'll be my son's problem, God help them."

They were married in August, on a plane to America less than a week later.

MENTOR HEADLANDS

On a snowy February Friday, Muneer awakens into darkness. He twists the lamp switch: bright, brighter, brightest, back to darkness, back to least bright. He closes his eyes and opens them until his pupils adjust. He feels this way in his marriage, in his life here—as though his eyes are constantly trying to accustom themselves to a too-intense light.

Saeedah sleeps with her back straightened against the wall, her mouth ajar, the corners of her lips glistening. He goes to the bathroom and pees, washes up, prays, dresses, eats breakfast, wrestles his comically enormous down coat out of the closet and off a hanger.

He hears her moving around upstairs, the old wooden floorboards of the house creaking. He places Saeedah's gloves, scarf, and hat on the folding chair. He feels optimistic for no reason whatsoever—other than his faith that God is looking out for him. Moved by this good feeling, he decides not to go upstairs and say goodbye, for fear she might ruin his mood. He knows it's wrong to feel that way, but he wants to go on with his day. Outside, he sticks his tongue out to catch the snow floating in the slanted orange-yellow light of street lamps. Snow still amazes him. He doesn't need Saeedah by his side to enjoy the snow.

He slides into the dark green Beetle's cold white vinyl seat and takes the car down the driveway in neutral before turning the key. The engine sputters. He steers widely around corners with his puffy ski gloves slipping on the steering wheel, keeps the engine in high gear, and avoids stops.

He feels oddly free.

The snow-covered pizzeria parking lot, not much bigger than a pizza pie, is nearly empty, too, except for a white Datsun delivery car. As Muneer drives into the lot, the VW skids suddenly and swings around 180 degrees. Muneer's heart thumps in his throat and his right leg shakes uncontrollably, yet he keeps his foot on the brake. The optimistic feeling dissipates. When the car stops, he is confronted by the silent side street, the shadowy porches of the houses on the other side, their windows' white curtains like starched ghutrahs. He gets out and trudges through the snow to where Jameel stands outside the back door, which is wide open to the cold and lets the shop's lurid neon light out onto the stoop.

Muneer isn't sure whether Jameel saw the one-eighty or not. If he did, other issues outweigh his concern for Muneer's safety.

"Roaches," Jameel says. "The health department is shutting us down."

"For how long? Is Tony going to pay us for showing up?"

"Tony! Muneer wants to know if he's getting paid," Jameel shouts in English through a tear in the screen door. He says it with an edge of sarcasm, like he already knows the answer. A ruckus from inside and some cussing, then Tony yells, "Shut the frigging door."

"Ya Allah," Jameel says.

Muneer digs his hands into his pockets, as though searching them for cash. His Saudi government stipend won't be enough once the baby comes, if he wants to keep sending money to his mother. But Jameel seems unworried. He's happy, smiling his blizzard-bright smile. With time to kill, they drive the Beetle to the Jewish greasy spoon on Lee Road, where they don't have to worry about whether or not they're ordering pork.

Muneer gives the cashier girl fifteen cents for the *Plain Dealer*, and he and Jameel sit at a table in the corner and order beef sausages, sunny-side-up eggs, and rye toast. Muneer pokes a yellow half globe with the blunt corner of his toast and watches the bright liquid seep out. Maneuvering his thumb and two fingers, he tears off a bit of bread and twists it to grab some egg and sausage. He holds the newspaper in his other hand, eating and reading at the same time. Juggling the two activities calms him, keeps him from obsessing about the pizzeria and the money he's losing.

"Get your nose out of the paper," Jameel says. They speak English to avoid curious, sometimes mildly concerned looks. "No wonder your wife's depressed."

Muneer jabs his other egg with another bit of toast. Jameel always thinks he knows something other people don't.

"She's fine, thank God."

Jameel folds his paper napkin into a small, fat square. "Ya shaykh." He takes a breath, as though putting mental effort into returning to English. "She's not fine. Something's gone wrong with her. And with you. You jump when she's near."

Muneer wants to deny it. But arguing is tiresome. "I'll stop reading if you stop talking about my wife like she's a bad piece of fruit."

"OK, habibi," Jameel says. He pulls a small velvet box out of his pocket with a twist of the wrist that reminds Muneer of the magician they saw last summer at Cedar Point. With one thumb, Jameel pops the box open. A diamond ring.

The room is steamy and overheated, the smell of grease cloying. They've both removed their sweaters and draped them over their coats on the backs of their chairs. Muneer waves the newspaper like a fan.

Jameel sets the box on the table, in front of the salt and pepper. "For Diane."

"I know," Muneer says, as though he anticipated this, which he did not. There are many things Muneer could ask: Has Jameel spoken to his father? Has Diane agreed to convert?

"What will you do with her dog?" he says.

"She's giving the dog to her sister." Jameel opens his palms as though he might slap Muneer on both sides of his face. Muneer flinches. Jameel brings one palm to his heart. "Come to the ceremony."

"At the mosque?"

"City hall."

"What if she doesn't want to leave Cleveland?"

"We've talked about it."

"She won't be able to drive, or wear that cross."

"It's halal to marry a Christian, Muneer."

"That's not what I'm talking about. I'm talking about will *your* wife be depressed if you take her to Jidda."

Jameel snaps the box shut and returns the ring to his pocket. "Let's go."

"Where you guys from?" the girl says when they pay.

"We're Spanish," says Jameel, laughing a little at his own lie.

"Beirut," says Muneer.

"My father-in-law's Moroccan," the girl says.

"Merhebeh," says Muneer, putting on a Lebanese accent, which is lost on the cashier. But Jameel laughs.

Free from work, they drive to the West Side to attend Friday prayer at a modest storefront mosque they've gone to once or twice before. The imam is an Indian South African, tall with broomstick limbs and a wispy-curly beard. Today's sermon rouses Muneer from the everyday and reminds him there are people out to get him and all other Muslims. People, the imam says, who want to steer them from God and tie them to Satan: Zionists and Hollywood producers and starlets and congressmen and regular Americans who offer Believers bacon bits on their baked potatoes and wine with dinner and Oreos that harbor lard in them. Judging by the rigid faces of the other men in the room, Jameel included, they also feel the sermon beating against their insides like a drum. They nod and murmur at the imam's aphorisms. Muneer leaves homesick and discontented and determined not to return to the mosque anytime soon.

Back at the house, he writes a ten-page letter to his father. He composes these letters weekly, folds them up and shoves them into envelopes. He addresses them before slipping the fat envelopes into a brown accordion folder he keeps on the top shelf of the bedroom closet.

Today, Muneer writes about the weather, Jameel's engagement, God, preparations for the baby's arrival (a classmate of his has offered them a crib, a stroller, boxes of baby clothes). He says Saeedah is in good health. He doesn't mention how his world seems to shift daily under his feet, like sand. His professors decry any sort of censorship—that of the state, the editor, the journalist himself. But he knows self-editing is sometimes a survival tool when writing to the dead. Why worry his dead father who, in an imaginary aerogram delivered to Muneer's mind, welcomed the news of Saeedah's pregnancy with these words: "Daily, I ask God to keep the three of you safe. Remember to observe your five daily prayers." Why admit to himself the five daily prayers have become 2.3 on average? That he can't keep Saeedah warm, let alone safe. That this marriage is more difficult than anyone could have warned.

Jameel and Diane are married in early March in the basement of the mosque—not a courthouse—and her uncle throws a small celebration in his living room. Diane wears a white lace minidress and a veil grazes her ankles. About two dozen people sit at card tables set up in the living room: Diane's aunt and uncle and cousins and a few close friends, Jameel's buddies from school, Muneer and Saeedah. Neither the bride's nor the groom's parents attend. Her mother and father will take several years—until the first grandchild's birth— to accept her marriage to a Muslim. His family will learn about the wedding in a letter accompanied by a green-tinged Polaroid of Jameel in his suit and tie and Diane in her minidress. For the intimate group assembled on this day, there is roast chicken and wine and the entertainment of Jameel getting a little sloppy. The bride's uncle makes a toast, and people clink their glasses, and Diane whispers loudly to Jameel that this means they are supposed to kiss. The clinking recurs half a dozen times, and Muneer is convinced there is one person at the other table responsible for instigating. He and Saeedah alone have water in their wineglasses.

After dinner, Muneer sits next to Saeedah on a rickety love seat with wooden legs and leans over to kiss her cheek. It is cold, and her fingers, which he takes in his hand, are icy.

"Do you want me to find you a sweater or a blanket?"

She squeezes his hand, braces her legs, and pushes up from the seat with both hands.

"I don't think Jameel knows what he's doing," she says. "This marriage is a bad idea."

"You don't know that," he says, though he thought close to the same thing when Jameel showed him the engagement ring. Though he, too, doubted this match, he doesn't want to agree with Saeedah. What is done is done. Jameel and Diane are married.

"She's Christian. He's Muslim. What will the children be?"

"They'll be Muslim, like their father, of course."

She holds her hair up in the back, twists it around and lets it fall back to her shoulders. "You should have told him not to marry her."

The girl's family drinks and gossips and dances. None of them speak Muneer and Saeedah's language. He is alone with her words.

Snow falls the next week. Muneer is tiring of this white stuff, and March snow seems worse to him than any other kind. It makes him yearn for spring, whereas April snow—that would seem like a fluke. Maybe it's the cold or the stone-colored sky, some weather-related discontent makes it hard for him to be alone in his annoyance with Saeedah any longer. He makes the mistake of telling Jameel what she said.

They're working a shift at the pizzeria, which has managed to stay open the past month, and Muneer tosses the elastic dough toward the buzzing neon lights of the kitchen.

"Do you agree?" Jameel asks. "That I shouldn't have married her?"

Muneer adjusts his plastic gloves and sprinkles flour on the board. He lays the dough on the surface and ladles tomato sauce onto the round.

"You're married, and God bless you," he says.

"You're a coward," Jameel says. "You won't tell me the truth."

"It's her opinion, not mine."

"You think marrying your cousin is a better idea than marrying a woman you love?"

Muneer wants to say he did marry for love, but is love what he felt at the beginning? "God knows what's best," he says.

Jameel doesn't talk to him the rest of the shift, or on the way to campus. When Muneer drops him off, Jameel shuts the car door too quietly, draws his hood up, and trudges away.

Muneer has half an hour until class, so he passes by the old yellow mansion that houses the ESL program. He parks the VW on the circle and walks into the wood-paneled hallway of the building. Two of Saeedah's classmates, Sonja and Weronika, are shrugging into their coats, their backpacks bulging and unzipped on the floor. Their faces are a question: What is he doing here?

He's not sure. Maybe he wants to test whether Saeedah would be happy to see him.

"If you're looking for Saeedah," Weronika says, "she didn't come to class today. We thought maybe she had the baby."

Outside, the temperature has suddenly plummeted ten degrees, and the wind has picked up. The top layer of snow swirls and scurries down the sidewalk. He curves his head into his neck and his arms into his torso and runs to the car.

It is barely three o'clock in the afternoon, but the sky has darkened as though night is coming. He pulls up to the house. The windows are dark, and he doesn't bother going inside. He drives. Something takes him to her. Intuition, love, God, worry—he doesn't know what to call it.

Today, the lake is muddy, the sky dark and dense like gray felt. The snow on the beach is ashen, and so are his thoughts.

When he sees her, he stops. He can't move, as though he's strapped to a chair, like a prisoner in a movie, watching her without being able to lift a finger to rescue her.

She stands at the edge of the water with waves lapping her bare feet. She slips off her jeans and white turtleneck and stands in her white bra and underwear. She walks into the choppy water, pauses, moves forward. As though overcoming the cold. The water envelops her body bit by bit, until it touches her shoulders.

"Come inside," he says, but of course she can't hear.

A small prick of shame, like the shock of touching a car door in the dry winter air: here is his wife taking her clothes off in public. But no one is on the beach, and he's too cold and frightened to care. To warm himself up, he pulls his arms out of his sleeves and into the body of his coat.

He walks to the edge of the lake, his boots leaving tracks in the thick, wet mixture of snow and sand. The air smells woody and wet, and someone must be burning a bonfire somewhere because he smells smoke. He turns toward the parking lot and squints to the left and right, searching for a lit fire, smoke, evidence of other humans sharing this beach with them.

He looks back to the lake. She has reached the sandbar about a hundred yards from the shore, and the water is at her waist.

He drops his coat onto the sand and wades into the water. It is so cold it might as well be a block of ice. He presses on. His jeans and long johns are so heavy. The water stings like peroxide on a wound.

Behind him someone is yelling. "What the hell! It's fucking cold."

Muneer looks back to the shore. A man has appeared out of nowhere, walking along the beach holding a metal detector out like a blind man's white-tipped cane.

"What the hell are you doing?" the man says. In his other hand, he holds a rusty tea tray—an odd thing to have found on the beach.

Muneer turns to his wife. She hasn't moved from the sandbar.

When he reaches her, her body is purple. He lifts her. He isn't sure he can reach the shore. Next he remembers, they are lying on the cold, cold ground.

The man is standing over them. He wears a ski mask, folded up to reveal a face that resembles Johnny Carson with a salt-and-pepper beard. His metal detector and tea tray lie on the ground, and he's holding Muneer's coat and a sand-colored blanket—pilly and rough, but better than nothing. He hangs the coat on Muneer's head by the hood and wraps the blanket around Muneer and Saeedah. They are too cold to warm each other.

"Do you need a ride?" the man says, picking up his things. He dangles the tea tray from one hooked thumb. "You're not from here, are you?"

Muneer rubs Saeedah's hands between his. He rubs her feet, her arms, her legs. She's made of chilled rubber, not flesh and blood.

"No, thank you," Muneer says. He doesn't think the second question deserves an answer. "Can we keep the blanket?"

The man shakes the tray in lieu of a nod and continues down the beach.

Muneer bundles Saeedah in the blanket and scoops her up. She feels heavy as anything.

This experience binds them together—or should. Because he has saved her and the baby, and tonight, she will be OK. The child will be OK, will be born beautiful and whole, will be named Hanadi. He will pray two raka'ahs in thanks tomorrow morning, and another two daily for a month. He will beg his professors to give him extensions on his coursework and to let him graduate if he finishes by the end of the summer, and they will agree.

But doubt will return bit by bit, like the whisperings of a devil. Aunt Faizah, who will need no convincing to fly across the world to help take care of her baby granddaughter, will yell at him for failing to prepare and boss him while he sets up a crib from Sears in the spare bedroom she and Hanadi will share. His mother-in-law will guide him toward the things Saeedah did not: blankets and onesies and tiny caps and socks with yellow ducks on them. Bottles and nipples and pacifiers and canisters of formula and boxes of diapers.

"Good God, the two of you, both so ignorant," Aunt Faizah will say. "Didn't you take care of your younger brothers and sisters? It never occurred to you that you needed these things?"

"The baby was not supposed to come for a month," he will insist, and in his mind he will place the blame on Saeedah. If she had been willing to talk to him these last months and weeks, she might have told him what they needed.

Aunt Faizah will wrap the baby so tightly the little thing can't move, can do nothing but sleep, and Muneer will wish he could be swaddled and kept safe from the world. He'll spend most of his time at the library, and when he returns home, Saeedah will usually be sitting in the rocking chair, holding the baby when her mother lets her, looking always like she is in shock. Jameel and Diane will come to visit, and the pity in their eyes will tell him the shell-shocked look is on his face, too.

After his mother-in-law leaves, he will muddle through the year of his internship, writing for a little local paper in Beachwood, covering shopping mall Santas and fire department fundraisers. He will inhale the fragrance that emanates from the top of his daughter's head, the essence of her, and watch her shove her fists in her mouth and grab her mother's dangling gold earrings so that Saeedah has to carefully extract them before Hanadi can tug them straight through her earlobes, as a thief once did to Saeedah's sister at the Haram Mosque in Makkah.

Muneer and Saeedah will sleepwalk through the year. One day, near the end of his internship, something in them will snap decisively, and the state of their marriage will revert to exactly what it was before Hanadi was born. Saeedah will say she would rather stay in America—a place she has never been drawn to, has not always seemed to like—than stay married to him.

He will feel the knife of her disdain turning in his stomach, though he feels the same. He will grant her wish of divorce and move back to Jidda without them, intending to find a way to bring his daughter home.

But he won't. Saeedah will shatter Muneer's life as though she were smashing through a sheet of ice. She will hide his daughter from him so well it will be as though the child were back in the womb, unreachable.

Leaving the beach with his wife asleep in the back of the VW, speeding to the hospital with the heater turned up so it whooshes and rattles, Muneer is blind to the future. He prays, "Oh, Protector, protect them. Oh, Protector, protect them."

God alone knows what lies ahead.

"YOU ARE DIVORCED"

1974–1975

WITNESSES

If anyone aims the sentence "You are divorced" at Saeedah three times, she is not there to hear it. Spoken or unspoken, the words must travel to her across continents, from Jidda to Cleveland Heights, as though transported by jinns or the world's most muscular carrier pigeons. The men of her family go about the official business of nullifying her marriage without her, same as they signed her marriage contract six years ago at the neighborhood mosque while she sat on her mother's bed with three sisters curling her hair and kohling her eyes for the wedding celebration.

"Your brothers Hazem and Mohannad were with me in the judge's chamber," her father says on the phone, describing the divorce proceedings. Three of Muneer's brothers were there, too, though the names go in one ear and out the other. Baba is trying to reassure her that the divorce has truly happened: male witnesses prove its reality.

Thank God? Thank you? Neither sounds correct.

"OK," she says.

Saeedah's mother takes over the phone with a rush of *habibtis* and *God protect yous*, and Saeedah wonders how vigorously she has pushed Baba aside with her hennaed palms, what kind of side glance he is giving her from under his shimagh, which he hardly ever takes off, even at home. Always professional, always ready for a journalistic scoop.

"When are you bringing my darling home?" Mama says, speaking of Hanadi.

"Maybe next summer, inshallah." Saeedah is finishing her psychology degree, paying for Hanadi's day care with money her father sends. After her long maternity leave, her grade point average suffered from the everyday skirmishes with Muneer in the final days of their marriage. She has had to retake courses and endure endless conversations with her advisor, Dr. O'Rourke, an Irishman with six children, a penchant for mixing plaid and tweed, and hair like streaks of rust combed over his bald head. He seems befuddled that a woman of her nationality could ever sit alone in a room with him and often wonders aloud if she might be more comfortable studying in her home country.

"Hanadi should be here," Mama says. "In her country, with both her parents."

Saeedah's temples throb because she knows she should agree with the divorce, but Hanadi's seventh birthday lies two and a half years away, a sinister finish line when Saeedah will be expected, by religious custom, to hand Hanadi over to her father.

"A mother is the best to raise a young child," Mama says. "Her father should finish raising her so he can fulfill his duty to find her the best match."

"Khalas." Stop. "She's four. Why are we talking about her marriage?"

"God protect her and bless her and shower her with goodness," Mama says.

Two and a half years will be gone in an instant.

Coming back to reality—the hum of the window air conditioner; the phone cord twisted round her finger; the neighbors' footsteps creaking above her, their rock music thumping—does not ease her anxiety. In a few weeks, Muneer is coming to see his daughter. Saeedah hangs up the phone and retches into the toilet.

She calls her friend Weronika, who's recently moved to Toledo for a nursing job. Having grown up in the Soviet Union, W gets the kinds of fear you can't explain to Americans.

"Just because you're paranoid, doesn't mean they're not out to get you," W says.

DRAEGER'S

Saeedah lets the doorbell ring and ring. She tells Hanadi not to answer it, though the four-year-old knows her Baba is at the door.

The ringer loses patience and presses the bell relentlessly; the rings jumble into one sound.

"It's too loud," Hanadi says. "Why won't you let Baba in?"

"OK, OK." Saeedah yells a lie as she rushes to the door. "We were in the bathroom."

Framed by the doorway, Muneer's younger sister Lujayn wears a fringed T-shirt and bell-bottoms, and her hair swirls in hot-curled, inky ringlets past her shoulders. Her face is frozen in annoyance—eyes squeezed, jawline tight. She kisses Saeedah on the cheeks and lifts Hanadi onto one hip.

Behind them, Muneer paces on the front porch. "Where were you?"

"I told you," Saeedah says. She's angry that he won't believe her lie.

Hanadi at four is too big to be picked up like a baby, but she lets her aunt hold her. She is in jean shorts and a white tank top embroidered with red and orange flowers. Her chubby bare legs hang down Lujayn's thigh.

"I love you, Baba," she says over her aunt's shoulder. It's the first time she's seen him in two months. Her smile is sunshine falling on the frozen adult landscape around her. "Mama wasn't in the bathroom."

"I know, love," he says.

Saeedah feels her jealousy in every fiber of her body, and she doesn't want to cure it with a prayer for forgiveness. Hanadi smiles adorably at her father and aunt, and subjects Saeedah to tantrums over the smallest things. The food Saeedah puts on Hanadi's plate, how long they stay at the ice-skating rink or at the shopping mall play area. Why should Muneer and Lujayn enjoy sweetness? Why should they not feel the impact of Saeedah's jealousy? She hopes for Hanadi to kick and scream at them today.

Lujayn and Muneer exchange a look. Do they think she doesn't notice? But they don't call out her lie.

"We don't need to waste time standing here," Lujayn says. "She's going to enjoy the rides at the amusement park. Right, love?" Lujayn kisses Hanadi on the cheek.

"Carousel!" Hanadi says.

"You're not taking her there."

"I told you not to say anything yet, Lujayn." Muneer puts a proprietary hand on Hanadi's head.

"What did you tell Lujayn not to say?"

"She didn't give me a chance to ask you. We want to take Hanadi to the amusement park."

The casualness of his gestures and his voice makes Saeedah want to scream. She fights the urge to yank her daughter out of Lujayn's arms. She and Lujayn played together as children, throwing and catching pebbles on the rooftop the way the neighbor girls here play with jacks on the sidewalk. Lujayn bossed the other cousins and lied about what was in front of them: a pebble she failed to catch, the number of pebbles in her palm. Always needing to go first, needing to win. It irks Saeedah that Hanadi seems content in Lujayn's arms—not giggling or flirting with her aunt, but not fidgeting, either. Muneer touches his forehead to Hanadi's and she puts her hand on his shoulder.

They are already cutting Saeedah out of the picture, and they haven't left the porch. She tries to remember why she'd flirted with him behind her parents' backs. He'd been curious for new places, willing to take a risk by driving alone with her, though he'd acted nervous the whole time. Why is he settling for going back to Saudi and telling the stories society will allow, like her father?

"If you'd asked me before, I'd have said no. You're going to take her an hour away? Or to the other park—two hours away?"

"I wanna go, Mama," Hanadi says. She wriggles down her aunt's leg. "Please, please."

"Never mind. We'll go for ice cream," Muneer says. He turns to his sister. "You've ruined it. I told you not to say anything."

"You say ice cream, but I know you're lying."

"The shop's down the street. You know where it is."

"Don't fight," Hanadi says, and Lujayn takes her hand and whispers something to her.

As Lujayn and Hanadi walk across the porch, Saeedah feels her anger like a separate being inside her—a child squirming in her belly or a jinni possessing her. She lunges for Lujayn and grabs her arm.

"Get away from my child!"

Not shocked or scared, Lujayn emanates angry heat. Her full weight rams into Saeedah, who has to catch herself from falling. Hanadi erupts in tears. Muneer takes her in his arms. The meter between them and Saeedah seems like an ocean.

"Lujayn!" Muneer says.

"You saw she came at me. I was trying to take Hanadi from the fighting."

"Let Lujayn and Hanadi stay outside while we finish talking." Muneer steps inside, ushering Saeedah into the living room, as though he's the one who lives here.

Saeedah resents his implication that she's failed to protect her daughter. Whenever Muneer comes back, these situations slip from her control. Nothing matters but Hanadi's tears, which sit on her cheeks whole and perfect, tiny reminders of everything Saeedah has ever done wrong as a mother. Through the bay window, she watches Lujayn and Hanadi in the yard, poking sticks in the grass.

"Are you going to keep us from seeing her? The thing we came here to do?" Muneer says to Saeedah. He's taken his boots off to come inside, left them neatly by the door, their toes and heels lined up perfectly. His socked feet seem too intimate. What's changed in her? In Jidda, it's customary to take your shoes off in someone's home. It's nothing special. Here, the sight of his shoeless feet on her wool carpet suggests a closeness they've lost.

She sits in the rocking chair. The urge to fight has leaked out of her.

"Fine. Take her for ice cream."

"We'll be back in an hour."

She doesn't believe him.

She has begun to tire of the phone calls. Once a week, during Saturday morning cartoons, he calls, as arranged. Hanadi lies flat on her stomach, legs kicking the carpet beneath her. She keeps her eyes on the black-and-white TV, barely larger than a toaster, that Saeedah bought at Zayre after Muneer took the color set.

Whenever the phone rings, Saeedah gives it to Hanadi without answering it. "Talk to Baba."

Hanadi hardly speaks. She listens to her father and nods. Saeedah hears his tinny voice, trying to keep the conversation going, like a cold engine sputtering in Ohio in January. In Jidda, engines die of heat, not cold. When she takes the handset from Hanadi, Muneer is always angry because his daughter won't speak to him.

"She's four," Saeedah says. "She's watching cartoons."

"Turn the TV off."

"She'd yell."

"What are you telling her about me?"

"Nothing. You'll see when you visit."

He comes every three months. They have agreed on this arrangement until Saeedah finishes her degree. Muneer has taken Hanadi to Draeger's, the ice cream parlor on Van Aken Boulevard, during past visits. But Saeedah trusts Lujayn less than she trusts her ex-husband. Lujayn will goad him. She'll complain about Saeedah's refusal to let them drive Hanadi to an amusement park. She'll insist it's his right to take his daughter wherever he wants.

Saeedah turns on the TV. Nothing but soap operas and *Leave It to Beaver*. She opens a textbook, reads ten pages, turns back to reread passages because nothing has stuck in her brain. What if they didn't go to Draeger's? It would be better to know now, rather than wait for them to be gone for hours.

After a week of thunderstorms, it's a beautiful, sunny, late August day. The heat doesn't bother her. She likes to let it soak into her skin, hoarding sunshine in preparation for the long winter that will arrive soon. But her Beetle, which sits in the driveway because the garage houses the landlord's rusted-out Chrysler, is blazing hot. The vinyl burns the backs of her thighs.

She rolls down the windows and drives through the leafy shade of the neighborhood, out toward Van Aken. A family of four walks home from the pool, damp towels hung over the crooks of their arms. Two boys race their bikes down the street toward her, veering over to the sidewalk when they see her car coming. Too late, she realizes she might miss Muneer, Lujayn, and Hanadi driving back along another route. She might as well drive all the way. If they arrive home before her, Hanadi will be home, and Saeedah will lie and say . . . She doesn't know what.

In the parking lot of the shopping center, she spots Muneer's white Chevy rental car. She lets the Volkswagen idle alongside the curb. Should she park at the far end of the lot and tail them back? Or leave, satisfied they are where they said they'd be?

Draeger's glass door swings open, and Hanadi skips out, a smear of pink ice cream underlining her smile. Muneer takes a napkin from his pocket and carefully wipes Hanadi's face with its edge.

Certainly they'll see Saeedah. She's a beacon of envy. She's meters from them. But they turn their attention to crossing the parking lot, avoiding a tan Corolla whose driver seems not to see them at first. The car brakes suddenly, and Saeedah's heart skids in her chest. Hanadi is fine, sandwiched between her father and her aunt, not noticing how they have shielded her. Saeedah smells the rubber of the Corolla's tires, sees the driver's stricken face and his shock at having nearly hit a family.

She steps to the curb and balances on its edge on the balls of her feet. Muneer, Lujayn, and Hanadi climb into the Chevy. Its engine growls and it begins to back toward her. It pulls up and passes her, so close she could tap on the window, but she is as invisible to them as a jinni.

GETAWAY

1975

Mama: You stole me. March 25, 1975. My fifth birthday. In broad day-light. You carried me to the car, in my purple giraffe pajamas and suede saddle shoes, through early-spring snow. I put my head on your shoul-der. The flakes settled like sifted flour over the hard-packed, dirt-crusted snowbanks. The car's seat was joltingly cold, the window icy against my fingers. The Bug was noisy, too, backfiring and sputtering. A terrible getaway car.

"This," you said, and the s went on forever, "is a terrible car. Some people say Beetles are reliable. Hah. A little snow and it falls apart."

Some people. Were you talking about my father?

I know that you stole me. If we had been moving like normal people do, the car would have been loaded full, the windows obscured by boxes and garbage bags and an overflowing laundry basket. You would have been forced to use the side-view mirrors because you couldn't see over the crap stacked up in the back. But we weren't moving, we were run-ning. We had one light blue hard-sided suitcase and matching vanity, as though we were heading off for the weekend.

Once in a while, I'll have this flash, and an object from the past will be illuminated in my mind. I'll read about some returning seventies trend—culottes, ponchos, hip-hugger jeans—or I'll be in a thrift shop and see a wild-eyed baby doll with a plastic head and oblong cloth body, and I'll remember something we left behind. I'll wonder, What happened to that oil painting of a crying boy?

You forced me to forget for so many years. I'm trying to remember. In my mind, I see the silhouette of the brick duplex in Cleveland Heights; the screened porch with a patch of mud underneath that never dried out; the rust-blemished, faded-blue swing set in the back; the lilac tree whose blossoms would, a month or so after we left, dangle like bunches of grapes; our down coats and snow boots and hats and scarves and the other odds and ends that might have kept us warm; your dishes and comforters and towels; the tulip-shaped Arabic coffee cups I used as teacups for my teddy bears; my books and Barbies and purple bicycle; the phone my father called me on; our memories of anything that had happened before you turned the key in the ignition that day.

Before I understood what happened, understood that you stole me, before I escaped you, I used to think about riding a purple bicycle. I didn't know I was having a memory. I thought I was daydreaming. Sitting on the stoop of a suburban Midwest walk-up apartment or the porch of a California one-horse-town bungalow, I'd touch imaginary tassels, flip the nonexistent bell, rest my foot on the back, and push off down the driveway in my mind. I'd peer back at an imaginary brick duplex shaded by maples. The trees' helicopter pods would twirl, hover, fall.

The car engine turned over for several minutes while you cursed. I put my fingers in my ears, and when the engine caught hold and sputtered to life, you had to repeat yourself several times and lean your whole upper body toward the back of the car to pull my fingers out of my ears as you waited for the car to warm up.

"For your birthday, we're going to McDonald's," you said.

"No friends?"

"*This is better.*" *The snow had stopped, and the windshield wipers squeaked against the salt-streaked glass. McDonald's was on the way to the freeway. We passed the big yellow* M *and the brick building and pulled onto the on-ramp.*

"*There it is! Mama, we passed it.*"

"*For your birthday, we're going to Cedar Point. OK?*"

You sped up to merge onto the freeway. I tensed my body and gripped the passenger seat in front of me to keep from falling. My stomach ached, like there was a big rock pressing against my insides, and the pain migrated into my muscles, and my arms and thighs began to ache, too. The achiness would stick with me, stuck with me more than anything or anyone except for you. In the years ahead, my stomach would learn to always brace itself against sudden disappointment, suck itself in so far it might have grazed my spine. With you, everything was always changing in an instant. I could never feel settled.

"*But I'm hungry.*"

"*We'll eat there.*"

I napped on the back seat. When I woke up, we were driving along the edge of the empty amusement park parking lot, as though you didn't see the vast space to our left, the faded lines of the parking spots.

The Bug swerved, though there was nothing to steer clear of, and I nearly fell off the seat.

"*We're here,*" *you said.* "*Look.*"

I sat up and fingered my cheek, where the seat cushion's patterned vinyl had left an imprint. I knelt at the window and pressed five fingertips against the glass. In the distance, Lake Erie shook its brown-gray fists against the color-leeched sky. We sputtered to the front gate.

You parked across two parking spaces, turned the ignition off, and got out, letting a frigid draft into the warm bubble of the car.

I put my whole face against the glass, felt the pressure against the bones of my nose and forehead. You walked past the ticket booths and up to a big gray gate. You shook the padlock and grabbed the bars of the gate, like a prisoner trying to break out. You walked back to the car, your mouth a straight line, your face a locked gate. Your hair had frizzed, and you held it behind your head with one hand. You wore jeans and a denim shirt buttoned to your neck, and sneakers that slid along the icy ground. You righted yourself, bent your knees, and held your arms like a surfer, gliding till you hit the car with your hip to stop yourself. You laughed, like you couldn't help yourself—it was funny, and you were going to laugh.

The laugh made me feel safe, and the memory of that feeling makes me realize how scared I was, how I must have known something was wrong.

You got inside the car, bringing the cold air with you. I crossed my arms tightly for warmth. You chewed your thumbnail for a minute, put both hands on the steering wheel. You didn't start the car.

"We can't have the heater, Mama?"

You faced the gates, relaxed and patient. As though you expected someone to come out at any minute and invite us in.

"I guess it's closed," you said.

You rested your forehead against the steering wheel, like you were so, so tired.

"I'm hungry, Mama."

My words animated you. You lifted your head slowly, at the same time reaching into a paper shopping bag on the passenger seat and taking out a plastic baggie of Fritos.

Accepting that bag meant giving up on my birthday. I didn't want to. I put as much perkiness into my voice as I could. "I know! Let's go to McDonald's."

You put the Fritos back and rummaged around for another baggie. "Grapes?" Like you'd prepared for a picnic.

You put the car into gear and swung back the way we had come. I climbed into the passenger seat, and you didn't stop me. Tapping the window with four fingers, I mouthed "Goodbye" to the roller coasters' prehistoric skeletons, the giant eye of the Ferris wheel, and the rocky shores of the lake.

The wooded back road leading from the amusement park was dark with mist, which hung like a curtain dividing where we'd been from where we were going.

"When are we home?" I said. And when you didn't reply, "When are we home, Mama?" As though the addition of that one word might make you answer.

Somewhere in your silence, I must have heard how alone we were.

"How will Baba know what number to call us?"

"Your father is dead," you said.

That was the first of many times you told me that lie. You insisted, many years later, that you never told me he was dead. But you did. You tried to kill my memory of him.

Of course, I believed you.

SUITABLE GIRLS

1975–1985

YA'QUB'S BLINDNESS

From the first Saturday afternoon Muneer hears "This number is no longer in service," it takes months to understand Hanadi is truly missing. Still, he knows something is different, wronger than usual. Saeedah has ignored his calls for weeks, and whenever he dials, his stomach clenches tighter with each ring. Now, Saeedah and Hanadi aren't there. His stomach has twisted so tight, he could pull it through a ring. Kneeling in his mother's sitting room after lunch has been cleared from the floor, with the ceiling fan spinning overhead, he swallows the bile in his throat and calls Saeedah's sister Randah.

Groggy from her afternoon nap, Randah swears to God she knows of no other number and asks if he's sure.

"Try it." His voice leaves his body calmer than he expects.

She calls him back.

"Wallahi, you're right. I'll try again tomorrow."

In a week, the number remains disconnected, and Randah has not heard from Saeedah.

"I'm sure they will call soon." She sounds uncertain.

"Has she called your parents?"

"No, they're worried. We're worried."

Muneer is holding the handset up for Bandar to hear. They huddle close and strain to listen to the tinny voice. He needs his brother as his witness.

"She's lying," Bandar says when the call is done. "How could Saeedah's father not know where they are? Go see him."

Muneer slams his fist into a cushion. How does a father lose his daughter as though she were a pair of socks under a bed, a toothbrush left behind in a hotel? No one asks the question out loud, but Muneer knows they think it, too. When his mother rails against Saeedah—"God damn that girl to hell"—and frets about her granddaughter surrounded by unbelievers in an unbelieving country and wonders why Saeedah would not want to come home where Hanadi could be near her father until she is old enough to live with him at age seven, he hears unspoken criticism of his own actions. *Everything is in God's hands, but Muneer did not do enough to bring his daughter home.*

Hanadi could be anywhere—anywhere in the States, anywhere in the world. She might be here in Jidda, hidden by her other family behind the mirrored windows of an apartment, though he doubts Aunt Faizah would be that bold.

Soon, his family's advice descends on him like Jidda rain—always a downpour.

Bandar wants to interrogate Saeedah's parents and her sisters until they confess to knowing where she is.

Salem offers to call the minister of the exterior. "I gave him the answers to our mathematics final in high school," Salem says. "He owes me a favor."

But what can the minister of the exterior do, says Lujayn. "You're better off calling the American Embassy. It's America's fault a mother and daughter can disappear. Why would a Jidda girl do such a thing?"

Bandar, on thinking longer, advises Muneer to hire an American lawyer and a private investigator. A few days later, he tells Muneer to fly to the States to look for Hanadi himself.

Mama says simply, "Make your family whole."

So much advice from so many people. It will be a full-time job to find his daughter. It will be expensive. His journalist's wages at *Akhbar al-'Urus*, the paper his high school friend Imad started to rival *al-Sharqiyah* and other bastions of Saudi journalism, are good but not lavish. Like his brothers, he helps support their mother. It was his idea to pay a double share on her rent because he lives with her. His brothers agreed reluctantly, and he has to insist monthly when the rent is due. The building is new, but the gated lift is rickety and smells like stray cats. His sisters sew curtains for the flat on their foot-powered sewing machine. On Fridays, he goes to prayer with his brothers and to the halaqah afterward for cartons of fruits and vegetables. They split up the contents in his mother's small tiled kitchen, a share for each sibling with a family, a share for Muneer and Mama and Lujayn, the last unmarried sister. His brothers refuse to take his money, insisting on paying for him and the women. Accepting gifts hurts his pride, but he's not the oldest brother, so his pride can withstand a little pain. He saves his money at the national bank, for a future trip to find his daughter in America.

He starts with the easiest, most logical, most inexpensive step. He calls Fareed and asks to visit on a Thursday evening.

"Of course, my son, you're always welcome," Fareed says, as though nothing unusual has happened, as though a hole has not been torn in their family and two people fallen through it. On the phone, he sounds like a radio announcer: in control of his words, on top of the story.

At Fareed's villa, Muneer is buzzed through the gate. In the courtyard, he leaves the garbage-ripe smells of the street behind. Here, jasmine and gardenia perfume the night. Fareed opens the villa door himself. He is casual, the collar of his thawb unbuttoned, the sleeves rolled up. As the two men lower themselves onto cushions in the family room, rather than a formal salon, Muneer feels the scratch of his own starched collar and ghutrah. Fareed settles in next to a shisha, its coals glowing orange, and brings the nozzle to his mouth. He exhales and offers the pipe to Muneer, who gestures no.

There are phrases of greeting people normally pass between them at the start of a conversation: "God protect you and yours." "How is the family?" "It's been too long." "How are the children?" These things go unsaid. Muneer sees no point in stalling. The awkwardness of his topic is unavoidable.

"Have you talked to them?" Saying their names would be painful. Besides, Fareed knows who *they* are.

"She told us she was going to California." Fareed says the words slowly, as though carefully lifting drinking glasses out of a cardboard box. "You didn't know that? That was more than a month ago."

He offers Muneer the shisha again. Muneer says no. Fareed must know Muneer suspects the family of covering up for Saeedah. But at first, Muneer can't keep himself from pretending he believes

Fareed. He feels the stress of playacting along his cheekbones, through his forehead and his jawline. His face wants to break into a grimace of disgust. But he can't call this man he's looked up to for years a liar. He searches Fareed's face for signs of distress. Perhaps the casualness of his clothing is a sign—perhaps his grief has kept him from getting dressed.

Muneer hates to be so charitable. He wants someone to blame. If Saeedah was going to California with his daughter, *someone* should have told him. Randah should have told him. Lie or omission, they have deceived him.

A young woman in a black headscarf and floor-length cotton dress comes in with a tray of sodas. Muneer was rude to say no to the shisha. To atone, he takes a glass, though he doesn't want it.

"Can you learn where they are?" Muneer's voice chips at the edges. "Saeedah can do what she wants, go where she wants. I want my daughter back."

"Young man, I want the same thing." Fareed sets down the nozzle and presses his fingers into the bones beneath his eyes. "We have prayed. We have spoken to private investigators. We have spoken to the ambassador in Washington."

"Thank you, Aminah," Fareed says as the woman leaves with the tray.

They're alone again. The privacy emboldens Muneer and dissolves his mask of respect for a man who raised a daughter who would run away from her family.

"It's not possible you don't know where your daughter is." He senses how wrong the words are as they leave his mouth, but he doesn't regret saying them. "You might not have spoken to her, but she must call her mother."

The shisha bubbles as Fareed sucks. In Muneer's eyes, the smoke he breathes out is an obfuscation.

"We're devastated. But at least we must believe your girl is with her mother, and that is a good place for her to be." He touches his heart. "As I said, we have an American looking for her. But there's no reason for the world to know they've disappeared. We'll find them soon, and this situation will be like nothing."

Muneer wishes he hadn't twice said no to the shisha. He inhales Fareed's fragrant smoke. He needs something to soothe his nerves.

Fareed laughs, a sound like a warning. What he is about to say is not what Muneer wants to hear.

"Don't forget, we fathers are fourth in respect, after mothers: your mother, then your mother, then your mother, then your father."

Muneer loves this saying of the Prophet. But he wishes Uncle Fareed had not spoken it, and asks God's forgiveness for the thought.

"Ya'qub went blind when he lost his child Yusuf," Muneer says. He understands the English expression of "blood boiling." Heat surges in his body.

"God forbid," Fareed says. "Thank God, we are healthy. We have our sight."

"Our sight, but not our children. Let me give you something for the investigator."

"I won't take your money."

Muneer sits a beat longer. "You have to tell me when you hear from her. Swear you will, Uncle."

"Of course. God willing, we'll tell you," Fareed says. "And may God give your upstart paper great success. Competition is good for us newsmen."

Fareed sucks on the shisha, and then smiles for the first time during this meeting. He lets the smoke come out the corners of his mouth and tells a story Muneer has heard before: how Fareed's father came up with the idea of an upstart paper in the 1920s while he was smoking shisha with fellow veterans of the Hejazi army, in the open air of a café in downtown Jidda, which was a small yet important port city at the time. Their breath infused with apple-scented smoke, their minds animated by camaraderie and regional pride, the friends imagined a broadside that would tell the truth about everything and reflect their cosmopolitan city, the most vital organ of their beloved Hejaz, which they saw as a strip of land containing everything: mountains, plains, valleys, coastline, oases, agriculture, and the two holiest sites in the world. An English merchant named Fitzworth financed the partners. They told him, "One day, one of us will own Harrods, and we'll pay it back."

"None of those guys ever owned Harrods," Fareed says. "The Egyptians beat us to it, like they beat us to everything else." He always tells this joke when he talks about the founding of his paper. Muneer found it funny once.

At first, they called the paper *Voice of the Hejaz*, but soon, the Hejaz belonged to the Saudi kingdom, and the paper belonged to the new nation. It became, in the 1930s, *al-Sharqiyah*.

"That was my father's idea, too," Fareed says. "A paper to unite the people of our whole region."

Many years later, Imad and Muneer had started *Akhbar al-'Urus—News of the Bride*—with big aspirations, too: a paper for the people of Jidda, where Eve was said to be buried, a city affectionately called the Bride of the Red Sea.

Muneer knows neither paper belongs to the people any longer. Both are bankrolled by the royal family, like every paper in the kingdom. But Fareed has deeper connections than Imad does. He can ask permission to say the things no one else is allowed to say, to say them in such a way that they ruffle no feathers.

He has money to find his daughter, and Muneer does not.

Fareed stands, a cue for Muneer to leave, but Muneer remains seated and Fareed is forced to look down at him. What should seem like a position of submission beneath the older man's gaze instead feels powerful to Muneer. He knows he has the higher moral ground.

ROUTINE

When the faithful are called to prayer, they must perform ritual ablution, and when a man is unmarried, his family must find him a bride. Muneer's family does not let the loss of his daughter keep them from encouraging him to remarry.

Muneer's brother Bandar favors a second cousin on their father's side for him, a tall girl with green eyes inherited from a Turkish grandmother. Marrying her would strengthen ties with that side of the family, which, everyone seems to agree, have weakened since their father's death.

Muneer's sister Lateefah wants his permission to share with her girlhood friend's younger sister a wallet photo taken of him soon after his high school graduation. The friend and her sister are from a good Jidda trade family, Lateefah says.

Muneer's mother comes back from women's gatherings and weddings speaking of some young woman, as luminous as the moon, who knows at least three Hadeeths for every situation: the importance of patience, forgiveness, cleanliness, privacy, moderation in food and drink, mothers, fathers, avoiding sin, charity, exercise, kindness to animals.

Lujayn has a new university classmate to recommend weekly, until she marries a second cousin, moves out of Mama's apartment, gets pregnant, and puts her studies on hold, against the advice of Muneer and their other siblings.

He would like his mother and siblings to stop fussing, but they don't listen.

The prospective brides are sixteen-year-olds, eighteen-year-olds, a few twenty-year-olds midway through university. Most Jidda women five or ten years younger than Muneer are married, and no one would recommend a widow or a divorcee.

"God protect you. You've suffered enough already," his sisters say.

Muneer might consider marriage under other circumstances, but he can't afford it yet, he tells them. He is saving his halalas for a round-trip ticket to America. After a trip, he saves again. The family keeps trying, though.

Soon after Muneer's visit—the last time the two men will speak—Fareed begins sending a courier to the four-room offices of *Akhbar al-'Urus* to deliver a PI's reports, monthly at first, then quarterly. The packets of typed records of the American's comings and goings across the United States come stuffed in heavy manila envelopes, the pages butterfly-clipped and accompanied by fuzzy photographs. Muneer carries the envelopes home in his briefcase.

"If that's a tip, I hope you're going to share it with me," Imad says the first few times.

Muneer wonders if Imad knows the envelopes contain something personal. They never talk about the contents, though sometimes Muneer thinks he would like to. Imad is a good guy. He shaves his face clean, unlike most of the other men Muneer knows, and keeps a fountain pen and a Bic in the chest pocket of his thawb, a pack of cigarettes in his deep side pocket. He speaks English, French, Spanish, and, as more guest workers arrive in Jidda over the years, picks up a little Urdu, Bengali, Tagalog. Sometimes Muneer thinks he catches a whiff of alcohol on Imad's breath, but he's never sure. Regardless, Imad talks to people easily, as a reporter should, while Muneer must bolster himself whenever he picks up his reporter's notebook.

At first, Muneer is jealous that the PI, a man he's never met, is doing the searching he daydreams about. He's ashamed to delegate this duty and not pay for it. Months later, he is angry: Hanadi's been gone for more than a year. The daughter in his memory and in the few photos of her he possesses stays four, while Hanadi, he knows, is growing older, taller, more out of reach.

Two years pass. Three years. Muneer waits and waits for real news, true news of his daughter. He would like to shrink, limit himself to his mother's two-bedroom apartment; his desk at *Akhbar al-'Urus*; and the fifteen-minute drive between home and work, past the green neon shop fronts of Tahliyah Street. Instead, in these early years of the separation, he wraps himself in other people's stories.

Assigned to cover the mayor of Jidda and the growth of the city, he files stories on high-rise apartments going up, the city's first department store, first shopping mall, first Safeway, first pizza parlor, first hamburger shop, first Henry Moore sculpture on the Corniche, first hotel buffet, first cappuccino.

Ikea, McDonald's, and Coca-Cola are years away.

He haunts the Old City, the gold souk, the perfume souk, the miswak vendors, the new discount souk with concrete stalls and no soul. He writes about a historic rainstorm that doesn't let up for half a day. The city floods, and *al-Sharqiyah* respectfully calls for King Khalid to remove the mayor. He simply covers the damage, naming no names.

"We're the new paper on the block. I don't trust our royal patron to cover our butts," Imad tells Muneer, using English idioms, while they're driving to grab lunch one day. In the car, he can say what he can't say in the newsroom, where they know there are probably spies and bugs. Imad switches to Arabic for a more heartfelt sentiment: "God is the Protector. I need this paper to survive."

So does Muneer. It is his life's dream to uncover the truth. Digging up half-truths is better than nothing.

Finding Hanadi matters more than anything. He dreams of a child who looks nothing like his memories of her, and yet he knows her to be his daughter. There is so much he no longer knows: How tall is she? How deep is her one dimple? She was learning her English letters when he last saw her. What books is she reading? How long is her hair? What phrases does she fall back on over and over? Where is she? What will it take to get her back?

He needs *Akhbar al-'Urus* to survive, and he needs Fareed to survive, too, to continue to be able to pay for the PI's search for their daughters.

Four years pass. Everyone but his mother stops urging him to marry.

In 1979, when terrorists lay siege to the Holy Ka'bah, no one, Fareed included, has the balls or the permission to run it in his paper. The secret police personally visit the kingdom's newspaper editors, telling them to keep it hushed until the government says so. As though no one listens to BBC Arabic. Imad never announces it to the staff, but the reporters gossip, and they know the newspaper editors of Makkah and Jidda are the ones who have leaked the news to the BBC and the foreign wire services. Muneer is happy to be a reporter, a lesser person who doesn't have to make such a tough call.

He makes a handful of trips to the United States over the years. Near the fifth anniversary of the disappearance—Hanadi's tenth birthday—Muneer's younger brother Tariq, newly at work for the airlines, helps him buy a discounted ticket. It is thin, wispy, but it feels like a million dollars in his hand. Muneer walks onto the plane in his thawb. A pair of khaki pants and a button-down shirt are carefully folded in his carry-on. Midflight, he washes up in the tiny lavatory, lifting his foot up and into the sink with his hand. He prays in his seat, though others pray in the aisles. The layover in Frankfurt is purgatory, but when he lands at JFK, he feels more hopefulness than he's felt since Hanadi's birth.

A few weeks ago, a friend of Jameel's younger brother Rami saw Saeedah and Hanadi in San Francisco. The friend-of-a-friend tip for once corresponds with something the PI sent: photos of a North Bay bungalow half hidden behind bougainvillea.

On the drive from the airport in Rami's tan Chevy, there are yellow ribbons on trees and lampposts. On the radio, there is talk of Iran. Rami likes the oldies station. Elvis croons, *I can't help. . . .* Muneer remembers the days of the oil embargo, how he'd hear the word *A-rab* floating in the air—at the grocery store, in the library, at the gas station and the playground—and wish he could shrink inside his clothes or hide behind a wool scarf.

"Americans don't know the difference between Iranians and Arabs," Rami says. "We've been keeping a low profile. But we don't feel safe on campus."

No one would bother a little girl? Would they?

At a red light, Rami maneuvers the slip of paper bearing the bungalow's address out of his back pocket. He hands the address to Muneer, who locates it on the road atlas with his finger. With the windows rolled down, the wind musses the pages. He holds the book open with two hands. The air smells something like licorice. Rami drives with one hand on the wheel, the other arm resting on the open window.

The whole scene is too relaxing, Muneer thinks, too much like a road trip and not enough like a mission. He thinks, *Inshallah, inshallah, inshallah,* but something tells him before they arrive that there will be no cars in the driveway, the lawn will be overgrown, the house empty.

BENEATH THE MOTHERS' FEET

Nearly ten years have passed without Hanadi when Imad hires two women to copy edit the paper. They have their own entrance through the back and their own office with two desks face-to-face, but they share the men's assistant, who distributes morning tea and daily copies of *al-Sharqiyah, al-Ahram, Asharq al-Awsat,* and Jidda's two English papers. Imad insists the women attend editorial meetings, and they choose to stand on the perimeter of the men's space, taking notes. The men joke among themselves that Azizah must constantly chew luban gum; they hear the occasional smack of it under her molars at staff meetings. Her red pen is fierce, but her bangs are artfully arranged and curled onto her forehead, her scarf wrapped loosely. Lamees, on the other hand, has a smoker's voice, but seems too pious to have ever lit a cigarette. Her edits are friendlier than Azizah's, filled with queries, yet her headscarf is sharply creased down the middle and tightly wound, letting not a wisp of hair out of its grasp. The scarf's dark outline accentuates her round cheeks and high forehead, the deep brown of her eyes.

The assistant, Jacob, is a smart-dressed Filipino man who, back in Manila, was a newspaper reporter for ten years. Imad recruited him to help start an English-language paper, but it failed after six months. Jacob, who reads enough Arabic to understand headlines, ferries pages between the women and the men. He can't jump ship to one of the two English-language newspapers that remain in the city because Imad holds his passport, as employers must do for foreign employees.

Jacob laughs in the Saudi men's faces as he hands them their marked-up copy.

"You can't be alone with your women, but my countrymen and I can. You don't think we're men like you?"

"This is our culture," Imad says. There is a shrug in the men's voices when they talk about the way things are: between men and women, Saudis and expats, Muslims and Christians, royals and everyone else.

"What would the women say to that?" Jacob says.

"We'll ask them," Imad says. And so the women's weekly column, "Daughters of Saudi," is born.

They write about too-lavish weddings and Saudi men's marriages to foreigners and non-Muslims, about Saudi mothers' overreliance on Filipina nannies, and the significance of Laylat al-Qadr. The one thing Imad tells them not to write about is the driving issue.

"People aren't ready for that debate."

"We weren't going to suggest it," Azizah says.

Muneer tries to guess which of the women the opinions belong to. He wishes he had a way to speak to Lamees, but she isn't forward like Saeedah was, so he keeps his eyes down and his tongue quiet on the rare occasions they cross paths on the way to their cars.

One late evening in the parking lot, she calls to him.

"Sayyidi Muneer, I heard you're leaving for a bit."

The moon is a pearl in an ocean of sky and the air is cool enough for a blazer over his thawb. He shivers a little. She appears to be in her late twenties, older than most unmarried women.

"Yes. Personal business in America." The PI's envelopes stopped coming four or five years ago. Clearly, Fareed thought the search had become hopeless. But Muneer will never give up; he saves up for one or two trips a year.

"You went to college there," Lamees says. "Godspeed."

"Would you like something from there?"

"No, no. You'll be too busy."

The urge to tell her the truth pushes him a step toward her. She jumps a little in surprise, smiles to cover up the awkwardness. Her driver is waiting for her. She disappears into her car.

That night, Muneer calls his latest informant in the United States from the phone in his bedroom. He tries to whisper, though Mama isn't home. She eavesdrops on him sometimes, presses her ear noisily against the door, as though she wants him to know she's listening.

"And the girl was wearing what? . . . How many times did you see her? . . . And the mother?"

He hears hope in his own voice. Yet he doesn't believe in hope anymore, God forgive him. The phone calls come in strings, and always the story is the same: a friend of a friend has seen Saeedah and Hanadi—or so they think. When he can afford to go, he goes. When he can't, guilt wakes him up at night.

He changes into a white T-shirt and a green waistcloth. The front door slams, and he hears puttering sounds: Mama taking her shoes off, Mama putting her abayah in the hall wardrobe. He opens the door, and, yes, there is Mama.

"You look like a Yemeni gateman," she says.

He rubs his face, runs a hand through the triangle of hair on his head. She tells him the skin under his eyes is dark and he looks weary.

"What do you want, old lady of mine?"

He calls her old as an endearment, but today he can tell it bothers her by the way she strings her fingers together and squeezes, a sign of annoyance from a woman whose face remains ever tranquil.

"Who were you talking to?"

"No one, old lady."

He kisses her on the forehead and slips into the bathroom. He senses she wants to fix whatever has gotten into him, the jinni that eats at him from inside.

When Muneer returns from his latest failed trip, there is a wedding invitation from his mother's cousin Lama in the post office box. He opens the envelope with a fingernail and reads to Mama from the pink and gold card without a hint of jealousy in his voice.

She has not stopped encouraging him to get married, but according to her he has been picky—no girl in Jidda has pleased him. Four—was it five?—years ago, she reminds him, there was an engagement to his father's sister's daughter. He phoned Mama from America to tell her to call it off. She did as he asked, but he suspected her anger boiled in her belly like coffee brewed in a metal pot. When he came home again, she had gathered his brothers, who told him, "You can't wait till you find Hanadi before you marry again. God willing, you'll be blessed with other children. Please do this for your mother's sake."

He never listened.

He laughs. "I thought marriage was for my sake. What about this invitation? Will you go four hours to Madinah for a wedding?"

He's a young man, but she tells him often that he is growing older than his years in front of her: his eyes sinking into his face like seeds in bread, his mouth collapsing, his cheeks drawing in between his teeth. He laughs her worries off.

"I can't possibly look as old as you say I do."

But she insists: Of her seven children, he is the one she stays up at night worrying about. Him, and the missing piece of him, Hanadi, she says.

No matter how often he tells her to stop this litany, she never does.

"I might go," she says, returning to the topic of the wedding. He sees on her face that an idea has come to her, and she clings to it, like Umm Kulthum clutching her famous handkerchief. If he will not marry any of their friends' or relations' daughters in Jidda, she will seek suitable girls elsewhere. Why didn't God give her the idea sooner? she says. There will be many girls at the wedding.

"That's not necessary, Mama," he says. "But go to the wedding if you want to."

The next day, while Muneer works at the newspaper office, Mama has their maid, Sara, find the little red address book filled with relatives' phone numbers. Sara is Indonesian and reads enough Arabic to look up the number and dial it. Mama herself is as illiterate as the Prophet.

When Muneer comes home for lunch, she tells him about the conversation with Lama.

"I had to make sure that awful person"—her sister Faizah—"will not be there."

"Will she, Mama?" He eats her green bean stew with a piece of bread.

"No. Lama told me, 'Darling Haleemah. I promise, we understand the situation. You're my favorite cousin. Who else from Jidda would I want to be at my daughter's wedding?'"

Mama appreciates that her cousin sees things her way. And if her sister *were* invited, Mama is certain Faizah would not make the trip to al-Madinah, where their relatives refuse to allow musical instruments at weddings—no lute, no dancing, no "Ya Layla Dana," no stereo, no songs by Amr Diab or Ragheb Alama. Only drumming and human voices, songs about God and the Prophet. Nothing about love, about eyes like a gazelle's, about longing for the stars.

"You should stop talking, old lady, and eat. God bless your hands that made this food."

"'Who has time for such boring people and their boring weddings?' Faizah would say."

Mama keeps going: *She* will attend her cousin's daughter's wedding because her son needs a pious, old-fashioned girl. Yes, let Muneer's bride be one of those women who wears a coat instead of an abayah, who covers her hair in front of other women. Let her raise daughters who cover their faces when they go out and never listen to music. The more religious, the better.

"Mama, be patient. God rewards the patient."

But Muneer is the one who must be patient, as Mama rails about her sister, a familiar monologue she trots out to prove to him that Hanadi's disappearance has affected her as much as it has him.

He listens because, as the Prophet said, "Paradise is beneath the mothers' feet."

Mama and Faizah haven't spoken in nearly ten years, and Mama can't banish the idea that her sister knows where Hanadi is and won't tell. Muneer has never told her about the private investigator.

In the beginning, Auntie Faizah swore to God three times that she had no idea where they were. Mama had tried to believe her—what a sin to think her sister would swear to God on a lie!—but one weekend soon after, as she was about to join a gathering at their younger sister Fahmah's apartment, she saw Faizah's black sandals on the mat outside. The sight of those shoes, of the imprints Faizah's toes had made in the insoles, caused hatred to possess Mama like a fever. The way to exorcise it was to never come within a centimeter of Faizah ever again, she has told him time and again. She didn't set foot in Fahmah's place that night, and everyone—Faizah included—knows she will not enter a room Faizah's perfume has wafted into.

At first, Muneer's grandmother tried to persuade Mama to talk to her sister Faizah. "You're both from my womb. You want me to die of sorrow because my daughters won't speak? It's not your sister who did this thing to you."

Mama refused to back down.

Tonight, Muneer lets her talk. One topic winds into the next. She is annoyed because he can't take her to the dressmaker. The wedding is in a week, but Muneer's mother insists there's time for a new dress to be made with the gray silk she bought a few months ago. Bandar's wife employs two Filipina seamstresses in an annex behind his villa. Muneer reminds her he will be in America, but he'll be back in time to take her to al-Madinah for the wedding. She pouts.

"Can't Bandar send you his driver?" he says.

She sighs and begins clearing the food, though Muneer hasn't finished eating. "My granddaughter, surrounded by kaffirs—to think of it makes my head throb. I pray to God you find her on this next trip."

"Maybe you should take a Tylenol or read Surat al-Fatihah," Muneer says. He separates a cinnamon stick from a green bean and mixes more sauce into his rice.

Mama sets a dish down and removes her glasses. She rubs her eyes, her temples.

"I should lie down. People say I should have found you a bride years ago. I pray for you every day. I've prayed for you at the Haram in Makkah, asked God to guide you. I've prayed for you at the Prophet's Mosque in al-Madinah. I've prayed for your daughter, and I've prayed for her mother. What more can we do? God will lead you to a bride."

He doesn't want to tell her he already has a bride in mind.

MADINAH WEDDING

The morning of the wedding Muneer has returned from another useless trip. When he wakes up, Mama has already zipped her gray silk dress into a garment bag, packed a blue tweed suitcase, braided and wound her hair in the back, and put on a black-and-white cotton dress with a high neck and long sleeves. She has already had Sara set out olives and cheese and bread and cream on a floor-cloth in the living room. She is not hungry, she tells Muneer. She is thinking about God's plan. But Muneer should eat.

On their way to the car, parked on the street outside, Mama adjusts her black scarf with one hand. He tries to help her into the car, but she pushes him. She lifts the door handle with two fingers and maneuvers herself into the front seat, pulling her cane in behind her and settling it next to her.

The air is hotter in the car than it is on the street. Muneer rolls down the windows and braces himself for hours of Mama's talk. With one hand, he steers through the neighborhood, its streets lined with apartment buildings with marble façades, tinted-glass doors, and barely used balconies.

She puts her hands on the dashboard and says, "God knows best, but maybe you should stop going to America. Maybe you should live your life here. A man needs a companion. A man needs children."

Muneer's mind wanders for an instant. He sees an empty bedroom, the tiny sneakers and cardigans and T-shirts left behind in the closet. He sees his daughter's face in black and white.

"God save you, don't drive so fast," Mama says.

"You have other sons. Let one of them drive you."

"Say a prayer for the Prophet," she says. "Calm yourself."

He breathes in, but he doesn't slow the car. Air whips past and into the window, blowing his ghutrah about. Her tightly wrapped scarf barely ripples.

The sky beyond their neighborhood is high and blanched pale as an almond. Palm trees and streetlights line the highway, keeping watch over it, separating them from the desert. As they leave the city, they pass a large sculpture of an open Qur'an and Mama begins to quietly pray. Muneer can't hear the words, but he imagines she is saying, *God save Hanadi from the unbelievers. God bless my son with a wife, children.*

Mama sifts through her big white purse. She hands a cassette to Muneer and he clicks it into the player. He rolls up the windows and turns on the AC.

Surat Yusuf begins. It is the story of a man who loses his child. The boy Yusuf abandoned in a well, rescued by strangers, raised far from family. The father, Ya'qub, gone blind with grief, thinking his son killed by a wolf.

Muneer stops the tape, clicks it out of the player, brings it up against the steering wheel, and stares at it. He flips it over and slips it back into the tape player. Another surah begins.

"Why did you change it?"

"Calm down, Mama."

"I'm calm." She stabs the dashboard with her fingers, but she doesn't know what button to push. "Stop it, stop the tape."

Muneer slides the cassette out and deposits it in Mama's purse. She turns to the window. They have left the city, with its ful mudammas and rotisserie shops, its marble façade apartment buildings and neon lights, its grassy boulevard dividers that smell of the sewer water used for irrigation. When Muneer was a boy, the city smelled more like the sea. Here on the outskirts, he imagines he could smell the clean sand of the wilderness. The road seems to cut directly into the desert, barely making a dent in its vastness. Sand has crept onto the shoulders. Road signs provide the only color; cars are the color of dust.

The plain gives way to mountains, low and brown, like the desert has pulled itself up to the sky.

Soon Mama falls asleep, slumped against the window. Muneer drives. Baboons sit on the low stone wall along the roadway. The monkeys are lined up, the babies on their mother's backs, watching.

The car comes into a valley, the next set of hills shades of brown and gray, hulking shadows against the sky. Muneer pulls over and gets out of the car before Mama can wake up and ask why he's stopping. At the side of the road, a man in a turban is selling cucumbers, laid out on an overturned wooden crate. The man sits on a large green cooler. He has a face like a dried date. At his age, he should have his sons out in the sun, selling for him.

Muneer buys yogurt in a plastic bag.

"How are we going to keep that?" Mama says when he returns to the car and heads off again.

"We can eat it," he says. But there's no spoon, and by the time they reach the hotel, the yogurt will be drippy and warm and clotty. This is what makes her worry about Muneer, she says, his impracticality.

He's regretting driving her. "You're worried because I bought yogurt, Mama?"

There's a sound like something is rattling up along the side of the car and inside where the wheel is, followed by a loud pop. The car lurches. Mama grabs the dashboard. Muneer veers onto the side of the road and gets out without a word. More monkeys appear. As Muneer prepares to change the tire, they watch, scratching their ears, sinking their sharp teeth into bananas someone must have tossed to them, and swallowing in a businesslike manner, picking at each other's fuzzy heads.

Mama taps the window and waves at them.

"Shoo. Shoo."

With the AC off, the car heats up. Mama fans herself with a tissue box.

Muneer takes off his ghutrah, iqal, and kufiyyah, and rolls his sleeves up. He gets the spare tire and jack out of the back.

"You have to get out, Mama," he says.

She doesn't want to stand by the side of the road, so he brings her a suitcase to sit on. She fans herself with the box, stops to pull a tissue out and wipe her forehead. Cars pass so close she can feel the hot air on her face. She flips the edge of her scarf across her face; through the cloth, she keeps her eyes on the monkeys. They make her nervous with their sharp teeth and big yawns. The monkeys gaze at her, wagging their chins and cheeping disapprovingly, as though they are telling her to climb back in the car.

When Mama and Muneer arrive in al-Madinah, the Asr call to prayer is sounding. They pass near the Prophet's Mosque. The green dome looks like something a child might paint. She remembers once that Saeedah got lost at the mosque—that child was always getting lost. Faizah found her at the prophet's grave, praying with worry beads she claimed to have found lying on the ground. Mama tells Muneer the story as they inch along in traffic.

"I always knew she stole those beads."

"I don't want to hear about her, Mama," he says. "I'm tired."

"That girl was trouble, I always thought so. She wasn't praying. She was pretending so her mother wouldn't spank her in front of the world. You never should have married her."

"You never objected."

"I did, I did object. I said marrying a cousin is a bad idea. I said find a girl with good manners."

"You must have said that to someone else."

They sit idling at a red light. He can tell she's offended by his comment from the way her silence sits between them, but she quickly becomes distracted by a little girl approaching on the median. The girl wears a headscarf gray with dirt and a long dress with ruffles at the wrists, a flounce at the hem. She doesn't smile; beggar children never do. She starts to wipe the windshield with a brownish rag. Muneer waves—"Go on, go on"—but she keeps wiping as though the car belongs to her.

That child could be Hanadi, Mama says. The girl's chin is dimpled, the little bulblike tip of her nose is sprinkled with perfectly formed droplets of sweat. The dark brown birthmark on her forehead looks soft as felt. Mama convinces herself that Hanadi had such a birthmark, though Muneer swears otherwise and reminds her that Hanadi is fifteen, much older than this girl.

Mama doesn't listen. She lowers her window and sticks her hand out with a riyal.

"What's your name?"

"Come on, Mama. The light will change any second."

The girl stares at the ground and reaches for the bill. Mama tugs it gently for a second, as though she could keep the little girl from going too quickly. But the girl wants the bill, and she takes it, leaving Mama empty-handed.

"God protect you, Miss," the girl says, moving to the next car.

The light changes to green, and they leave the girl and her median and the Prophet's Mosque behind.

The hotel is hidden by fig trees and bougainvillea bushes, pink flowers flaming. Muneer drives back and forth several times before he finds the gate into the parking lot, which is quiet and nearly empty, shaded by hills.

"We're not late," Muneer says. "We're early."

"You drove too fast."

In the hotel room, before showering, Muneer eats the warm yogurt with a spoon room service delivers. He swears the stuff is delicious. They pray, nap, pray again. Mama puts on her gray dress, oils her hair and braids it again, coiling it the way it was before. She applies sandalwood essence behind her ears. She pulls the kohl rod swiftly over her closed eyelids. She calls Muneer's sister Aaliyah. "Your brother drives too fast," she says.

He looks up from fastening the collar of his thawb with studs. "Old lady, I can hear you. What are you talking about?"

"Not a thing."

She says goodbye to Aaliyah and puts her scarf on, drapes her abayah over top of her head. She sits on her bed while Muneer drapes his mishlah over his shoulders. He goes to the mirror to carefully lay a clean ghutrah and his iqal on his head. Perfectly adjusting the crease of the starched fabric at the crest of his forehead takes him a few minutes.

"Let me help you," his mother says. "The girl should have used more starch."

"Don't blame it on poor Sara," he says. "What does she know about ironing ghutrahs?"

The wedding hall is set apart from the hotel, on the other side of the parking lot. Cars have arrived. The white lights strung across the building switch on as they approach, and the place transforms from a plain box into a neck with a woven necklace of pearls.

He leaves her at the door of the hall and kisses her on the cheek before heading back to the hotel, where the men's gathering is being held.

Later, Mama tells Muneer everything: How the hall was bright white, high ceilinged, full of women she didn't recognize. How she wished she'd brought Aaliyah or one of her other daughters. Sitting down at a table in the far corner of the room, she tried to smooth the creases in her gray silk dress, but they obstinately stay put.

In her white satin purse were photos of him. She scanned the room for girls of appropriate age and family.

At a Jidda wedding, young women would have cinched scarves around their hips; they would have danced Egyptian-style with one leg poised outward, or flipped their long hair side to side. Here, the girls sat demurely at the round tables, their purses set in front of them, chewing on mints and pieces of allspice they'd plucked out of the bowls on the tables. Mama set herself down at a table where two girls, one in a dress the color of the bougainvillea flowers outside and the other in peach and green, took turns whispering to each other.

"They were too made up," she says.

As she inspected the guests, Mama took several mints and cupped them in her hand, closing her fingers over them and slipping them into her purse. A woman in green sequins and bright blue pumps grabbed her by the shoulders and kissed her cheeks. Lama's sister Lena.

Mama shows Muneer where Lena's lipstick rubbed off on her skin.

"God bless you for coming. You are the only one from Jidda who has blessed us," Lena said.

"Oh, of course my dear, it's nothing. Where is your sister?"

"At the hotel, getting the bride ready. God bless you for coming." A little bit of the lipstick had come off on Lena's front tooth. She kept licking it but her tongue didn't budge it. She moved on to the next guest, repeating her kissing performance and her lipstick-fixing.

On the stage, women in white were singing songs about the prophet and beating drums. Mama sat for a few minutes, but her legs wanted to move. She floated around the room, among the tables, leaning from time to time on her cane, staring openly at the young women. A few stared back.

"Which family are you?" Mama asked, and if she liked the answer, "Who's your father?"

She set her sights on two young women holding hands, their hair curled into ringlets and held back with garlands of white flowers, gardenias Mama could smell three tables over. Their fingernails were unpainted, their faces fresh, with a hint of rouge, no lipstick or mascara or eye shadow. Their modest satin dresses fell to their ankles. Was it the bougainvillea outside or the gardenia in the girls' hair that caused Mama's nose to itch, her eyes to water? She instantly knew she'd found perfect brides-to-be, the way she knows how much rose water to put in syrup, how much spice lamb soup needs. Mama could see they were pious, modest girls, suitable for Muneer.

Mama does not believe, as some people do, that girls should not wear makeup until their wedding days, or that listening to music will send you to hell, where hot lead will drip into your ears. Her own father, she tells Muneer, was a music lover who kept a horse-hair violin in a red velvet–lined case. But Muneer's divorce was a disaster, a catastrophe, and she blames herself. She isn't going to let that happen again. He needs a girl who won't make trouble or gossip too much, will not smoke shisha, will be devoted to her husband and family, covers her face and does not mix with other men—not brothers-in-law, even with her scarf on—and prefers listening to the Qur'an over listening to music.

This is the kind of girl Mama was looking for at the Madinah wedding.

Either of these girls would do.

"Who are those girls?" she asked a woman sipping orange soda at the next table.

The girls were first cousins from a well-known Madinah family, the woman said. The father of one owned a date factory on the outskirts of the holy city.

Midnight had slid by. The drums were *dun-dun*-ing and women were trilling for the entrance of the bride, who wore a beaded white dress with puffy lace sleeves. Her bangs were curled and teased, her lipstick orange-red. She followed an entourage of women and little girls carrying ribbon-wrapped candles that dripped wax on their delicate hands.

Mama sat. The two suitable girls were two tables over. One tapped her foot in time with the drumbeat. The other sipped coffee. The girls removed pink and white candy-covered almonds from little mesh bags tied with ribbons, popping the candies in their mouths and snapping the clasps of their purses in time with their chewing.

The trilling in the room rose to a crescendo, and Mama's temples throbbed. The bride arrived at the stage, her closest family members gathered round her as she sat, stiff as a doll in a gold-and-white armchair, for everyone to gaze upon.

Mama spat the clove she had been chewing into an empty coffee cup and moved to the girls' table. The candied almonds had sweetened the girls' breath. The young ladies smelled like sugar.

"Is your mother here?" Mama said.

"No, Auntie," said the foot-tapping girl.

"Over there," said the other. She pointed her little porcelain cup, embellished with delicate roses and a gold rim, toward a woman in a golden dress at another table.

"You're like twins," Mama said. "Neither of you is married?"

The mother of the one girl gamboled over. She had a big gap between her upper front teeth, deep pink lipstick, and silver eye shadow. To Mama's chagrin, she knew this woman. Karamah was a grade-school friend of Faizah's who married a man from al-Madinah and moved here years ago. She kissed Mama on the cheeks, back and forth several times.

"Haleemah! How are you? How is your family? God has blessed me with seeing you!"

Mama shows Muneer the second stain on her skin, this one from Karamah.

"Your daughter—how old is she?" Mama asked.

"Seventeen. Graduating from high school this year."

Mama said her son was thirty-two.

"That's not how old I am, Mama," Muneer tells her.

"Oh?" she says. "I confuse you and your brothers sometimes."

Mama wondered if Karamah had heard about her feud with Faizah, but the woman seemed open, friendly.

"Can we meet your daughter?" Mama said.

"Ah. Yes of course. We can welcome you tomorrow afternoon."

The girl was whispering something to her friend.

Muneer stops Mama's story. "She's too young."

"That is not the end of it," Mama says. "Something else happened tonight."

She goes on: Karamah squealed. Confused, Mama touched the corner of her own lips, rubbed her lips against her teeth. Was something the matter with how she looked? But it was a squeal of delight. For what?

"Your sister! Shall we greet her?"

Faizah. Mama's heart flattened. Her limbs moved as though stirring thick syrup. Karamah rushed to the far side of the hall and embraced Faizah. Muneer's aunt wore a sequined peach dress, Bahraini freshwater pearls at her throat, large gold earrings that nearly reached her shoulders, high-heeled shoes that matched her dress.

"She looked so tacky! So badawi!" Mama tells Muneer.

Mama, in her plain silk, made her way to Lena. Mama took a deep breath and said a quick prayer before speaking. "I thought my sister was not invited."

"God protect you. I hope we haven't offended you."

Before Mama could say anything further, Lena caught the arm of a woman she apparently hadn't greeted yet and left Mama behind.

Mama didn't want to leave until they fed her. But she guessed the food wouldn't be ready for at least an hour. Her belly tight with hunger, she opened a mesh pouch and chose a smooth silver almond. It tasted like nothing until the sweet coating began to dissolve in her mouth. She bit, and pain shot through her gum. She heard the crack of her tooth and grabbed her jaw. No one noticed her wincing, though her face felt transformed by the pain. Her sister and Karamah sat at a table in the far corner of the hall. What were they talking about?

She found herself caught in her sister's gaze.

Faizah's eyes were hard as date pits. Mama looked away, as quickly as she might jerk her hand from the sting of a jellyfish. She brought her eyes to the bride sitting alone on the kosha platform. The pain in her mouth became too much. Clutching her jaw, she left quickly so she wouldn't have to speak to anyone on her way out. She was barely able to tell the doorman to fetch Muneer. As she waited at the door in her abayah and tarhah, Faizah came toward her carrying her purse.

"So rude of me not to say hello," Faizah said, moving in to kiss Mama. "You're leaving already?"

Mama had to kiss back and accept her purse from this sister she hated.

"Aren't you going to thank me?"

"My tooth." Mama moved her jaw as minutely as possible as she said the words.

The doorman called Mama's name, and she slipped outside to where Muneer waited to walk her to the hotel room.

She tells him everything later, after he's rushed her to the emergency room and they're back in Jidda, having missed the appointment to meet the young bride-to-be.

She's angry at how everything has turned out, though she knows it's God's will.

"It was rude not to go. I told the mother we would come."

"Mama, you were in pain. It's good we came back so Jameel could fix your tooth. That girl was too young for me."

The words gush out of him like Zamzam water from the spring in Makkah. He wants someone who will understand heartbreak, sorrow. Not a callow adolescent girl. Sadness springs forth with his words, and he feels like Hagar trying to stop the water from coming as she carries her infant son Ishmael between two desert mountains: "Zam! Zam! Stop! Stop!"

The water was a blessing for Hagar, of course, and no one but God can end our sadness.

"We rely on God," Mama says. "Pray to him."

"There's a woman at the newspaper, a female journalist."

"You chose a bride for love last time," she says weakly. "Why would you do that again?"

TOLEDO

1975

From Cedar Point, we drove an hour to Toledo, where we stayed in the spare bedroom of Weronika, your friend from English as a Second Language classes. W, she liked to be called. Her thick Eastern European accent made her sound like she was gargling some delicious, thick liquid—chocolate syrup or caramel sauce. Her cluttered house had light blue walls and deep blue shag in most rooms, including the bathrooms. She had bought the house that way, she told us, and she would sit in one of her green-and-peach wing chairs, her feet resting on a stack of magazines on the marble coffee table, and say, "I work hard. I don't have time to change anything."

There were two rooms that didn't make me feel like I was underwater: First, the oak-cabinet kitchen with an antique white stove, checkerboard-tile floor, and a breakfast nook with white café curtains that left the top of the windows bare and streaming with light. Second, the wood-paneled basement with a wet bar, a red vinyl barber's chair inherited from the previous owners, a lumpy sofa whose arms and back had been shredded by W's cat, and rows of paperback sci-fi novels in a built-in bookshelf along the far end. The whole house smelled of cough lozenges, raisins, and cigarette smoke. W, who in my child's mind was ancient but was thirty-five years old, always seemed to be hacking up a lung, leaving wadded-up tissues and full ashtrays around the house.

When W was at work the first day of our stay, you put on a pair of hot-pink dish gloves you found under the sink and traversed the apartment with a wastebasket tucked into the curve of your arm, plucking trash from the carpet and coffee table with two gloved fingers. I followed you around, bumping into you whenever you paused to stoop and reach for something. You put your pink-gloved fingers around my waist and set me on the arm of the living room sofa.

I slid off and leaned against the arm. "Why do we have to stay here, Mama?"

"Few weeks," you told me. You went into the kitchen, removed the gloves, and pulled things out of the refrigerator: a tomato, half an onion wrapped in cellophane, three eggs.

"Can we go home after the weeks, Mama?"

"Maybe," you said. "Sure."

I flopped on the floor crying, and you tripped over me on your way to the counter, landing on your knees, the food clutched to your chest, the eggs miraculously intact between your fingers.

"No crying. I didn't say no." You lifted yourself without using your hands, your eyes closed, like you couldn't look at me. When I didn't stop, your voice rose. "Stop crying, OK? You want lunch or no?"

I nodded, cowed, my heart in my knees, and climbed onto a chair to watch while you chopped an onion. You spread the onion along the bottom of a cast-iron pan coated with hot, shiny, smoking olive oil. While the onion sizzled and its fumes burned my eyes, you peeled a tomato with the point of a paring knife and squeezed the seeds out between your fingers, like you were squeezing a washcloth. You chopped the tomato with quick flicks of your wrist and tossed it into the pan. The phone rang and you ignored it. Steam rose. You reached your hand into it to break three eggs into the pan and stir them with a fork. We ate the eggs in folded English muffins, like tacos.

I liked watching you cook and eating with you. In the heat of the kitchen, tendrils of black hair curled off your face. You seemed certain when you were making a meal for me, no matter how simple—and the meals were always simple: open-faced cream cheese sandwiches softened under the broiler, long strips of hamburger fried in a pan and served with mint and yogurt, rice tossed with chickpeas.

When we weren't tossing out snotty tissues and cigarette ash or making a meal or a snack or afternoon tea, we watched the ten-inch black-and-white TV in the basement, where the reception was terrible. We never left the house. No preschool, no walks, no trips to the grocery store. If I wanted to pretend I was playing outside, I'd skip around the coffee table in the living room, humming that jump-rope song: "My mama and your mama were out hanging clothes/My mama punched your mama . . ." *Except I thought it was "hugging clothes" and "jumped your mama," and there was no one to correct me.*

The living room had a bay window filled with plants, a little jungle. There were ferns and creeping things with heart-shaped leaves, a ficus pruned like a huge green lollipop, orchids with petals like candy hearts, velvet-leafed African violets, a shock of gangly mint. The plants were in fake terra-cotta pots that were cracked on the sides and crammed close together, some of them half stacked on each other. Renegade clovers grew along the edges of the pots. W's marmalade cat, Poppy, slept in the one narrow space left on the floor.

You fought with W about the blue damask drapes that hung ceiling to floor. You wanted them closed. She wanted them open. She left for the hospital intensive-care unit before we woke up, and when we went upstairs for breakfast, we would find the curtains open. You made me sit at the kitchen table, out of sight, while you swiftly drew the drapes closed and flicked on the lamps. The yellow light turned the carpet greenish.

In the afternoon, I would sit in the swivel chair closest to the front door, waiting for W to arrive in her white cardigan and slacks and white leather shoes with piping around the edges. She would clink the metal mail slot cover on the front door, and I'd run over to see her face through the slot. I'd run back to the chair before you could drag me from the door. W would tramp inside, stomp the snow off her boots and tug them off, lay her cardigan in my lap, walk straight to the window, and tug the pulley.

W told me to turn the lamps off while she bent down and caressed the leaves of her plants as though they were kitten ears. "Look," she said. "They're reaching for the sunlight your mother deprived them of."

I sidled past the plants and displaced Poppy, who hopped up, licked a paw, and slinked off. I scooted as close to the glass as I could, catching a glimpse of a twist of coral-colored light illuminating the rain-beaded branches of a maple tree like a giant candelabra.

"Come from there, Hanadi."

I crawled to the swivel chair and rested my elbows on the seat. You picked up the white cardigan from the floor where it had fallen, folded it, and laid it on the chair back.

After several days of this, W put her hand on my shoulder. Like she was claiming me for her kickball team. "Who's gonna be outside to see?" She started to cough.

"You know," you said.

You were everything to me. I wanted to be on your team. But I also wanted to go outside, and I sided with W.

"Who's gonna see?" I said.

Behind your back, W smiled and clapped her fingers together, like she'd won a prize. I felt like I'd won one, too.

You won the battle, though. You sidled along the wall to the edge of the window, like a spy staying out of view, and pulled the drapes closed, arm over arm. W winked and shook her head to the shoulder on either side. I understood her message: arguing wasn't worth it.

On W's days off, she tried to convince you that we should go to the mall with her, or the grocery store, or the movies. You said no, so she went by herself and I yearned to be with her.

I felt drawn to the window. One day, while W was at work and you watched The Price Is Right, I sat among the plants and carefully snapped their leaves off at the base. I stacked the leaves like blocks, unstacked them, spread them around on the carpet, and set them one next to the other, making a pathway toward the window. I moved plants out of the way, and the path led to the middle where the curtains parted. I poked my fingers between the drapes and stood like a statue, not actually looking. When I heard you coming upstairs to go to the kitchen, I plopped on the floor with my back to the window.

You leaned against the doorway between the living room and kitchen, a glass of water in your hand.

"What are you doing?" you said.

"I don't know."

"Come from the window."

I inched forward. "The curtain's closed, Mama."

"I don't care." You leaned back into the kitchen to set the glass on the counter, readied yourself to step toward me and force me to move.

"Why?"

I didn't know why I wasn't supposed to sit there, not exactly. I imagined someone outside, spying on us, a monster with many eyes and hands and legs. And your voice, stretched almost to anger, brought me to my feet. I took a few steps, halfway toward you.

"Better. Put these plants back, and make sure you stay out of the window."

You got your glass and disappeared into the basement. I went back to my leaf path and made car noises for a while. When I went downstairs to see what you were doing, I took my time, sitting on the stairs and bumping down them one by one. At the third-to-last step, I stood up, swung my arms, and jumped, landing as loudly as I could so you'd notice my arrival. You didn't. When I thudded onto the basement floor, you were cradling W's phone to your ear, your free hand pressed against your forehead, your eyes closed. You sat with your feet flat on the couch cushion, knees up under your chin, fingers twisted in the yellow phone cord. You were the opposite of those old pictures of 1950s American teenagers yakking on the phone, chewing gum, their legs limber and draped over the side of an easy chair, their faces filled with contentment.

"Who's that, Mama?"

You glanced to the side as though searching for the person I'd referred to, put your hand over the mouthpiece, and set your feet on the floor.

"Come here."

I crawled into your lap and put my head on your shoulder. When you began to talk on the phone again, your jaw moved against my head. You must have been speaking Arabic, because my grandmother didn't speak anything else, but I only remember in English.

"I miss you, too, Mama," you said into the receiver. "Swear to God you won't tell anyone you talked to me."

Evenings, W let me dress up in her cardigan and shoes and clomp around pretending to be a nurse. Sometimes we played Boggle with rules I made up—like, shake the letter-dice onto the carpet and see who could find the Z first. At bedtime, I would lie in my twin bed, humming to ward off thoughts of the monster beyond the window. W usually went to bed when I did, but one night before a day off, she stayed up past her bedtime talking to you. Your voices came to me through the vent.

She said my father's name. She said, "No one's going to take her from you. He can't. The rules are different here."

"He'll take her," you said. "He'll take her back to Jidda. I don't want to go back there."

"OK, OK," W said. "Don't worry. No one's going to find you here. You want to go to the middle of nowhere? This is nowhere. Stay here."

That's how I knew he was alive, and he might one day come back. I wanted him back. When you came upstairs, I pretended to be asleep, but I was thinking.

At breakfast the next morning, I said, "When will Baba come?"

W was drinking a cup of coffee, tapping it with a fingernail. I looked at her, because she'd talked about him. She'd said his name. She mimicked blowing a raspberry at me, a silent warning that I'd said something wrong.

You held my chin and turned my face to you. Your eyes were cracked like China bowls. "Don't talk about him."

I ran upstairs and burrowed under the comforter, where it was dark and muffled and I couldn't hear anymore. My warm breath settled onto my face, and my tears disappeared into the flannel sheets. I fell asleep. I dreamed I died. I dreamed you died. I dreamed my father lived and didn't want me. He was happy we were gone.

After my nap, I steered clear of the bay window, sat next to you, followed you into the bathroom, nuzzled your leg whenever you stood still, swung my leg over yours, and snuck myself into your lap whenever you were sitting, as though I were a neglected cat.

We ate lunch with W in the round eating nook in the kitchen, at a metal patio table laid out with olive-green place mats. The nook looked out onto the driveway and the chain-link fence separating W's yard from the neighbors'. Spindly rosebushes leaned into a peeling white trellis.

"You've been here six weeks," W said. "You must be dying to get out. Let's go to the movies." She spooned into her mouth leftover rotisserie chicken and the rice with almonds and raisins you had cooked the day before to supplement it.

"We can't go," you said. "You know why."

W stared you down, unblinking. You told me to put my hands over my ears. Your lips moved.

W turned her head from side to side like an owl. She pushed my hands from my ears.

"Come on, let's go. You can't stay inside forever." She sawed the flesh off a drumstick, speared the meat with a fork, held it up in the air, and waved it around. She liked to be dramatic. I don't think you liked that side of her. You took her plate of bones to the sink and slid them into it. W got up and with two fingers removed the bones and tossed them into the trash can. After she sat down again, I walked over and stepped on the foot pedal, listening to the lid slap-slapping.

"You should cut your hair." W shook her cupped hand, and I realized she wanted me to come to her. I shuffled over, sliding along the tile with my socks. She patted the top of my head. "Both of you."

"I don't want it." I'd never had my hair cut before. It came to the middle of my back and you had to spray it with soapy-smelling detangler after baths and tug a comb through it while I squeezed my eyes and complained about how much it hurt.

"A disguise." W held her hands out, like she was presenting a painting. "She can pass for a boy. You'll be able to leave this house and not worry. Send her to kindergarten in the fall. No one will recognize her."

Your cheeks moved side to side, swishing unspoken words around your mouth.

"Why do we have to worry, Mama?"

"You didn't finish your rice."

"I don't want to look like a boy."

"OK, sweetie," you said, the endearment three syllables, in that funny way you had of pronouncing it.

You and W must have repeated the conversation, because the next day I followed you obediently into the basement, where W had stacked towels on the bar and spread newspaper on the floor in front of the barber's chair. The light in the basement was dim, so she carried lamps down from the living room and set them up on the bar. Too much brightness. I held my hands above my eyebrows, like a visor.

"It's not that bad," you said, prying my fingers from my face and pressing my hands to my sides.

W cut your hair first. With the flourish and seriousness of a bull-fighter, she draped a pink towel over your shoulders and ran her fingers through your hair.

You looked like a queen to me, in the barber's chair.

"How do you want it?" *W eyed your head expertly, like a real hair-dresser would.*

You straightened yourself in the chair and looked directly ahead. "It doesn't matter how you do it. Go on."

The metallic sound of the scissors slicing through your hair made my skin go cold and goose pimply. I covered my eyes.

"Go watch TV, sweetie," *W said.* "If it bothers you."

"No." *I opened my eyes. If I let you out of my sight for too long, you might disappear. It had become a recurrent nightmare: me, alone in the Cedar Point parking lot, walking in circles in the snow.*

I split my fingers on my face like I was watching a scary movie as W snipped, at first hesitantly, gaining momentum and confidence, whirring around you, comparing lengths on the sides of your ears, pinching your chin between her thumb and fingers and staring at your bangs. After a while, I focused on the newspaper beneath you, where the hair fell in a pile, transformed into something different—uglier—than it was on your head.

"Done," W said. "We should dye it, too. Blond. I'll buy hair dye tomorrow."

"How does it look?" You touched your shoulder and bare neck, as though missing something. The new haircut made you look like a teenager, and I was a little afraid of you. You seemed like a stranger. You wore a black turtleneck and mustard-colored jeans. You tugged at the shirt's neck.

"You don't look like your real self," I said.

"Good job, yeah?" W reached over her own shoulder and patted herself on the back. She swept the towel off your shoulders. A flurry of your hairs floated to the newspapered floor. "You look completely different."

You stared at the mirror behind the bar. Did you see what I saw?

"I don't want to look different," I said.

"This is what we have to do," you said. You got down and lifted me onto the barber's chair. It was my turn. The two of you debated cutting my hair very short—shorter than yours—with an electric razor W said had been her ex-husband's. She was happy to have a use for it, she said.

When she turned the razor on, it buzzed like a saw.

"Nononono!" I yelled, as though she were trying to kill me or cut me.

You hushed me. W dug around behind the bar and unearthed a jar of chocolates. The jar had once had a large gold-foil label, but most of that was peeled back, leaving the white paper backing.

"Honey, take one," W said. "And have as many as you want when we're done."

I scratched the foil off a ball of chocolate and put the candy in my mouth, sucking on it. First, W braided my hair, quickly and deftly, her fingernails tapping against my neck. She cut straight across the back and gave you the plait.

"I don't want this." You dropped the plait like it was a rat.

"You will one day, or she will."

You picked up the braid and stuffed it into the pocket of your jeans, where it bulged, like you had too much cash in there.

"You need new names, too." W pointed at each of us. "How about Amy and Sheila?"

My mouth was clammy with chocolate. I reached toward the jar and grunted. W put a new chocolate in my hand.

"Amy and Sheila?" Mama rubbed the bridge of her nose, like she was trying to erase her features, as well as her name. She didn't sound convinced.

As W clipped the hair at my neck, I closed my eyes and watched yellow and red blotches dance around. Chocolate slid down my throat. It was peaceful with my eyes shut. For a few seconds I was somewhere else.

You startled me awake. "Don't do that!" I had wiped my nose with my fingers, which were sticky. I sandwiched them between my legs and stared at them so I wouldn't have to see your face transformed by the haircut, by your anger.

"Let her be," W said. "Stop wiggling, little girl."

When it was done, W lifted me and set me on the bar, facing the mirror. "What do you think?" she said.

She'd given me bangs and cut straight across the top of my ears, trimming it shorter in back.

"Samantha," you said, touching the ends of my hair gently so that my scalp tickled. Where in your brain did that name come from? You touched yourself at the base of your throat. "And Theresa. Like Mother Theresa."

"OK." W hugged me, and I thought she was going to lift me off the bar, but she didn't. "We'll call you Sam, for short."

"I want to go home," I said.

"This is where we've always lived." You ran your fingers through my hair and grabbed a handful. You smoothed it down and kissed the top of my head, a hard kiss that made me draw my elbows together and push you off me. "Sam," you said, trying it out.

My anger was a knot at the back of my neck. I wanted to keep my name.

Hair had piled up on the floor. Your black hair, my black hair—who could tell the difference? W folded up the newspaper and swept up the hairs that had escaped its borders. She squatted and held the dustpan between her feet, the long handle of the broom bobbing above her head. Tiny hairs stubbornly stuck to the vinyl floor. I pressed my finger against one. On my skin, it looked like a paper cut. You blew, and the imaginary cut was gone.

"Make a wish," W said.

ASPIRATION

1980

HACIENDA ROAD

In Aspiration, California, Theresa changes her name to Lara and Sam's to Emma. She gets a job working the register at the plant nursery on Hacienda Road, and from Jimmy, her boss, she learns to grow succulents and how to break the tip of the aloe and rub its gel onto the sunburned skin at the edges of Emma's tank tops. She rents a yellow bungalow with green trim and a weedy front yard, and from the hippie couple that lives next door she learns about the other kind of weed, which they grow in a hidden corner of their backyard.

"Shhh," the husband says. "We call them 'Mexican tomato plants.'"

The smell of those plants.

The hippies are welcoming. They invite Lara and Emma over for dinner and let ten-year-old Emma hold their baby and carry him around in a Guatemalan striped sash wrapped around her torso, not too different from the muslin wraps Lara's mother and sisters used years ago to tote infants in Jidda. The hippies' house is full of sun. The bead curtain between the kitchen and the living room clicks

like a misbahah when they pass through to drink sun tea at a table
the husband, Toby, made out of the kitchen door. The pots of basil
and rosemary on the windowsill above the sink smell better than
the marijuana the hippies grow, Lara thinks. Dog hair drifts along
the hardwood floors, but the hippies keep their golden retrievers in
the bedroom after they see the panic on Lara's and Emma's faces at
the sight of the animals.

"They're real gentle," says Eleanor, the wife, as she leads the
dogs away, her fingers hooked into their collars.

Lara doesn't tell her that she and Emma have never been so
close to a dog in their lives.

They ask a lot of questions about where she's from, and she
smiles and pretends sometimes not to understand, sometimes not
to hear. They make guesses: Guatemala, Honduras, Mexico.

Emma tugs Lara's jeans. "Is that where we're from, Mom?"

Once, Eleanor says how much she admires single mothers, who
cares what people say, and asks Lara if she's divorced. Lara lets
Emma answer. "My Daddy's dead."

"Oh, I'm so sorry," Eleanor says, and the next day leaves a basket
of tomatoes at their door.

After a month, Lara decides the marijuana in the hippie backyard is a bad influence on Emma and the neighbors are too nosy-
friendly. She and Emma move over a brown hill to a beige shotgun
house with a stone patio in the back and a cherry plum tree in the
front. She smells weed. The town is full of hippies, it turns out. On
the weekend Lara and Emma run into the original hippies in the
tiny downtown. They coo over the baby.

"You're here," Eleanor says.

"Right on," Toby says.

In Aspiration, Lara trims her own hair every six weeks. She takes the heavy scissors from her sewing basket and sits on the toilet with the door closed after Emma is in bed. She doesn't have to look in the mirror. She cuts a straight line across the back of her own neck with her eyes closed. Having kicked around the West Coast for a couple of years, Lara has learned some things. Don't get familiar with a hairdresser. Word always gets back to someone about where she and Emma are. In other towns, before Aspiration, it happened time and again: A Buick or Chevy—some car that could be her neighbors' but definitely wasn't—out on the street several days in a row. Or some Saudi she didn't know watching her in the grocery store. She always knew they were Saudi before she heard them speak, by the particular blackness of their hair, the way the women wrapped their headscarves or didn't wear them at all, the smell of the men's cologne, some specific note in a child's whine that reminded her of her childhood. When they recognized her or almost recognized her, she and Emma had to move again. One year, they moved four times, and in between she had the mole on her cheek removed in a dermatologist's office. She has learned to avoid towns with universities or flight centers, the types of places Saudis go to study or train for the national airlines. She watches out for an American man in a baseball cap and sunglasses, reading a newspaper. That's what a private investigator looks like. When she catches a man like that watching her, she knows how to pick up and leave. She's not tired of leaving. Behind her eyelids, when she's snipping her hair, she sees the possibility of weariness edging toward her. The possibility she'll one day want to find a place she never wants to leave. Will want to chisel her home into a rock face. But the fear of being found stays with her, the wanting to put on her own cap and sunglasses, hide behind the paper's A section, and spy on Emma at school so no one can snatch her.

Emma has refused to have her hair cut for years. It wraps itself around her as though protecting her, covers her face and her shoulders, her little-girl chest, her back, nearly reaches her butt. Her fingers are long and elegant, her hands nearly the size of Lara's already, but her little-girl feet haven't caught up.

Once when Lara was small, when she was Saeedah, her father slipped two gold bangles on her wrists while she slept. The next morning the bracelets surprised her. How tight they were. How she couldn't slip them off without bending them so that they were lopsided, no longer perfectly round. But they reminded her of Baba, so she kept them in a velvet box and one day brought them to America, where she sold them to pay for the mole removal.

In Aspiration, a landscaper named Chris Tanaka steals her heart.

The town is home to a grocery store, a department store, an army surplus store, three bars, a Greek pizza place, a drugstore, two Mexican restaurants, Jimmy's Nursery, and a vacant elementary school. Aspiration enjoys 269 sunny days a year, according to a sign outside town. It has one radio station and no banks, but that doesn't matter to Lara, because she keeps her savings in cash in an envelope in her sewing hamper.

In Aspiration, she realizes it isn't her black hair and brown skin that has invited men and women to speak Spanish to her at city bus stops and in the aisles of grocery stores and in doctors' waiting rooms, but also the way she rolls her *Rs. Redondo, Aspiration, RC Cola.* She used to resist the identification, but here she goes with it, not letting the fact that she doesn't speak Spanish impede her. She nods yes, as though she understands. This gesture of acquiescence gets her in trouble one time, when a woman thinks Lara has agreed to bum her a smoke. Lara sticks her hands in her pockets and takes them out, empty. Shakes them. The woman angrily walks off.

Sometimes white men in Aspiration and nearby towns whistle at Lara, and she ignores them. Sometimes they ask if she's a Native American. Sometimes they catcall when she is walking to or from the bus stop alone on her way to work and call her "mi corazon" and chuckle and say, "Talk to me, beautiful. No habla Englais?"

She never tells Jimmy, the nursery's owner, about the idiots at the bus stop. He must explain to customers and delivery people ten times a day that he is Indian-from-India.

He looked at her funny when she asked for the job and first told him her name.

"You look Indian, like me. I guess Lara could be Indian."

His brother teaches at San Francisco State, and Jimmy could, too, he says—he has a PhD in linguistics—but he prefers to be in the middle of nowhere with dirt under his nails.

"I much prefer plants to people, as you can see."

She never finds out if his name is adapted to English, shortened.

Letting people come to their own conclusions, rightly or wrongly, is the best way to hide. Whether or not she's Indian doesn't entirely matter; she senses Jimmy hires her because of some sort of affinity he feels.

Six months pass quickly, a long time for her at any job. Jimmy's a kind boss. He lets her leave for fifteen minutes in the middle of her shift to pick Emma up from the school bus stop, and he doesn't mind if Emma roams the rows of indoor and outdoor plants like a shop cat. He lets Lara take home finjan-size pots of cacti with delicate spikes and six-packs of waxy begonias for her yard.

"I thought you hated plants," Emma says one day while Lara lets her water a row of Jimmy's herbs with a long wand-like hose. Lara breathes in mint, sage, cilantro, basil. Citronella tries to crowd out the other scents. She's surprised Emma remembers such a small detail from five years ago. It had been true that Lara had no appreciation for greenery. It had been true that she didn't understand why W cared for so many houseplants in Toledo.

In this desert world, different than the one Lara grew up in, she craves the tiniest, crankiest bit of green, of life.

EVERYTHING

Once a month, while Emma is at school the next town over, Lara calls her parents from the phone booth on the corner of Main. Rolls of quarters weigh down her purse, and the booth heats up like the inside of a greenhouse. She'd stay cooler using the pay phone tucked inside the grocery, but this one is more private. These phone calls to her parents are less frequent than her haircuts and often a waste of money. Nothing said. She can't let them know where she is, can't trust them with her secrets.

The pattern has persisted for years: For months she won't call them. One morning, without fail, she wakes up barely able to breathe, needing their voices if she is to go on.

Today was one of those mornings. Emma didn't want to go to school. She refused to get up from the floor in front of the television after Lara switched it off. Minutes later, she put on her shoes and backpack and walked out of the house in the opposite direction from school.

"I'm running away!" She slapped her backpack as she walked. "I've got clothes in here."

Lara followed her down the sidewalk. She glanced over her shoulder. Behind them a few kids were gathering at the bus stop. She couldn't make a scene. At times when she is losing control, the words accumulate in her brain in Arabic, but she can't speak them out loud. In the process of translating her anger, something gets lost. Maybe that's a good thing. In English, she sounds more reasonable than she feels.

"Come back. Emma."

Emma stopped. "No."

"Go to school please."

"*Never.*"

"They'll take you from me if you don't go. They punish the parents when children don't go to school."

"I don't care."

"Come on. Please, habibti." She let herself say that one word in Arabic; the likelihood any of the bus stop kids would recognize the language was slim.

And it worked.

Whenever Emma melts down, Lara has to try a different method of calming her. Promises of ice cream, television, a new Barbie they can't afford. Nothing works twice. This morning, a simple endearment.

They held hands walking to the bus stop, and they were a block short when the bus slammed its doors shut and rumbled off. They ran-walked back to their car, Emma crying the whole way. Late again.

The hanging phone book knocks against Lara's knees. Black blotches of chewing gum mar the metal writing surface. The phone booth is a space where she can speak Arabic safely, but she feels exposed speaking whole sentences of it. She wonders if anyone looking in through the plexiglass could lip-read and realize she's not speaking English.

She doesn't need to say her name. They recognize her voice.

Talk of God flows from her mother's mouth. *God protect you, God assist you, God keep you and your girl.*

Mama says, "Saeedah. Darling. Where are you?"

Habibti her mother has called her.

"We're here." She wishes those words were enough.

Baba asks more insidious questions. About the weather. About what they do on the weekends. Trying to trip her up, solve the puzzle. She never tells him about the man looking for her.

"Thank God, we're fine." Her hand is sweaty on the handset. Her mother rattles on like a child learning to talk, infatuated with the sound of its own voice. Getting off the phone is like cracking ice cubes out of a tray. It takes three or four tries to find an opening to hang up.

Chris strides by, a bag of groceries under one arm. She's learned enough in her ten years in America to look for a ring.

Chris Tanaka is a regular at the nursery. He comes most often for mulch, loading the bags into a black Chevy pickup. He tells Lara about a customer of his who looks like Jimmy Stewart.

"It's not him, of course."

"Who's Jimmy Stewart?"

"Don't you watch TV at Christmastime? *It's a Wonderful Life?*"

Lara rings up the mulch. No reason to explain why she's never watched a classic Christmas movie. After Chris leaves, the shop interior smells like his aftershave. She rushes outside to escape the scent, pretending, for Jimmy's sake, that she's worried about having left Emma alone for too long.

Emma has opened a bag of gravel and is leaving rocks in a trail along the aisles of plants.

"I'm being Hansel and Gretel," she says.

Lara doesn't know what that is.

When Chris comes back, he says, "When are you going to let me take you out?"

She doesn't have a babysitter. She's never been on a date.

"Never?" His smile is somehow both dazzling and shy.

"I'll tell him to leave you alone," Jimmy says after Chris leaves. "Next time he comes round."

Jimmy reminds Lara sometimes of her father, the way he has made the nursery his kingdom, as the paper is for Baba. His crown is his thick black hair, barely graying despite his age, maybe five years younger than her father.

"You don't have to say anything," she says. "I can handle him."

"Maybe, maybe not," Jimmy says.

Jimmy knows what he's talking about. The next time she sees Chris it's on Main Street again, and he's walking toward the drugstore. His hair curls against his shoulders and his clean-shaven face reminds her of velvet. He sees her and she is overcome by a feeling of want. She's never been surer of anything.

"Everything OK?" he says.

She straightens her spine and her lips, offering him an almost-smile. She and Emma have been arguing about sleepovers. Emma has to explain this tradition to her; it is not something Lara grew up with. And Emma won't take no for an answer.

Lara asks Chris what he thinks. Emma rolls her eyes, pulls one foot out of its flip-flop, and drags her toes back and forth along the sidewalk.

"Put your shoe back on," Lara says.

"I can't quite place your accent," Chris says.

"We're from Ohio," Emma says. Exactly what Lara has told her to say.

Chris's laugh pulls Lara closer to him. "Well, OK," he says. "Let her go to the sleepover."

Emma steps so close to him her fingers nearly touch his arm. "Listen to Chris, Mommy," she says.

It's like they're both taking sides with him, when they barely know him.

She wishes they hadn't left the hippies, who would have agreed to watch Emma for an evening. They would have been pleased to hear Lara was going on a date, would have said, "That's great," as though she'd done something worthy of congratulations. Who else can she ask but Jimmy? She lies and says she's going out with "girlfriends."

"No problem," Jimmy says.

His wife, Sima, is a pharmacist with henna on her nails. The orange dye has faded from her palms, but Lara knows it must have been there a few weeks ago. She has memories of afternoons with her mother and sisters, sitting on the carpet grasping thick, cool handfuls of henna and scraping it off later, after it had dried. She'd hated the smell, but today she feels an unexpected nostalgia. Jimmy and Sima's house smells like onions in the pan and something else Lara can't place. Coming out of the kitchen, Sima asks Emma if she's hungry.

"Not really."

"She could stay home alone, but I don't like the idea of it," Lara says. "At night."

"I could have slept over at Jennifer's. But you wouldn't let me."

"Our children are grown," Jimmy says. "We'll let her watch something on TV."

"We'll play UNO," Sima says. "Or do you want Scrabble?"

"I guess," Emma says.

Lara meets Chris at a roadside bar near town. When he kisses her on the cheek, the smell of that aftershave defeats the beery, smoky atmosphere and any hope she has harbored of not wanting him. It's the first time she's ever left Emma, outside of school or work hours, and the fear of what might happen while she's gone sits on her shoulder whispering into her ear. It's always there, the fear, urging her to move on rather than be found. But it's louder tonight, bolder, than it has been in at least six months. She's never had anyone she trusted to watch her daughter, never left Emma at other kids' houses. Her fingers drum against the menu; Chris thinks she's nervous about the date. She can tell by the way he asks what she wants and offers her a beer.

"I don't drink," she says, and regrets it. She's never met an American who didn't drink.

"You a Mormon or a Lutheran?" Chris says.

"I don't think so."

"I like your sense of humor. I'll drink for both of us."

They order wings that burn her fingertips, and he says how impressed he is with a woman willing to eat with her fingers.

Should she worry that she's revealed something, about who she is and where she's from? She picks up a fork and knife, wanting to prove she knows how to use them.

For the first time in her life, here is someone she wishes she could tell everything.

They kiss outside in the milky moonlight, serenaded by the sound of cars crunching through the parking lot gravel. She wishes she could tell him everything—she's not ashamed of any of it—but she has seen parked across the lot a man wearing mirrored sunglasses, reading a paper. It's like something out of a detective show. A realization hits her: it can't be a coincidence that she called her parents a few days ago and here he is. Does it always happen that way? She'd thought the men were sent by Muneer.

She tells Chris she's not ready for the night to end and they go inside. She leaves him at the bar, saying she needs to use the ladies' room. Her nerves are elastic pulled tight, by her need for him on the one side, by her fear of losing her daughter on the other. If her parents and Muneer find Emma, they'll want her back in Jidda. And that will mean Lara will have to go, too.

She's tasted too much freedom to go back to Jidda, or to share her daughter with Muneer again.

She walks out the back door, drives home, packs the car. She drives to Jimmy's praying the whole way that the man hasn't arrived there first, vowing to do a better job of disappearing.

FOUND

1987

APPARITION

When Jameel calls to say he's seen Hanadi in Cleveland, Muneer is in the *Akhbar al-'Urus* newsroom. He grips the phone uncomfortably between his neck and shoulder, to keep his hands free, though he's not taking notes on this call and questions evaporate from his brain.

He concentrates his thoughts into the front of his forehead, and the din of the newsroom recedes. As Jameel relates how he saw Hanadi sitting shotgun in a rust-colored Corolla—how he saw a girl he's certain is Hanadi—Muneer's heart stops. His vision falters. He can't handle the stress of uncertainty, but he finds himself wanting to believe.

"Black hair with dyed-blond streaks. A nose with a bump like a knuckle. That's your nose." Jameel recites the details and analysis as though reading from a journal. She wore a black T-shirt. The fingernails that came up to brush the hair behind her ears were painted black. Jameel says Hanadi hovered in his vision as the cars moved in tandem for long enough for him to paint her face in his mind before the Corolla sped up and she was gone.

"Are you sure? She was in a moving car. You haven't seen her in sixteen, seventeen years." In a way, Jameel has *never* seen her because when he did, she was a baby Muneer transferred into his arms.

She is seventeen, old enough to drive in the States, nearly old enough for college. A different child than she was the last time either of them saw her.

Jameel swears to God it was Hanadi. "I wouldn't call you if I wasn't sure. I know the mother"—he doesn't say Saeedah's name throughout this whole conversation—"she was driving. And the girl in the passenger seat was your daughter. I told you. She had your face."

Jameel admits he hesitated. It was a strain at first to see who drove the other car but he kept looking till he could be sure. His wife, Diane, was at their rented Chrysler's wheel, they were en route from Hopkins Airport to his mother-in-law's duplex, and he was jet-lagged. His eyes felt like someone had poured sand into them. He hadn't gotten any rest so far this summer.

Muneer already knew the story: To everyone's chagrin—except her younger sister's—Jameel's fifteen-year-old, Summer, had flunked one of her religion exams at the end of the school year in Jidda. Which meant she'd needed to retake it and pass to avoid repeating tenth grade. Diane had refused to stay while their daughter studied. She'd gotten on a flight back to the United States with Lulu, the twelve-year-old, leaving Jameel to deal with Summer.

Jameel hadn't had to tell Muneer why. It was an unspoken agreement between Diane and Jameel: school months in his country, summers in hers. Diane never stayed in Jidda longer than she had to. Muneer had teased her about it once, years ago.

"I miss my mother," she'd said. "You should understand that."

He'd swallowed the words he wanted to say to her. How she had her daughters, and he . . .

Muneer brings the phone close to his lips. "You're sure it was her?"

He would have preferred Jameel not call him at work—in the past, he's asked people to relay messages through his brother Bandar. But here is better than home. He doesn't want Lamees to know about this tip until it's more certain. She's not back at the newsroom yet, after the latest baby's birth.

"One hundred percent," Jameel says. At the time, he rubbed his eyes, he says. Maybe his grogginess had made him see something that didn't exist. Maybe Hanadi wasn't in that car.

But in case, Jameel sat bolt upright and peered around the driver's seat. And wouldn't you know, at the stoplight, they came upon the Corolla again.

"We don't believe in coincidence, right?" Jameel says. "God put me on that road at that time to find her."

Muneer fishes in his pockets and scans his desk for a misbahah but comes up empty. "Subhan Allah," he says out loud. Like Jameel, he believes in messages from God, and clearly, God is telling him something.

"Tell me the rest. Where did the car go?"

Jameel says the Corolla zipped ahead, merging into the left-turn lane. He told Diane, "Follow that car," like he was in a cop show, but Diane drove along like she hadn't heard him. Maybe she hadn't. He pulled himself forward with his hands on her headrest. "That car, the orangey-red one. Follow it."

"She said, 'What the fudge—Jameel, you're going to make me crash,'" Jameel tells Muneer.

"Thank God you're fine," Muneer says.

"The girls asked what the heck we were doing. I screamed at Diane, 'Turn left!'"

Jameel thought for sure the girl and the car had disappeared. But miraculously, Diane made the left turn, and up ahead was the Corolla.

Jameel gushes, and though he means to show love, solidarity, understanding, Muneer wants to hang up the phone and not have to be grateful. Jameel says, "Since Hanadi disappeared, whenever I come to the States, a sliver of my brain wonders if I'll finally see her."

He'd never expected to *actually* see her—especially not in Cleveland. Why would the girl and her mother come back here?

"Keep on with the story," Muneer says, though he wonders the same thing. Wonders if this is another apparition, a doppelganger jinn sent to confuse him.

On his desk is a photo of his two older boys dressed in feminine ruffles to ward off the evil eye, when Fouad was an infant and Fadi was one, and another more recent snapshot, with the boys at two and three years old. He doesn't yet have a picture of the new baby, Hatim. Muneer keeps the pictures slightly behind his typewriter. Lamees is superstitious. She would worry about the eye if she knew the photos were out in the open for people to see.

His photos of Hanadi are safely stashed at home.

"So, we chased after the car," Jameel says. "You should've been with us."

He tells how they followed the Corolla down an avenue lined with old, oversize colonials, and around a wooded pond. Muneer knows this family so well, he almost feels he *was* there with them.

Saw how the girls looked out their windows expectantly, their hands slightly lifted, as though they were eating popcorn and watching a movie. Heard how Diane worried: "What are we going to do if it's her?" Witnessed her knuckles whiten as she tightly gripped at ten and two.

The Corolla pulled into a driveway, and they drove past. Jameel says he needed another glimpse of Hanadi. "To make sure. Because I don't want you to come here on a wild duck chase." He says the idiom in English.

"Goose?" says Muneer.

But Jameel didn't see. Diane hit the gas, rather than the brakes, and the car squealed down the street.

"What the hell?" Jameel said.

"She would have seen us. Duh, Dad."

"Turn around."

"What are you going to do, Meel, go inside?"

"3555 Woodland," said Lulu, because she's the smart one in the family, Jameel says. She memorized the car's license plate, too.

They drove out of the neighborhood. Muneer knows that place. He imagines billowy summer oaks and maples giving way to low blond-brick strip malls and cement-colored synagogues. They passed the shopping mall, nearly home. In the silence, Jameel says, he almost heard his wife and daughters, like he was, repeating the address over and over so they wouldn't forget.

Their four minds churning together, Muneer thinks, and his throat aches. He swallows painfully. His years of sorrow, held back by a gate inside his esophagus, are threatening to burst through.

After work, he finds Lamees in the kitchen, showing Mary, their nanny and maid, how to stuff zucchini. Somehow the boys are napping. Lamees senses his presence, looks up, and catches his eye. She starts to smile, but her mouth straightens when she sees his face. She knows better than anyone that Muneer has become jaded; time has eroded his hope of finding his daughter and built a wall around the section of his heart that belongs to Hanadi. His love for his wife stands strong, though. She saw him cry after she gave birth to Fouad, their oldest, who is four. Though Muneer never said it out loud, he thinks she knows that the rush of joy he felt welcoming his first boy into the world was followed by a sharp pain, a knife severing the umbilical that connected him to his first child. When Lamees leaves the kitchen to check on the boys, he kisses her discreetly on the cheek as she passes, so Mary won't see. His wife touches her cheek where his lips brushed, then touches her heart.

TRESPASS

Muneer can't grab a flight for five days. He is determined to find his daughter. He despairs he ever will. For years he's had these feelings in his liver. Now they lurk beneath the surface of his skin. He's on edge with Fadi and Lamees, who keeps saying, "God willing, God willing, God protect you and guide you," and so on. He starts praying extra Sunnah prayers throughout the day, and Lamees prays with him. He can hear her muttering du'aa behind him at the end of prayer. She is asking God to guide Hanadi back to him—to them.

They are between drivers. Lamees, the boys, and Mary go to stay with Muneer's in-laws so Lamees will have someone to drive her to work.

Before he leaves, Muneer plays a finger game with Fadi and chants the little chant that goes with it. Nicknames for the five fingers: *small mind, wearer of rings, big crazy, scooper of stews, crusher of lice.*

Fadi barely smiles when Muneer tickles his armpit at the end of the song. Muneer can't remember if he ever played this game with Hanadi.

Lamees asks, "Will she know Arabic?"

Being in Ohio brings back an ice-cold feeling in his limbs, although it's a rainy summer afternoon when he arrives. The clean-shaven, jowly, balding taxi driver who takes him to the Cleveland Heights townhouse appears Egyptian—the name on his ID placard pasted on the back of the passenger seat is Hani Abdul Qadir—but Muneer does not attempt to speak to him in Arabic. He doesn't want to have to talk about why he's here.

In a fabric pocket inside his suitcase, Muneer has stashed a small white envelope into which he's slid a crisp stack of hundred-dollar bills. Next to the envelope is an open-ended ticket to Jidda with Hanadi's name on it.

Jameel is frantic, his hair a curly mop, not the usual wavy pomade. He starts talking before he's done kissing Muneer's cheeks. "We have to go look at the house. If they saw us, they're long gone."

It feels as though he's stolen Muneer's right to fret. Muneer sits on a white leather couch and says, "God forgive me," to himself.

Diane asks Muneer if he's hungry, if he wants to lie down. No, he says, but water would be nice. She gives him a weird thumbs-up as she disappears into the kitchen. For the water request? For the potential of finding his daughter?

"That house in Shaker isn't going to vanish into thin air," she calls.

"We've got to go back before they disappear," Jameel says. "They've vanished a million times, right, Muneer? Slippery as a worm, that woman."

"Worms are slimy, Dad," Lulu says, appearing in the living room. "Who are you talking about?"

Muneer gives her a hug and kisses her cheeks. She and Summer are as fair as their mother, with nearly blond hair. Muneer knows the story of how once, in a Jidda corner store, three-year-old Lulu toddled among the aisles of Kit Kats and chips, and the shopkeeper thought she belonged to a white British woman who was leaving the store.

It's never been clear to Muneer whether Jameel wanted him to laugh at the shopkeeper's ignorance or take the situation as a cautionary tale of what could happen if you married a blond American: foreigners could take your daughter.

Like Jameel, he doesn't want to dally, but he wants to pray first.

"Get 'Ammu a prayer rug," Jameel tells Lulu.

"We have prayer rugs?" Lulu says. "Where are you going?"

Diane hands Muneer a glass of water.

"Where's Summer?" he asks.

She straightens already straight magazines on the glass coffee table. "She's at a friend's. Lulu and I are getting her after we go to the mall."

Muneer senses something held back; he's not sure what.

Jameel says of course they have prayer rugs, and goes to find one. Muneer wishes he'd brought one in his suitcase. He tries to determine which way he should face when he prays. Where was the sun when he was in the cab?

No one answers Lulu's question about where they're going.

When Jameel shows up with two prayer rugs, Diane says, "You're praying?"

"Five times a day!" he says.

After Diane and Lulu leave, the men pray with Muneer leading because he is a few months older, and afterward Jameel makes Turkish coffee in the French country kitchen.

"If Diane hadn't made me quit, I'd want a cigarette," Jameel says. "Because I'm nervous for you, friend."

He tells Muneer he hasn't smoked this summer, but Diane will be pissed if she finds out Summer spent June and July sleeping and watching videos while Jameel was at work. He knew his daughter was lying when she said she'd studied, because Roseanna, their maid, told him what she was up to. In the evenings, he drilled Summer on the Hadeeths she had to memorize, and she stumbled through them. Afterward, he took her out for shawarmas and strawberry juice and long sessions watching Egyptian soap operas and professional wrestling at his parents' house.

Summer begged not to have to go to her grandparents'.

"'You're home all day. You have to get out,' I told her." But if he had to sit around while she moped, he'd rather do it with company, he says. And the way he sees it, making her sit with her grandparents was as big a part of her punishment as having to stay in Jidda most of the summer and review her religion textbook.

"Girls!" Jameel says, in Arabic. And in English, "Teenagers!"

The words carry everything Muneer has lost.

Jameel seems to have forgotten his earlier urgency. But though Muneer has come across the world to find Hanadi, he doesn't want to be rude. He drinks the coffee down to the sludge.

This is Diane's mother's place. She lends it to Diane and Jameel in summer when her student tenants leave. The living room is furnished with white leather couches and glass coffee tables.

"Diane says this stuff is terribly impractical for a rental, but I love it," Jameel says. "When I crank the central air the leather gets cool, and my mother-in-law complains about the bill."

To offer someone your generosity and then be stingy about it is foreign to the two men. It's very American, but neither of them says so out loud.

Jameel says, "We should go?"

Muneer wants nothing more than to leave this living room, but staying here delays disappointment. He uses the sofa's armrest to push himself up slowly.

"We should go."

Jameel drives the second car, his mother-in-law's white Chevy, to the neighborhood the Corolla had led his family to the week before. On the way, Muneer asks about Jameel's father, though he's too distracted to listen to his friend talk.

"My brother is telling him to lease a shop in that big new shopping center. I told my father to do whatever Fahmi says. How is your mother?"

"I didn't tell her I'm here."

"God protect her. When you tell her you've found Hanadi, God willing, she'll forgive you for everything you've ever done to her."

When they reach the Tudors of Shaker Heights, they immerse themselves in silent concentration. Muneer feels like he's at the start of a roller coaster, not knowing what to expect. The green of the trees is calming, a mosaic of light and leaves. But soon it's clear Jameel can't quite remember the route. He turns down a street that leads into a park, past a picnic shelter and a duck pond. He grumbles after they've gone around the pond twice. This isn't the same pond. They spend half an hour turning onto cul-de-sacs, and Jameel never apologizes or admits to being lost. Muneer offers to look at the street atlas, but Jameel says, "I forgot the address. But I know I can find it."

Muneer begins to lose hope they'll ever find the house. If he
grabbed the wheel, could some homing instinct, some biological
connection, or God's will take him to Hanadi? What if he recited
the Fatihah?

"*Al-hamdu lillahi rabul 'alameen*," he intones hastily.

"Don't worry, brother, we'll be there soon." Jameel's voice is
level, like he's calming a patient before drilling a tooth.

Around and around Jameel goes. The houses are so open to the
world, their lawns expansive and green despite the heat, and yet
they also seem closed off, as though hiding valuables and family
secrets from the eyes of the street.

"I don't know where the hell it is," Jameel says.

"What the fuck, Jameel. God forgive you. We've been in the car
an hour."

"I've got to call Diane. Lulu will know the address."

"Where are we going to find a pay phone?"

"This is it!"

The house is medium-size, with one or two additions. It is
smaller than a Shaker Heights mansion and larger than those ubiquitous postwar boxes, and it looks as if it popped out of the ground
but didn't want to rise too tall, like a colony of mushrooms. A thick
oak with a broken swing hanging from it leans toward the house. A
fence goes halfway round the yard, as though someone had run out
of money to finish it.

"Are you sure? Keep on driving. I don't want Saeedah to see me."

"Look, no cars in the driveway. She's probably not here."

The beige garage doors are closed. It is summer, but it is the
middle of the week, the middle of the day. Everyone must be at
work. Most likely the garage is empty.

"How do we know this is the place?"

"This is it. I remember. I want you to stay in the car until I know the mother is not there."

Jameel parks three houses down and gets out. Muneer watches him walk over to the swing. The bumpy oak roots, thick as biceps, nearly trip him. Jameel touches the frayed end of the swing-rope, the busted wooden seat. Scrapes the flaky red paint with his fingernail.

He approaches a window at the side of the house closest to Muneer. He cups his hands against the window, presses his face to his hands, and peeks inside.

Muneer rolls down the car window when he sees a neighbor watching shrewdly from across the fence, an older woman in green Bermuda shorts with short gray hair. A phone rings inside the house, inside where his daughter might be. It stops. Muneer calls to Jameel, "Ya sheikh, hurry back here."

He wants to barrel forward, but if Saeedah takes Hanadi again, God knows if he will have a second chance to find her.

"What are you doing?" A teenager comes down the front steps in blue plaid pajama pants and a baggy white T-shirt with the words *Howard Jones* on it.

Hanadi. Muneer is out of the car, standing on the front lawn, in the middle of a flower bed, saying her name.

"What?" she says. The side of her head is shaved close, but the rest of her hair hangs to the middle of her back. If only he could see through her skull into her thoughts.

"Hannah, go back inside," the neighbor says. "Arnie and I will call the police."

Hanadi's jaw moves side to side, and she looks straight into Muneer's eyes. "What do you want?" she says.

He's bowled over by the shock of recognition and burst of love, like looking into a newborn's eyes. Jameel is by Muneer's side, an arm around his shoulder, holding him up. He whispers into Muneer's ear in Arabic: "Tell her you're her father. Tell her.'"

"I am your father." The words come out in Arabic, and she doesn't understand. He says them again in English.

"No." The girl touches her ear, as though not wanting to hear. "No. You're supposed to be dead."

The neighbor shouts at them. "No trespassing. Scram. Leave. Her. Alone."

"Don't call the police," the girl says to the neighbor. "Don't call my mom."

She steers her gaze between Muneer, Jameel, the neighbor. He wishes she'd let her eyes land on his again, so he can see the dark brown he's missed.

"Wait," she says, her face turned up to the sun, like a flower. He takes it in. Her cheekbones, her earlobes, her widow's peak, her lips, her chin, the curves of her nose. Muneer feels another surge of love, a happiness he hasn't felt since he lost her. She goes inside, and they wait. The wave of goodness stays with him.

The neighbor pretends to pull weeds out of her lawn, and Jameel rocks on his feet.

"Should we knock? Should we ring the doorbell?"

"She's here," Muneer says, and it's what he's wanted, to know where she is. But of course it's not enough. Worry creeps in. He prays she's not escaping through a back window.

The screen door creaks open, a sound like heaven. She comes out with a palm-size sketch pad and a charcoal pencil and asks him to write a number. Muneer doesn't have a number to write. He holds the pencil till it tumbles out of his trembling fingers and onto the grass. Jameel picks it up and writes his mother-in-law's phone number on the pad while she holds it.

"I'll call you tomorrow," she says.

"What's your number?"

"You can't call here."

Clouds appear when she goes inside. The neighbor slams a door.

Jameel steers Muneer to the car, practically pushes him along the sidewalk, opens the passenger-side door for him, and settles him into the seat. Muneer's a shell. His organs, his spirit, the blood that pumps through him are left behind, with her.

LA SAMAH ALLAH

At the townhouse, Lulu is tucked into the corner of the white leather couch, her hair spread over the arm and a white coverlet pulled up to her chin. Her shoes lie haphazardly on the carpet. Remote in hand, she watches music videos with the sound off.

Jameel takes the remote and switches the channel to CNN. There was a hijacking over the weekend, and the crisis has not yet ended, but there's nothing to see but an unmoving airplane on tarmac.

Lulu holds her palm out, waiting for her father to return the remote. He does, and she goes back to MTV.

Diane hovers in the kitchen doorway, drying a plate.

"Well?"

"We found her."

"That's amazing," Diane says. Her eyes are wet and shiny. She wipes them with the dish towel. "That's my idea of hell, what you went through, Muneer, and now it's over."

"Alhamdulillah," Muneer says. But is it over? He hasn't *found* Hanadi. He is finding her.

The long flight and time change are catching up to him. It's three o'clock here—a good time for a nap. They've got a pullout sofa for him in the basement. First he asks if he can use the phone to call Lamees. He promises to use his phone card to pay for it, but Jameel insists it's no problem to use their long distance.

Diane tells him to use the phone downstairs, "for privacy." He sits on the sofa, which has a set of folded sheets and a towel neatly laid on one end. He holds the phone on his lap. It's heavy against his thighs. When he picks up the handset, he hears two voices: a deep young man's and Summer's.

He hears dissembling in her voice, and over-enunciation, as she says, "OK, see you tonight, Jenny."

She heard the phone pick up, and she's covering up. She was speaking to some sort of a John, not a Jenny, he thinks.

The dial tone sounds in his ear. He dials the phone card number and calls Lamees. She's surprised to hear his voice. He imagines she's eating late supper with her parents, or watching the news, though she doesn't say. She's waiting for him to give her some news.

"Alhamdulillah," he says. "She's living in Shaker Heights. I spoke to her."

"Bring her home," Lamees says.

The next day, Friday, Muneer racks up a dozen hours watching CNN. The jumbo jet does not move. Its doors remain sealed closed, and the hijackers' requests remain unrequited. Muneer has nothing else to do. He can't leave the house, because he might miss Hanadi's call. Jameel takes breaks to run errands, chauffeur his daughters to camp and the mall, but he doesn't go far or leave Muneer alone for long.

Muneer holds Summer's secret in his palm. She barely interacts with him, but he senses she's not wary of him. She thinks she fooled him, or she thinks someone else picked up the phone. The secret seems harmless enough to Muneer. Don't all American girls talk to boys? But he doesn't know how Jameel would view the situation. She is his Saudi daughter.

Anyway, she can't speak to the boy today because her parents shoo her from the phone when she tries to pick it up. The line must be left open for Hanadi.

"What if she doesn't call?" Muneer says at dinner that night.

"*La samah Allah*," Jameel says. May God not allow it.

"Go back to the house," Diane says.

The girls are reading fantasy novels at the table, pizza limp in their hands, while the grownups eat roast chicken. Muneer wishes he were home eating rice and lamb on the floor with Lamees, his mother, and his boys. Hanadi, Hanadi. His mind can't fit her into the scene.

After dinner Diane takes the girls to the movies and Muneer and Jameel take a break from CNN to watch a Clint Eastwood western on cable.

At nine o'clock, Diane comes back with Lulu. Summer is spending the night at Jenny's.

"She doesn't have her toothbrush or anything," Jameel says.

"Her teeth will be fine," Diane says.

"Why do they need to sleep over?" Muneer says.

"There's not much sleeping that goes on," Diane says. "They push the boundaries, stay up till dawn, in the safety of someone's home."

"It's not fair I have to stay home," Lulu says.

"Fair, shmair," says her father. "You'll live."

Muneer wakes up at the break of dawn. The pullout couch's thin mattress has been poking him in the spine. The basement is cold and moist even in summer, the dehumidifier noisy, the blanket Diane gave him no thicker or warmer than a sheet. Since he's wide awake, he might as well wash up and pray. With his hands folded over his stomach, he recites Surat An-Nas: *Say: I seek refuge in the lord of humankind. The king of humankind. The god of humankind. From the evil of the slinking whisperer.* After turning his head right and left to say salaam, he cups his hands before his face and asks God for guidance.

Jameel's family has not woken up. "Go back to the house," Diane said last night.

Outside the sky hovers between dark and light. Muneer considers going back to bed or making coffee. Instead, he retrieves the cash and airline ticket from his suitcase. He finds car keys hanging on a hook near the front door, which he opens slowly and shuts as quietly as he can.

As he starts up the Chrysler, he remembers frigid mornings waiting for the VW to warm up. And Saeedah, pregnant with their daughter and already far from him. In this warmer weather, no need to wait.

He remembers exactly how to reach the house where Hanadi lives. The trip takes twelve minutes. The driveway is empty. A deep crack runs up one side of it, and green weeds have filled in the blank. The garage doors are closed. He waits. At eight forty-five, the garage doors slide noisily up, and the Corolla backs down the driveway, listing to one side as it drives along the crack. Two heads are visible in the front seats.

He follows the car to University Circle, careful to stay a little ways behind. It is early on Saturday, little traffic on the road. The sun burns in a hazy, no-color sky.

The Toyota pulls into the nearly empty art institute parking lot. Muneer parallel parks on the street. Hanadi gets out of the Toyota. She wears black jeans, a black T-shirt, ugly black lace-up shoes.

The woman in the car, is she Saeedah?

A jolt of anger bursts through his arms, and he tightens his grip on the steering wheel. He recites Surat An-Nas again to calm himself.

Hanadi slings her backpack on one shoulder and trudges inside, hunched over as though it were raining.

He watches the glass doors close behind his daughter and waits for the Toyota to leave.

He could leave the car and follow her, but it seems like a creepy, rather than fatherly, thing to do.

She said she would call, and she didn't. What does that mean? He lays his head on the steering wheel in weariness, and it accidentally honks. He startles and bumps his head on the ceiling of the car. No one else is on the street or sidewalk to hear.

After about an hour, she comes out, eating potato chips from a small bag. She stands to the side of the doorway, waiting for a ride, perhaps.

He gets out of the car and walks across the parking lot toward her. She recognizes him from the other day. He doesn't like the look on her face, a panic in her eyes like a child in trouble. Why can't this reunion he's longed for be joyful?

This is not their reunion, though, he reminds himself. That was two days ago. Coming back to her is harder than he expected. Like learning a new language. You can't flip a switch in your brain and understand English or Swedish or Bengali or Swahili.

"I said I'd call you," she says, defensively, her arms across her chest, chip bag crumpled and mostly hidden in one hand.

"I have to go back to Jidda soon," he says. But that is not the reason it hurt that she hadn't called.

She tosses her chip bag toward a trash can and misses. "I knew it. I knew Mom was lying. I knew you weren't dead."

The faint sound of geese quacking comes to them from the Museum of Art lagoon. Had she known, or hoped? Either way, the idea that Saeedah could not cover the truth bolsters him. He imagines if his own father came back from the dead, how he would feel. He would be thanking God for blessing him with a miracle.

He picks up the crumpled bag, squeezes it in his fist, and throws it in the bin. The first time in many years that he's cleaned up after her.

"Here I am," he says. "Alive."

Hanadi seems to shake her head, but really, her whole body is trembling. He wants to hold her tight, carry her backpack for her.

A two-door Pontiac pulls up. Hanadi moves to hop in, head bent to avoid looking at him.

"I'll take you wherever you're going," Muneer says.

"My boss will kill me if I'm late." She's speaking into the open door of the car and he has to strain his ears to hear her.

"I drive fast," he says. "Faster than Americans."

"It's a long drive," she says. "I don't know you."

"I'm your father."

She closes the car door. He comes closer and bends a little, like he would have done to talk to her when she was little, but he doesn't have to bend far.

An American girl in a white polo shirt and khakis gets out of the car, leaving it idling.

"Hannah, what're you doing? We're gonna be late."

"I'm going to ride with him," she says. "I'll see you there."

He puts his hand out to shake the American girl's hand. She has green eyes and freckles, feathered sand-colored hair.

"Hello. I'm Hanadi's father."

Hanadi's mouth twists, and she seems to be biting her own tongue to keep the words inside. He keeps himself from telling her not to do that. She relaxes her mouth and breathes loudly, a swimmer coming up for air.

The American girl holds her car key between two fingers, like a dagger. Her face is doubtful.

"Nice to meet you?" She shakes Muneer's hand, but doesn't squeeze back, and turns her head toward Hanadi. "I thought you said your father . . . I mean, you probably shouldn't—" As though suddenly remembering he's standing there, she says to Muneer, "I'm sorry, sir. I'm sure you're not some kind of murderer."

Hanadi does a half shrug, rolls her shoulders forward. Muneer is surprised at how attuned he is to the two girls' movements, the way he pays attention to his sons' pouts and stomps, their smiles and quietudes, the tiniest signals they give of distress or contentment.

The American girl stands with one hip out, rolls her eyes at Hanadi. "So, like, I came over here to pick you up for no reason?"

"Buy you a Coke?" Hanadi seems ready to hug her friend, but instead she stuffs her hands into her pockets.

"Never mind," the friend says. "See you there." She stands straighter, puts her keys in her pocket, takes them out again as she gets into her car.

On the drive, he has so much to say that there is nothing to say. Hannah—she asks him to call her that—directs him to drive north, through Little Italy, out of the city, farther than he expects, though she warned him it would be a long drive. She turns on the radio, as though they were cruising together in their own family car, and expertly tunes it to something loud and thrashy, adjusting the balance for maximum thump. The whole routine involves her for a minute or two.

"Could you turn it down?" he says.

She turns the music off, and the silence is worse than the noise was. He keeps waiting for words to come out of his mouth, but he feels like the Prophet Zakariya, ordered by God not to speak for three nights.

Hannah punches the radio back on and tunes it to classical. She doesn't adjust the volume. Chords swell between them.

Twenty minutes in, at a stoplight, he forces words out.

"What do you want to know?" he says.

"I didn't ask you to come here. I mean, I'm glad you came, I think. But I don't want anything from you."

She speaks above something that sounds like Beethoven, but he can't be sure. Mozart, that's the other one. Jameel would know, but Muneer has never known too much about European composers. The drama of swelling violins fits.

"You're my daughter."

"I don't know you. You're not going to try to take me with you or something? I'm tired of moving. I want to stay here."

It puzzles him that she wants to stay with the mother who lied to her, dragged her from place to place, robbed her of everything. The envelope and the ticket are in the glove box, but he truly doesn't know the answer to her question. He'd thought he would find her when she was little. She's nearly grown, and he hasn't come up with a different plan than to bring her home. What will she do in Jidda? Study at the American school?

What will her mother do to keep her here?

"What should I do?" he says. Words that have been stuck in his throat for years tumble out like a confession, as though he were the one who'd done something wrong. "Your mother took you from me. She made up a story that I was dead. She tricked you."

"Stop the fucking car. Pull over."

"Watch your mouth," he says, and immediately regrets it.

"I will jump out of this car and walk home."

He pulls into a strip mall parking lot. "You're going to be late."

"Don't talk about my mother. You don't know anything about us."

He begins to swear in Arabic, and he can't stop the torrent coming from his mouth. "God take her, God damn her, God forgive me."

Tears coat her cheeks in a sheet. "Stop yelling at me. I don't know what you're saying."

"I'm sorry. I'm sorry for the years we were apart."

"Why now? Why did you come back now?"

"I prayed to God to bring us together. I looked for you. Your grandparents looked for you."

There's no box of tissues in the car to hand her. No way to change this series of events that God wrote for them. But God brought them back together, and Muneer has to be thankful for that.

He asks if she wants him to drive her the rest of the way or find her a taxi.

"Drive," she says.

He thinks of her mother and the fateful drive that led to their marriage.

"I'll understand if you don't want to see me again." Though he wouldn't understand. He would truly go blind with sadness this time. After seeing her, nothing in life will be enough without her. Not his wife and sons. Not the paper. He's sure of that. He puts the car in gear, backs up. "I hope you'll let me stay in touch."

"The store manager's gonna dock my pay," she says.

He lets her out at a convenience store that sits alone on an island of concrete. He has a hundred-dollar bill in his wallet, and he tries to hand it to her. She slams the door behind her without saying goodbye or taking the money. As she walks from the car, she pulls a polo shirt out of her backpack and pulls it over her T-shirt, shifting the bag from one arm to the other so she doesn't have to set it down or stop.

She is everything he sees until the sliding doors close behind her. His vision expands, and he sees the haze has lifted and the sky transformed into a bright ocean blue that reminds him of home. There's a rainbow of spilled motor oil on the asphalt ahead of him. He pulls ahead, repeating God's name over and over: *Allahallahallahallah.*

He's left without her again.

WHERE DO WE GO

Muneer chooses prayer as his coping mechanism. He unrolls one of the prayer rugs Jameel never uses and spreads it in a corner of the basement. Lulu's on the sofa. She seems to migrate from space to space in the house, even though she has her own bedroom. Her headphones are clamped on, her eyes closed.

The air smells like dryer lint.

After he prays, he sits for a while, hands before his face but no request for God on his lips.

Footsteps come down the stairs.

"Oh," Diane says. She's carrying a basket of dirty laundry. When she discerns he's done with his prayer, she apologizes. "I didn't know you were praying down here."

"I saw her again."

Diane's eyes flit to Lulu. "That's wonderful."

"I don't think she wants to see me."

"That can't be true."

"It's been too long."

"We'll help you figure this out. We'll find you a lawyer."

She puts the basket down and says, "Lulu."

Lulu moves her head to the music, seemingly unaware of the adults. Her mom taps her legs. The girl brings her knees up so the mother can sit.

Muneer stands and begins to roll up the prayer rug. Diane's hands are flat on her thighs, as though she were kneeling in Muslim prayer, paying her respects to Abraham. But she's Christian. He doesn't know how or if she prays.

"I need you to help me convince Meel of something," she says. "I think Summer and I should stay here when he takes Lulu back to school."

"You told him that?"

"I will."

Summer has two years left of high school, Diane says. She isn't being prepared for college well enough by her school in Saudi. Diane has done the legwork. She has school brochures hidden in her nightstand. She talks about the SATs and college admissions. She says the people at the private school love Summer, and she could learn French there.

"When did you take her there?"

"Last summer."

"When she wasn't flunking yet."

Diane starts folding a T-shirt, returns it to the basket. "These are dirty. I've got to throw them in the washer." She lays her hands back on her thighs. "I don't know where to go from here, Muneer. It's not a new problem. The school in Saudi is OK for Lulu, but Summer won't learn anything if she goes back. Your kids aren't old enough yet, but you'll see. Can't you talk to him?"

He hopes she can't see how the empty chasm of lost years has opened up in his chest. Other people can forget Fouad was not his first child, but he never does.

"I don't think Jameel will listen to me," he says. The words come out lullaby-quiet, and he realizes he's holding the cylinder of prayer rug in his arms as gently as an infant. "I'm not the one to tell him *not* to keep his babies close to him for as long as he can."

Diane squeezes Lulu's ankle, leans over, gives the girl a hug that isn't returned, rises from the couch, and steps toward Muneer.

"I'm sorry." She carefully removes the rug from his grasp. "You should go tell Meel you saw Hanadi. We want the best for you, and for her."

The next day, Muneer looks up the convenience store in the Yellow Pages and dials the number on the basement telephone. He asks for Hannah. She's not there, but the voice on the line sounds young and female.

"Are you the one who drives her to work?" he asks.

"Who's this?"

"You saw me yesterday. Her father."

"She didn't show up today."

"You didn't drive her?"

"I'm sorry, sir. My boss is calling me."

He replaces the handset on the phone and lies on the couch, stiff as a board. He feels old. Through the windows up near the ceiling he hears rain. The basement mildew stokes an itch in his eyes and throat. Diane and Jameel are at the mall with the girls. When they come home, they're carrying big paper bags full of clothes for Lulu and Summer, a bread maker some relative in Jidda asked for, and a red Michael Jackson jacket with many, many zippers for one of Jameel's nephews.

Muneer wonders if Diane has talked to Jameel.

"We should have asked if Lamees wants anything," Diane says.

"I think it's time for me to go home," Muneer says.

The doorbell rings, and Diane worries that it's Jehovah's Witnesses or Mormons, out to save souls despite the pouring rain.

"I'll scare them off," Jameel says. "There's got to be a Qur'an somewhere in the house."

Diane puts a hand on his chest. "Leave them be. I'll tell them we've already found the Lord." She touches the cross at her neck and goes to the door.

Watching Jameel put items back into shopping bags, Muneer considers what he could possibly say about Summer's schooling. He doesn't think it's his business, but what's worse—a family choosing to be apart for a year, or a wife and daughter who resent their husband and father for a lifetime?

"Muneer!" Diane calls.

He trades places with her at the front door. Standing under a black umbrella is Hannah's friend from the convenience store. She's wearing her uniform and her eyeliner is smudged into angry storm clouds around her eyes.

"Hannah's in Toledo," she says. "She didn't want to tell you, but I told her she should. So she said OK, I could tell you even though she didn't want to."

"How'd you find the house?"

She shivers from the shoulders up. "Can I come in?"

They sit at the kitchen table and Diane makes individual mugs of Lemon Zinger, sets a saucer in the middle of the table for their tea bags. Jameel puts baklava on a plate; the girl has no idea what it is.

"What did you say your name is?" Diane asks, though the girl hasn't said.

"Joanie. I'm so sorry for bothering you. Hannah gave me your guys' number and I got the address from 411. I thought it was better to come in person. She ran away. She says she's never going back to Miss Sadie."

"Miss Sadie," Diane says. "Her mom?"

"Uh huh." Joanie pulls apart a diamond of baklava and picks at the nuts inside.

Diane fishes the tea bags out of their mugs. "Hannah's confused. Can you blame her? Her mom was her world, and she has to confront the lies."

"I should go to Toledo," Muneer says. He would walk there, if he had to.

"Let her figure it out," Jameel says. "In a year she's eighteen. She'll be free to live wherever she wants."

Muneer wants to keep chasing Hannah, but he's also tired, and he knows where she is. He asks God to keep her safe. There's the five hundred dollars and the ticket in the Chrysler's glove box. Tomorrow, he'll have Jameel take him to the Saudia Airlines office and have the ticket transferred to "Hannah."

"Will you tell me where she is?" he says to Joanie. "So I can stay in touch with her until she's ready to see me again?"

She writes an address on a notepad Diane ferrets out of a drawer.

"Thank you," he says. "Could you write her name at the top?" He doesn't want to admit he doesn't know what last name his daughter's mother has given her. The girl writes it out in cursive. It's not his name, but it belongs to his daughter and therefore is beautiful.

"MY NAME ISN'T SALLY"

1975

We had new hair and new names, but we didn't go to the movies. I didn't go to school. As the weather got less cold, sometimes you let W leave the upstairs windows open, the blinds up. From W's bedroom, I glimpsed green buds growing wart-like on the tree in front of the house. Spring was starting without me.

On a warmish day when the leaves on the tree had poked out, waxy and curled at the edges, you got sick and slept for hours. I watched cartoons and crawled around the basement meowing like a cat while Poppy eyed me with concern. I wanted to make a peanut butter sandwich. The jar of peanut butter was way up high in the cupboard. I dragged a chair across the vinyl floor and climbed onto the counter to reach the jar. I got the jar open and a scoop of peanut butter into my mouth, but as I sucked on the spoon, the jar slipped out of my hands and crashed to the floor. I cleaned up some of the peanut butter with a dish towel, but left the glass shards. My brain felt thick and slow, like my tongue did when it was coated with peanut butter. I cut the crusts off slices of white bread I'd already laid on a napkin, and rolled the bread into doughy balls before eating it.

I let myself out the side door and wandered into W's backyard, where I stepped on the cracks in the fractured pavement. I knew the rhyme "Step on a crack, break your mother's back." I pulled my fingers along the chain-link fence, stopped and pushed my sneakered toes into the holes, climbed halfway up and back down. The neighbors' rosebush, budless this early in the season, had trespassed through the fence. When I pressed the thorns against my thumbs, they budded with blood.

Being outside felt strange after being inside for two months. Like eating peanut butter after not having eaten it for months and forgetting how sticky it was, and at the same time how much I liked it.

I ran inside for a bandage and back out again to sit on the cold stone of the front stoop. A woman passed by pushing a red carriage, her two babies sitting face-to-face inside it. She waved and smiled, and it scared me. Maybe this lady was a spy, a monster in disguise.

The babies stared at me. One of them giggled. The other drooled, its expression serious, unreadable. I liked babies, always wanted to touch their soft faces and fuzzy hair, but maybe these were baby spies.

I stood up, brushed the dust from my butt, faced the door, and scurried inside. The basement light was off, and I felt my way down the dark stairs. You lay on the couch. When I straddled your bony legs, your eyes fluttered open.

"What is it, Sammy?"

"Hanadi," I said, sensing you didn't have the strength to argue. In the space of time it took me to say my real name, you fell back asleep. I watched you for a few minutes. Your hair was matted in places and tousled in others. Your breath whistled in your nose.

"Mama," I said. I got off you, and the outdoors drew me like a magnet for a third time. I walked down the driveway and turned right. The street was lined with aluminum-sided houses. I'd forgotten my jacket. The sun warmed me at first, and then it skittered behind a cloud and the air chilled. At the end of the block, I turned around and looked up the street to W's house. It seemed very far. I wasn't ready to go back.

"I'm running away," I said out loud.

W's street dead-ended at an elementary school. I looked both ways and crossed the street. The kids were out for recess, and I heard their shouts and squeals, like bird calls. I walked across a field to the edge of the blacktop. Two little girls with pageboys and bell-bottom jeans were peering at me sidewise, as though we were on either side of a fence, or a cage.

"How old are you?" one of them said. She wore big glasses that swallowed her cheeks. When she smiled, I saw her tongue through the gap her front teeth had left behind when they fell out.

"What's your name?" the other girl asked. Her baseball-sleeve T-shirt had a name on it in glittery rainbow colors: Katie.

"Sally," I said, after the Peanuts *character. I didn't want to get in trouble for saying my name to someone other than my mother or W, but I hated Sam.*

My eyes were drawn to the other kids—swinging, hopscotching, sliding, roughhousing. The sound of their voices made me want to whoop and call. A scene as mundane as kids playing on a playground—dozens of kids—frightened and thrilled me.

Katie watched me watching a gaggle of boys kneeling around an object I couldn't see. "We don't play with those boys."

"My name isn't Sally."

Katie sneered. "But you said."

"Jessica!" said the girl with the glasses. "Is your name Jessica?"

"How come you won't say your real name?" Katie said.

The boys had started tossing stones onto a metal slide. I wanted to throw things, too.

"My name is Sam."

"Are you a boy?

I rotated my arms like a windmill. "No."

"We don't play with boys."

"Me neither."

"Aren't you cold?"

A teacher noticed our conversation and came over. She was small, not much taller than the girls, a dwarf. I had never seen a grown-up that small before.

"Sweetie, where do you live?"

I pointed up the street.

"Do you know your phone number? We'll call your mom."

She took me to the office. The hallway leading there was quiet, no sounds but our footsteps and the squeaky wheels of a janitor's cart. The cinder block walls were lined with bulletin boards decorated with construction paper flowers, art projects, and drawings of famous grown-ups.

I sat in a padded chair with metal arms that chilled my forearms.

"Who's this?" the secretary said.

The teacher squeezed my fingers. "You're in good hands with Mrs. James."

"Does she speak English?" Mrs. James said.

"Of course she does."

After the teacher left, I sat for a long time. Mrs. James brought me a crayon and scrap paper and a magazine to lay the paper on so I could draw. She opened her purse and fished around with her arm immersed up to the elbow, till she found me a rustling, half-crushed packet of saltines.

"What's your name, young lady?"

"I'm not supposed to tell strangers."

"Well, that's a good rule. Where do you live?"

"I don't know."

"OK. Don't go anywhere while I speak with the principal."

Mrs. James disappeared. The clock on the wall ticked hollowly. Mrs. James returned to her desk and made some phone calls. I tuned them out, because she was talking about me and I was tired of people talking about me—you and W, these ladies at the school. After I'd drawn a purple VW bug and trees and a sun, and started drawing a house and crossed it out, and licked the cracker crumbs off the plastic wrapper, and peeled the paper off the crayons, and sucked on the neckline of my T-shirt, and kicked the metal legs of the chair for a while, I lolled in the seat and sighed loudly.

"When can I go?"

"Do you need the bathroom, sweetie?" Mrs. James said.

She must have asked me other questions, because somehow they got word to W, who showed up as Mrs. James was jingling her keys and trying to argue herself out of taking me home for dinner. W had her down jacket on over her uniform, and she'd changed her shoes to fur-lined, olive-green rain boots. She was carrying an adult-size hooded sweatshirt.

"This is your daughter?" Mrs. James put her keys in her purse and sat down, like maybe she thought she would have to stay there with me longer, since this blond Polish woman couldn't possibly be my mother.

"They live with me. Her mother's sick." She held the sweatshirt upside down for me. "Here, Sammy."

I slipped my arms in and flipped the sweatshirt over my head. Our shared familiarity with the ritual (which we had never done before— we were good improvisers, I guess) convinced Mrs. James to let me go with W, though the sweatshirt hung to my knees and its arms dragged on the ground.

I liked wearing the sweatshirt. It made me feel like a big girl.

Outside, raindrops the size of silver pebbles were falling. W picked me up and bent her head over mine and ran with me to her burgundy Buick.

"God, you're heavy." She set me on the back seat and got behind the wheel. The car smelled like W's house. We sat idling for a little while until the rain died down.

"Busy day, huh, Sammy girl? I nearly lost my mind with worry."

"Is Mama mad?"

"Your Mama's dead to the world."

The word dead made my stomach curl into a fist and punch me from the inside. W must have seen panic on my face.

"Sleeping, Sammy, she's sleeping."

I growled. "I don't want you to call me that."

She adjusted the mirror so she could see me in the back seat. I covered my face with my arm—I wanted to disappear, to not be somewhere I didn't want to be. I wanted to be nameless so no one could call me the wrong thing.

"Time is the answer, Sammy." W rocketed out of the parking lot and up the street, the windshield wipers going crazy and the rain a sheet. In less than half a minute, we'd pulled into her driveway.

"We'll be soaked on the way in. Let's wait." W left the ignition on and watched the windshield wipers go back and forth, and it was like sitting in the Cedar Point parking lot with you. I didn't want to be where I was, but I didn't know where else to be.

"I want to go home."

"I know. This can be your home. Like I told your mother: You guys'll be safe here."

When the rain tapered off, W lifted me out of the car. I squirmed in her arms.

"I want to walk."

She put me down. "Sorry, honey. You're like my own little girl." She paused on the stoop, fumbling with her keys. "I won't tell her. I won't tell your Mama that you ran away."

Inside, you were sitting in the middle of the living room floor, wrapped in an afghan that was usually draped over the basement couch.

"It's cold," you said. "Where were you guys? Where did you take her?"

"You need broth." W tossed her coat on the floor and went straight to the kitchen. "Ah fuck—who made this mess?"

"What mess?" you said.

"Nothing," said W. "Talking to myself."

The phone rang. I'd never heard it ring before. No one ever called W.

"Someone's been calling," you said. "Don't answer the phone. Where were you?"

"At the movies," W said. "I'll be in the kitchen. Call if you need something."

I stayed with you and listened to W as she cleaned up the mess I'd made. She was singing a song I'd heard on the radio, something about Sailor Sam.

"A song for you, Sammy," she said.

You sipped the Lipton's cup of soup she made you. W and I spread jam on toast—there was no more peanut butter—and chewed it slowly. When you trudged downstairs with the afghan draped over your head, I followed you. I put my giraffe pajamas on, and once you'd nodded off, I crept upstairs to sleep among the plants. Poppy was already nestled between a fern and the ficus. I pushed pots aside and lay my head on Poppy's ginger-colored side. She lifted her head, bit my cheek, decided she didn't care, and curled her head into her paws.

When I think about home, I think about that spot, Poppy and the pots, the low leafy canopy of houseplants that made me feel like I was not stuck between four walls. And W taking care of us, though I hated the fact that she cut my hair. I was learning to forget my father. I was learning to sleep wherever I needed to.

In the dark night, I heard you calling me, and W whisper-shouting, "She's up here. Let her sleep."

When I woke the next morning, I was staring at the burgundy ceiling of W's car. Classical music played on the radio. Potted ferns crowded the seat next to me and the foot wells, and W's afghan was wrapped around me several times. I wriggled out of it to sit up.

You clutched the steering wheel like a life preserver. The bench seat beside you held our suitcase and vanity and more plants. We were on the freeway, semis passing us on either side, and as they passed, their absence revealed an overcast morning, clouds so low they seemed to erase the sky.

"Where's our car, Mama? Where's W?"

"Let me drive. I'll tell you later."

"We took her blanket. And her plants. The police will catch us for stealing."

"You like the plants. I brought them for you."

My sobs burst out of me.

"W gave the blanket to us, Sammy. And the plants. She wanted us to have them."

"You're lying. You stole them."

"We can't take them back. We have to go."

"I don't want this stinky blanket. It smells like cough drops."

I opened the window to the cool, early morning air and stuffed the afghan through it. The blanket plopped onto the cracked, potholed asphalt and lay there.

I felt strong, as though purposefully leaving something behind was like Popeye's spinach, pumping my muscles up. I punched the back of the passenger seat a few times, until my muscles deflated, and I was back to being regular me.

The sky was pale; the day was going to become sunny and warm. We would see fiery rhododendrons at a rest stop on the interstate, dogs on leashes yipping crazily at the joy of being let out of the car. For now, you kept your eyes straight ahead on the drab gray road.

"Close the window," you said.

I tried to tell you to stop the car and go back—back to the blanket, back to W's house, back to where we'd started—but the words flew out the window and disappeared on the relentless wind as we hurtled forward to a place neither of us knew.

DESERT SHIELD

1990–1991

YOU DRIVE ME CRAZY

Hannah pulls the Fine Young Cannibals cassette from the shelf and remembers she has nothing but dollars in her purse. She should go ask Muneer for riyals. Put the tape back and walk from the music shop to the Safeway, where he and Lamees are buying groceries. Or better yet, come back another day with her own money, converted into the correct currency. Either option should be easy, as sending a letter to Malik or calling her mother should be easy.

Ever since she arrived in Jidda less than a week ago, leaving Cleveland a month and a half into the fall semester at the art institute, she's felt restless, listless, rudderless. She's questioned whether it was a good idea. She needs to grab onto something.

It's not that she expected to feel instantly at home. She's moved too much with her mother to think she'd settle into a new place, like putting on a spiffy new outfit and loving how she looked in the mirror, how the clothes made her feel. No, she'd known she would need time to acclimate to this place her parents "came from."

The cassette tape is solid in Hannah's hand. She slips it under her abayah and into her jeans pocket. Keeping her hands hidden under the black robe—which she can't get used to wearing, but is useful for shoplifting—she pats the little rectangle. It feels like a piece of home.

The whole tape shop feels familiar, with its smell of plastic, though the tapes are not the same as the ones in the United States; they are cheap and black-marketed, in thick, soft, unfamiliar packaging with typos on the song lists. The shop is darker and smaller than the Sam Goody in Ohio, too. Instead of carpet, her footsteps land on black and white tiles, mottled like birds' eggs. But the place is full of music she recognizes. FYC and the Smiths and Kate Bush.

To take that familiarity out of the shop with her, she is absconding with a buck or two worth of merchandise. So what?

She feels her femaleness constantly here in Jidda, in a way she occasionally does in America. For example, though she isn't the only woman in the shop, she's the one woman alone. The one person alone. Two teenage girls with fuchsia lipstick and teased, frosted bangs poking out from under their black headscarves brush past her and giggle. Two young men in jeans and knockoff-looking Levi's T-shirts hold hands in the M section. She's curious: Are they Arab or Indian? Are they gay? Up at the cash register, a group of American soldiers in desert camouflage and brown combat boots negotiates with the shopkeeper.

One soldier has mirrored sunglasses, a crooked smile, and a black crew cut. Later, at an underground party up the coast, Erasure in the background, she'll learn his name is Zee. Surrounded by drunk and flirty European and Arab expat high schoolers, and a few Saudis thrown in—pretending, like her, not to be Saudi—she'll tell him, "I had a feeling I'd see you again. I had a feeling we would meet one day soon."

He will tell her she's making it up, and she'll try to convince him. "No really, it was like a waking dream. I saw you in my mind without those glasses. I knew it was you. I knew I would see you again."

She can't see his eyes the night she steals the tape, but she can tell he's watching her. *What's with the sunglasses?* she thinks. *Don't you know it's nighttime, buddy?* As though he has heard her, he gives her a little salute. Is that kosher? Kosher isn't the word. Is that *regulation?* She salutes back and regrets it. She shoves her hands beneath her abayah to keep them from stealing or saluting anymore.

The female soldier next to Zee elbows him hard, and it occurs to Hannah that they don't know she's American, like them. Hannah's stomach twists. She thinks they noticed her stealing. Will they report her to the shopkeeper?

She considers returning the tape to its shelf—the right thing, the honest thing. She thinks about saying something to the soldiers in English. "Thanks for your service" or "How long you guys been here?" or "Whaddaya think of this place?"

Her father appears at the door. Three years since their reunion and he is almost as much a stranger to her as the soldiers are. She came here to get to know him better. It seemed like the fastest way.

"Lamees is in the car," he says. "Yalla." Probably the word slips past his lips involuntarily, without him thinking about whether she'll understand. *Yalla* is one of a few words Hannah has picked up so far. *Yalla:* hurry up. *Ahlan:* welcome. *Akhuya:* my brother. *Abuya:* my father. *Ummi:* my mother.

She's learned the words' meanings, but she hasn't spoken them.

As they walk to the car, the humid night air warms her face. Her headscarf presses against her hair and summons her sweat. She hates wearing the scarf, but she doesn't want to break the rules. The parking lot and streets are crowded with honking cars. Why do men drive angrily here, as though cutting someone else off is the only outlet for frustration?

Hannah's father keeps his eyes on the Americans, who have finished their negotiating and are piling into a Jeep. He seems especially to be watching Zee, who among the tall Americans is the tallest.

Or maybe it is Hannah who is especially watching Zee. She touches the stolen tape again.

"The king asked them to come, but they walk around like they own the place."

"They're my age," Hannah says. She doesn't know enough about the politics to understand any of it, or enough about her father to guess the true sentiment behind his words. Does he oppose the Americans coming here, or is he wary?

Her own reasons for being here seem trivial compared to young soldiers "fighting for freedom"—if that's how they see themselves. If she were being honest, the reasons she has come to Jidda are, in order: to piss off her mother, to meet her siblings, to avoid a semester of art school and her job at the art supply store, to see her father.

"You don't have to work, Hanadi," her father said as they sat in a car outside her Cleveland Heights apartment a little over a month ago, an international airline ticket on the armrest between them. If she were a better person she would have argued with him. But she's been low on money, and her mother found her number over the summer and started calling her several times a week to tell her to come home.

She is twenty. She can live wherever she wants. Go wherever she wants. She doesn't have to go "home" to her mother's lies.

Her father picked up the ticket with his index and middle fingers and held it in the space between them.

"Your brothers can't wait to see you."

The idea of brothers never occurred to her.

She always wanted a sister, someone to share in-jokes with, to repeat lines from movies with, to be the other person in the world who knows what it was like to be her mother's daughter.

She ran away. She looked up W's name in the Toledo phone book, which they had at the Cleveland library, and called four people with the same last name until she heard the familiar Polish accent.

"Of course I remember you," W said.

So Hannah bought a Greyhound ticket to Toledo with her paycheck from the convenience store where she worked at the time. She finished high school in Toledo, living with W and W's boyfriend, Tod.

When Hannah got into art school in Cleveland, but not in New York, Rhode Island, LA, or DC, W told her not to go back.

"Your mom will find you."

Hannah didn't listen. She moved back to Cleveland, into her own apartment. She gave Muneer and W her new address. But she didn't tell her mom.

Being here, she has a weird, admittedly vindictive urge to tell her mother where she is. "Here I am, in the place you kept me from, with the father you said was dead."

Hannah slides into the crimson-vinyl back seat of her father's white Chevrolet sedan. It smells like some sort of woody incense.

Sitting in the front, Lamees turns her veiled face toward Hannah. "Did you find what you were looking for?"

Lamees and Hannah's father are the first people Hannah has ever met who sound like her mother. That thin membrane of accent that makes her mother a mystery is normal here, is how English comes out their mouths. This place—this bride of the Red Sea, as her father calls the city—is the origin of her mother's phonemes. The blue sky like a vat of dye, the air like steam in a bathroom, the promise of sea to the west and carpets of sand to the east, somewhere over there past the city limits. These things gave birth to her mother's *p*'s that are not quite *p*'s, her *v*'s that bear passing resemblance to *f*'s, her insistence on opening lights rather than turning them on.

And so there is a strange familiarity she feels with these two, while at the same time she finds it disconcerting to speak to Lamees in public, to speak to someone whose eyes and mouth she can't see. Disconcerting to speak with her father, who was dead, who claims one day Hannah disappeared with her mother in a poof. *Like I was some sort of five-year-old genie*, she wrote to Malik in the letter she's been working on since she boarded the plane in Cleveland. She's already written five pages, front and back. *Is that what happened?* Whatever the truth, she blames her mother for lying about her father's death, which suggests she lied about so much more. Sometimes Hannah blames both her parents, but mostly her mother.

"They didn't have what I wanted," she tells Lamees. It's a white lie. Hannah is not an incurable liar like her mother.

The neon ads of the city are reflected in miniature in her car window: tires, soda, furniture, fresh juice. Her father stops at a shawarma shop, the spit directly outside manned by a guy with a carving knife and a chef's hat and patches of sweat on his back and under his arms.

Alone with Lamees, Hannah starts to hum. She's ruined things for herself; she can't listen to the tape because she's lied. Why did she lie?

"I stopped listening to music," Lamees says. "I used to love it, but the Prophet told his followers only the human voice and drums are halal."

What kind of person doesn't like music? About her stepmother, Hannah wrote: *It would be weirder if my father and I had any history together. As it is, she's some stranger. She can't figure out what to make of me. Maybe that's not fair. Maybe that's my problem. I want to get to know her. Really.*

FIRST IMPRESSIONS

Since she arrived, Hannah's days have gone by one like the other, identical pencils in a case. There's not much to do while her father works. She'd like to explore the city, but they don't have a driver, and women are not allowed to drive, so they can't go to the mall or the grocery store till he's done with work. It's frustrating and not what she expected, as someone used to coming and going as she pleases.

So Hannah spends long stretches of time drawing. The day after the shoplifting incident, she sits on the low cushions of the family room and props the hard, flat pillow from her bed on her lap to make a desk. The air conditioner hums, a constant sound. It's October and balmy outside. Lamees and Mary—the young Filipina woman who cooks, cleans, and helps take care of the boys—are making lunch. Hannah would like to click the FYC tape into her father's Sony stereo system, but there is the thing Lamees said about music.

The pillow is from the two older boys' bed, a full that they usually share. These days, her three brothers—six, five, and three—sleep with their parents. And Mary doesn't have her own room.

Her contract is with Lamees's sister, but she came to help take care of the boys after the littlest, Hatim, was born. She sleeps on a mattress in the formal living room, with the folding doors closed. There are too many people in this apartment, and Hannah wishes she'd known that before she agreed to fly thousands of miles to a country gearing up for war. The other day Muneer showed Hannah the blueprints for a villa he's having built in a newer part of town. Everyone, he said, will have their own room.

"How soon?" Hannah asked.

"Next year, I promise."

Does he think she'll be here next year?

In the margins of her journal, Hannah sketches her toes, a minaret, a bowl of black olives. She finds a dull charcoal pencil at the bottom of her backpack, twists it in her knuckle-size sharpener, and sketches a pair of mirrored sunglasses with her own face reflected in them.

Five-year-old Fadi, the middle of her father's boys, doesn't think too much of her drawings. He climbs onto her lap, grabs her pencil, and scrawls on the page, embellishing her careful cross-hatching with swooping loops. He's autistic and only speaks a few words of Arabic, her father told her, fewer than Hatim.

Fadi adds a layer to my sketches, she wrote on page seven of the letter to Malik, a few days ago. *It's a collaborative process.*

Hatim is not interested in Hannah; he loves Mary best. But she is trying to win him over by folding things for him: notepaper fortune tellers, gum-wrapper swans, a hat made out of their dad's newspaper.

The oldest brother, Fouad, drags her outside to make her watch him ride his bike around and around the courtyard. He knows "On your mark, go!" in English. They go down in the evening, when it's not too hot, and the air smells like flowers she can't name.

Hannah didn't think too much about Kuwait or Iraq or Operation Desert Shield the day Malik drove her to JFK in New York because her father had neglected to buy her a connecting ticket and she couldn't afford it. Malik waited until they parked in the garage to start freaking out about the war, telling her she was crazy to board the plane. He didn't understand why she couldn't wait until next summer, when the war might be over.

"If you go, I'll lose you," he said as he pulled her luggage out of the trunk. "Why can't your dad visit you here?"

"I'm going to Jidda, not Kuwait City."

"Maybe you'll stay there. Maybe your dad won't let you leave."

"I'm an adult. I can do what I want. I'm an American citizen. Although my mom would kill me if she knew what I was doing." Hannah stood on tiptoe, put her arms around Malik's shoulders, and kissed him. "Come with me."

Of course she didn't mean it, standing there with the ticket her father had bought her. Except, she did mean it. She wanted to fold Malik up like a letter and carry him in her back pocket.

"Your relatives will love that. A boyfriend. A black, American, Christian boyfriend."

"You don't know they'd say that."

They had walked to the Saudia Airlines counter. Women in black robes and scarves sat near the windows. At their feet were suitcases several small children could fit into, and in their arms they held expertly swaddled babies with thick, Muppet-y black hair. Their older children climbed on the luggage.

Hannah decided not to kiss Malik again, not in front of these conservative, likely disapproving-of-public-affection-and-dating women. She felt as though she were already in another country. Malik's last words to her were, "Write me, OK?"

On the airplane, with stale air hissing down at her, she started the letter. It has grown over the days into a fat stack of pages. She doesn't know how to transport herself to a post office, and she doesn't want to hand her father an envelope with a man's name on it. So she keeps the letter in her purse, next to the FYC tape.

The first place Hannah's father took her after she arrived at King Abdulaziz International Airport was her grandmother's flat. Almost the first place. They stopped for hot pita bread on the way, Hannah waiting in the car while her father hopped into a hole-in-the-wall bakery and emerged with a steamy blue plastic bag. As they drove down a quiet residential street toward her grandmother's house, the two of them, the bread smell made her giddy and intensified her feeling of displacement: Was she in a car, or a bakery? How had she come to be in this city and country she'd barely known until her father showed up three years ago?

She'd tried to find out about where she was going before she left Ohio. But the books about Saudi Arabia in the library were about oil and history. She'd had no way to start to comprehend what life would be like here.

Muneer had not brought Lamees or the boys to the airport. He wanted Hannah to meet her grandmother before anyone else, he said.

"I'm so happy you came." He tapped his horn as he steered the car through an intersection with no stop signs.

Hannah wasn't sure yet if she felt the same. She always reserved judgment on new situations: a new job, art school, a new boyfriend. Why should visiting her homeland be different? In any circumstance, things could go to crap, or be OK. Best to go in with low expectations. She gripped the handle on her door and pressed her foot to the floor, as though she were braking the car. She closed her eyes and imagined a bumper sticker: "I brake for stop signs." She opened her eyes and sand-colored apartment buildings marched past.

She could tell, being here for less than half an hour, that she was a different person than she might have been if she'd grown up here, with her family intact. There was no changing that. Her father had a black abayah thingy and scarf sewn for her and sent to Ohio so she would have them to wear when she arrived. One of the stewardesses—none of them were Saudis—had shown her how to put the abayah and scarf on.

Her grandmother's building faced a block of empty sandlots, as though the builders of the neighborhood had suddenly run out of steam and given up on trying to populate the desert. In front of the building, a leggy bougainvillea bush grew in a square of dry soil surrounded by sidewalk. The bright pink blossoms burned Hannah's eyes.

"Hellfire flowers," Hannah's father said.

Two men sat on the curb, their white robes tented over their knees. She had never seen anything like them, and at the same time, they were as familiar as her own hands. What other lost elements of herself would she find here?

A grandmother. A family. The thoughts took her breath away.

Outside the car, the air was greenhouse hot, the sun brighter than anything she'd seen.

Her father had a key to the front door of the building. The hallway leading upstairs smelled of cumin and onions and ground beef. Hannah's grandmother waited at the door—she must have been peering out the window for the car's arrival. She was a small woman with thinning black hair streaked with white, plaited and fastened to her head with U-shaped pins. Her cheeks, probably full and round when she was young, were wrinkled and flabby like deflated balloons.

She kissed Hannah enthusiastically on both cheeks. Her skin was soft and familiar against Hannah's. Her scent was sautéed onions and what Hannah would later learn was mastic gum.

"Hanadi!" she said, and other things Hannah wanted to understand but couldn't. It was strange to be called by that name, like she was being pulled into the alternate reality in which she'd lived here since her father returned from his studies in America.

"She's happy to see you," Hannah's father said. "She says she wants to eat up your sweetness."

"It's nice to see you, too." Tears blurred her vision.

Hannah's grandmother nodded, as though she understood. But she didn't, of course. She went on in Arabic. Her voice sounded like gum cracking in her cheek.

"She says, 'God bless you.' She says, 'God has blessed us by bringing you back to us, like the Prophet Yusuf returned to his father.'"

"Yusuf?"

"Joseph. His brothers threw him down a well and pretended he'd been eaten by wolves. His father went blind with grief."

"That sucks."

"Later the father regains his sight. It's a happy ending."

"Tell her this is a happy ending. Meeting my grandmother."

In the small living room, plastic had been laid out on the floor and covered with plates of meat pie and white cheese and sliced peppers and the hot pita bread her father had brought. It was four o'clock in the afternoon.

"Is it dinnertime?"

"No, but she's been waiting to feed you. Fifteen years. Aren't you hungry?"

When they left, Hannah's grandmother hugged her tight. If she'd wanted to, Hannah could have rested her chin on her grandmother's head. She kept her chin up, though, afraid her grandmother's skull might have a soft spot, like a baby's. The hug went on for a long time, till Hannah sought her father's eyes, asking for help.

"Ummi," he said.

Hannah's grandmother stepped back and touched Hannah's hair, petted it like she might pet the small round head of a parakeet.

"We'll come back. Tell her that." What Hannah almost said: "Tell her that, *Dad*." But the word stayed inside her, between her ribs and beneath her heart.

TAIF

Two days after the tape incident, Hannah's Aunt Randah shows up uninvited and presses the buzzer outside.

"What the heck is she doing here?" Hannah's father says when Randah's upturned face appears on the closed-circuit screen by the apartment door. "I didn't tell her you were here. Who told her?"

The question is not for Hannah. The tension in the air pulls through the middle of her stomach, though she doesn't know who she's looking at until her father tells her. She could have guessed. On the tiny black-and-white screen, her aunt's expectant face looks so much like Hannah's mother's or her own.

Hannah's father buzzes Randah in. As they wait for her at the open door of the apartment, her footsteps echo in the stairwell. She comes round the bend and floats up the last half flight like a black ghost, kicks her shoes off at the threshold without waiting to be invited inside, and sets down a large pink shopping bag with gold lettering. She hugs Hannah and kisses her cheeks, as though they've been parted for a week, rather than years.

"Your mother's sister," Lamees says in English.

"Ya shaykhah, she knows who I am," Randah says.

Hannah has no memory of her. Here is a person who knows who her mother was in the beginning, someone who might give a clue why she would hide Hannah from the family and the family from Hannah.

Randah keeps her headscarf on and gives her abayah to Lamees. She looks *Little-House-on-the-Prairie*-ish in her pink long-sleeved blouse and a plain brown skirt that grazes the tops of her bare feet.

Lamees ushers them into the sitting room and instructs Mary to bring refreshments: a tray of Pepsi and orange soda in bloodred goblets. Randah, Hannah's father, and Lamees exchange what seem to be pleasantries in Arabic. They sit on floor cushions placed around the perimeter of the room. The television is on, tuned to news on the English-language channel. Fouad and Fadi lounge on their stomachs on the floor. Hatim naps in another room.

"How are your children, Randah?" Hannah's father says in English.

"Your father is worried I'll take you," Randah says. "Like your mother did. But I'm not my sister. He has nothing to worry about."

Hannah can hardly believe how quickly the hostility between Randah and her father has come to the surface. She wishes to be anywhere else but here. And yet. It is the first time anyone has confirmed her father's version of things.

That ubiquitous air-conditioner noise fills the room, like ice water in a glass. Hannah's father sits straighter. Hannah sits straighter, too.

"I'm surprised you're here," he says. He is taking care to speak in English, Hannah thinks. He wants her to hear his disapproval.

Randah takes a stack of wrinkled blue aerograms out of her bag. "The letters my father sent your mother," she says to Hannah. "Returned by the postal service." She places the letters in Hannah's hand.

Hannah holds the stack between her palms. The addresses are in English, but of course the letters themselves are in Arabic. She won't be able to read them without someone to translate, and that means she will never be able to decipher for herself her mother's relationship with her grandfather. She tucks the letters under her thigh, as though they are bookmarks and her legs pages, as though she can flag this time in her life.

"Come visit me this weekend," Randah tells Hannah. "Come meet your grandmother and grandfather."

Bubbles pop on the surface of Hannah's soda. She sips. The carbonation tickles the top of her mouth. It never occurred to her to want to meet her mother's parents, or that her mother *had* parents. She can't recall them ever being spoken of when she and her mother were alone together in various American towns and suburbs, the kinds of places where people mistook them for Mexicans or Dominicans and Hannah's mother didn't try to convince them otherwise.

Hannah's father says something in Arabic, and Randah tilts her head toward Hannah.

"We're going to Taif this weekend," Hannah's father says.

The conversation teeters on the edge of argument. "Ah, Taif is very nice," Randah says. "But you can go later."

Hannah doesn't know where Taif is or why they are going there, but she wants a say in this matter. So she says the word she hasn't spoken yet. It tastes metallic and hard in her mouth: "Dad. I want to meet my grandparents."

Her father's eyes cloud. "Weekend after next," he says.

"Wonderful, I will send the driver."

Before Randah leaves, she hands Hannah the shopping bag, which contains a red velvet jewelry case, a floral skirt, a yellow blazer, and white flats. So many gifts! Hannah lays the clothes on the seat cushion beside her and opens the case. Inside is a small turquoise amulet with gold calligraphy. She rubs the smooth surface with her thumb.

"It's beautiful. What does it say?"

"'Oh, Protector,'" Randah says. "Put it on!"

"She can wear it later," Hannah's father says. Hannah freezes. Should she put it away? Should she put it on?

Randah decides for her by grabbing her hand, gently lifting her fingers, and filching the chain and pendant from her.

"Very simple to put it on," Randah says, looping the chain around Hannah's neck. She's wearing a V-neck tee, and the pendant adheres to her chest.

Hannah loses her abayah in Taif. On Thursday, the first day of the Saudi weekend, her father drives the family out of the city, up a mountain, past a rock perched over the road, into a park of low, bushy evergreens. As they ascend, Hannah's stomach somersaults and her mouth fills with saliva. Her father pulls over against the side of the mountain so she can spit into the dirt.

The park revives her. It smells like pine, like an Ohio hike, and oddly, that makes her happy to be here, in Saudi. The picnic area smells like a summer barbecue. Families have spread cloths along the sparsely grassy edges of the path that winds through the park. Though the late-October air is mild and breezy, people are dressed in layers, as though for a chilly fall day in Ohio. The fathers, wearing blazers or cardigan sweaters over their white thawbs, grill pungent lamb, and the mothers, draped in black, pour tea out of thermoses and set out trays of dates. Little girls of eight or ten, wearing black headscarves and colorful dresses under cardigans, cradle babies and run after toddlers. Older boys kick soccer balls on patches of dirt.

After lunch, Hannah, her father, and Lamees go for a walk, leaving the boys on a picnic blanket with Mary.

"I'll stay with them," Hannah says. The three boys might be a handful for Mary, she tells herself.

Muneer insists Hannah come along.

"It's fine, Miss," Mary says. "Go with your parents, please." Mary has a small daughter at home in the Philippines, she told Hannah a few days ago, though she doesn't seem much older than Hannah is. It's not till now that Hannah wonders how hard it is for Mary to be separated from her own child.

Lamees wears white sneakers under her abayah, and Hannah's father wears a blue polyester track suit he changed into when they arrived at the park. Once they pass the picnickers and there's no one around, Lamees lifts her veil from her face and drapes it over the top of her head. One side of her mouth dimples when she smiles, and her front teeth jut toward her bottom lip. They walk up a rocky path that slopes gently. Beneath them, patchy terraced farmland is scrunched into a narrow valley.

Hannah keeps tripping over her abayah. It never wants to stay closed, and her scarf never stays put. She feels foreign to herself wearing them.

Underneath is the real her: jeans and a gray Gap T-shirt.

She wraps the one side of the abayah around the other side of her body and tucks the fabric tightly under her arm.

"You see." Hannah's father coughs. He knocks his fist against his chest as though it were the door to a place he wants to go. He sweeps his arms open. In his track suit, he is a blue silhouette against a blue sky. "Our country is not only deserts and camels and oil sheikhs and Mercedes-Benzes. We have mountains and family picnics and trees and goats."

Two young men with the hems of their thawbs tied round their waists, revealing white cotton pants and leather sandals, saunter down the path toward them. Lamees flips her scarf back over her face and walks a few paces behind her husband.

The men stop to talk to Hannah's father. The three kiss on the cheeks and bring their hands to their hearts.

"How does he know them?" Hannah asks Lamees.

"He talks to everyone, know them, not know them." Lamees keeps her voice low. "Don't talk too loud, and cover your hair."

Hannah tightens her scarf under her sweaty chin.

"I think I'll go sit with Mary and the kids," she says.

Walking back, she breathes the scent of pine needles and thinks of forests and Malik.

Branching from the main trail, a little goat path leads down to a cliff that overlooks the valley. Weeds that smell like basil grow along the path. Hannah removes the abayah, folds it, and stuffs it under her armpit. She slides sideways down the incline. Rocks tinkle under her feet. On a small overhang, she lands on her knees in the dust, stands up, and brushes herself off awkwardly with the abayah. She doesn't need it. She places it against the trunk of a tree.

Beneath her, down a steep incline, is a field of low green plants. She can't go any farther.

She picks her way back up the rocks. When she reaches the top, she lies on her back, out of breath. A hawk flies through the cloudless sky. Malik flits through her mind. She wants to find a way to call him when they return to Jidda.

A man comes up to her talking frantically.

"English?" she says.

He keeps talking.

"My father's over there."

She wishes she had the abayah. Her arms are bare. After the man leaves her, she tugs off her scarf, drapes it over her shoulders and arms, and walks bareheaded to the picnic blanket, where Hatim sleeps with his head in Mary's lap and Fouad is showing Fadi how to kick a soccer ball. Mary's scarf is loosely draped over her hair— can she do that because she's Christian? Foreign?

Hannah kicks the ball a little with the boys, but Fadi would rather pick it up and throw it, which makes Fouad mad. He scolds his brother in Arabic, and Hannah tries to calm him, but he doesn't understand what she's saying. When Hannah's father and Lamees arrive a few minutes later, Lamees is practically jogging, her face covered.

"Where is your abayah?" Lamees says. Though out of breath, she has the fire of anger in her voice.

"It slipped off."

"Time to go," Hannah's father says.

"I should find it."

"We'll buy you another."

SOCIAL LIFE

After Taif, Hannah tells her father, "I need to meet someone my age." It's not that she wants friends so she can stay here forever, more that she can't learn about this place completely through her father's male eyes or in the living rooms of her relatives.

He arranges for her to go shopping that week with Summer, his best friend's daughter, whose mother, he tells her—as though it were a formula for friendship—is American. The younger girl shows up with an extra abayah and scarf draped over her arm. "My mom told me to lend these to you," she says.

Summer wears a striped Benetton sweater and faded jeans under her abayah. She slides into the back seat of her father's Nissan SUV and Hannah follows. Summer sits toward the middle, leaning between the front seats to give her driver, Nasser, directions. She adjusts her headscarf, pulling the ends wide and exposing her short Winona Ryder haircut before wrapping the scarf tightly over her hair.

"What music do you like?" she says.

Hannah brings the Fine Young Cannibals tape out of her purse, where she stashed it and forgot about it.

"I stole it."

"Ha!" Summer takes the tape and shifts forward so she can reach the dashboard and put it into the tape deck. Nasser doesn't seem to notice as he zips in and out of lanes like a race car driver. Hannah wishes she could lay her hands on the steering wheel, but she's not sure she could drive crazy enough to not get run over.

Over the music, Summer tells Hannah she spent her last two years of high school in Ohio and a year at a small college in the States. She decided to come home when Iraq invaded Kuwait.

"Why'd you come back with a war going on?"

"Pot, kettle, or whatever." Summer grabs the front seats as Nasser speeds through a red light. "Hang on to your headscarves! We're going to a party! Don't worry. Nasser won't tell your dad."

The party is in a walled beach villa forty-five minutes up the coast. The pink marble entryway is littered with shoes. Abayahs and scarves fill two coatracks. Loud disco-like music beckons from the second floor. Derobed, they climb the spiral stairs to a sitting room with no furniture. Big windows face the sea, a dark gleaming in the distance. A kidney-shaped pool, empty of swimmers, fills most of the courtyard beneath them. After she has taken in the landscape outside, Hannah looks around the room. Summer deciphers the crowd, pointing out factions. There are a few young Saudis, gel-haired boys in baggy jeans and Guess T-shirts who smell like cologne and cigarettes. A couple Kuwaitis whose families fled the invasion—"You can tell by their accents," Summer says. Some girls from the international school, a few of them wearing cat-ear headbands.

Hannah had forgotten it was Halloween.

And there is the guy from the tape shop, leaning against a wall sipping nonalcoholic beer. At first she doesn't recognize him without his sunglasses and fatigues. He salutes her.

"I've seen you before. Remember me?"

"Who?"

"It's Zee. How's that Fine Young Cannibals album?"

"Where are your friends?"

"Water pipes." He points toward the yard and the pool. "They're out there smoking bananas."

"It's apple tobacco," Summer says.

"I thought Saudi girls weren't allowed to socialize with men."

"I'm not a Saudi girl," Hannah says. "I'm visiting my dad."

Summer points to red punch in a big crystal bowl. "That's the booze."

"Isn't that against the rules?" Zee says.

"Ever gotten a speeding ticket?" Summer ladles punch into three plastic cups.

"Nah, I'm a total rule follower." Zee pulls out his sunglasses and puts them on the back of his head.

Hannah gulps too much punch; it's like drinking a cherry lollipop. "This is terrible."

"Nice red mustache." Zee winks. She wipes her mouth with her arm, and he winks again and says, "Still there."

"He's joshing," Summer says.

What a dumb joke, Hannah thinks. Doesn't matter. She wants to stay close to him. She tells him she's dying to see the beach, and they retrieve their shoes from the entryway and stroll down through the night, leaving Summer with the shisha-smoking Americans. They remove their shoes again to walk on the sand.

They're holding the shoes in their opposite hands, as though they'd planned it this way, to let the backs of their hands brush. Ahead of them, the water is darker than the sky. They sit at the border between wet and dry sand, at the edge of the foamy waves. Zee rests his chin on Hannah's shoulder. She smells the punch on his breath.

"I'm buzzed," he says.

She touches his fingers, not quite holding hands. A shock of heat zips up her arms and through her ribs.

He's from Kansas City, his parents from San Juan. She's never been to either place. He doesn't ask how long she's been in Jidda.

"Girlfriend?" she asks.

"Never."

He has a habit of winking when he says something jokey or sarcastic. He holds this wink for a few long seconds. She almost reaches to his forehead to stroke his crooked eyebrows.

"How does she feel about you being here? The war." The word *war* feels as strange as *father* in her mouth.

"It's not a war yet. Not too happy, I guess."

The kiss that comes next tastes as surprising and unsurprising as spiked punch. A little too boozy. A little too sweet. She likes it the way she likes spiked punch: with a nagging sense she may later regret the sips she's taken. She pushes the thought of Malik to the borders of her mind. This is an innocent kiss, and Malik is so far away, and Zee isn't looking for anything serious, and he is another solid thing to grab onto. Otherwise, she could imagine herself floating out to sea.

The rest of the week, Hannah reads and writes and sketches. Watches bootleg videos of movies with the sex scenes and the kisses excised by government censors. Sometimes the picture freezes but the audio continues. Smooching noises, sighs. She thinks about Zee when that happens and also whenever an air-raid test siren blares. She writes Malik about the test sirens, the beach house, her aunt, the feeling that everyone is on edge waiting for the war to start but also that life is incredibly normal, where normal means boring.

Certain things, she doesn't mention.

Late in the week, she realizes she's double-booked herself. At the end of the beach party, she promised to meet Zee on the Corniche the same evening she is supposed to visit Auntie Randah.

She phones Summer to ask what to do, speaking as quietly as she can in the bedroom. Summer advises to have the rendezvous first.

"No one shows up on time for anything here. Your aunt won't notice you're late. You can borrow Nasser."

But that night Summer calls to say Nasser has to take her mother shopping. Hannah has already told Auntie Randah not to send her driver.

Hannah's seen yellow taxis pass by on the wide boulevard two blocks from her dad's apartment. While her father and Lamees are performing sunset prayer, she tells Mary she's leaving for her aunt's house. At the bottom of the stairs, in the dark entryway with tinted-glass doors, she turns, thinking she's forgotten her keys. But here they are in her jeans pocket, and there is Fadi, holding onto the balustrade.

"Bye, Fadi. Go back. Yalla," she says, though she knows he doesn't understand.

Taking him with her would be a terrible idea. She would never. She's tempted, though. Having company is nice.

"Upstairs, Fadi. Or your mother and father will yell at me." She tries to say "up" in Arabic. He grabs her hand. She marches him upstairs and nudges him inside the apartment.

Outside, sunset prayer is ending, and down the street, the corner shop's metal accordion gate shudders open. Crossing the intersection, she stumbles on her abayah—again!—as she lifts her foot to the high sidewalk. A group of men walk toward her. To appear less conspicuous, she pulls her scarf across her face, the way she's seen Lamees do.

She treads carefully, because wearing the veil is like wearing dark glasses. What she sees are shadows of cars, but no taxis, passing by on the main road. As though her body has turned to sand, she drifts aimlessly down the sidewalk, past apartment buildings with aluminum balconies, vacant lots strewn with rebar and worn-down tires, yellow dogs sniffing at banana peels. The grass median smells like sewage. The trees' feathery leaves and coral-colored blossoms appear shrouded.

The taxi driver she hails wears his red-and-white headcloth piled high, so it nearly touches the ceiling. He speaks urgently through yellow teeth. He expects her to understand Arabic. In English, he knows "Where?"

She shows him the address of the restaurant Zee picked, jotted down in her notebook.

The cabdriver speeds up a ramp onto the freeway. After ten minutes or so, they descend another ramp into the streets of the city, hitting traffic that slows them down. The driver leans into his horn often. Hannah concentrates on the green neon signs that flash by on squashed white shops, advertising Pakistani food and tailors and shawarma.

The drive to the Corniche takes forty-five minutes. The cheesy-looking restaurant is made up of huts on stilts in the water and a series of bridges in between. She tells the taxi driver to wait for her. Her face uncovered, she holds onto the handrail as she crosses the first bridge to the maître d' stand. When the maître d' speaks to her in Arabic, she feels herself blushing. Not knowing the language that is her birthright is a special kind of stupidity.

With his bouffant black hair, European suit, and bow tie, the maître d' seems to be looking down on her. Zee is around somewhere, but she made a terrible mistake coming here. How would it look for her to appear in public with an American soldier?

As she walks back to the cab, the water beneath floats dark as a veil. If she threw off her scarf and abayah, they would disappear into the sea.

The cabbie loses his way, and the drive to Randah's villa takes forever. Hannah doesn't arrive till nearly ten o'clock, and just as Summer said, Randah doesn't care. Shoes are piled in the entryway, a warning that many people have gathered. Randah brings Hannah into a room with a gauntlet of people standing, waiting to meet her.

"Your aunts and uncles," Randah says. "Your grandmother, your grandfather. Your cousins." She explains each person's exact relation to Hannah, but the words are as foreign as if she's speaking in Arabic. Hannah can't tell these people apart, and yet they seem part of her. They've missed her, and she has no idea who they are. They kiss her on both cheeks. The women touch her sleeves, her hair, her cheeks, her ears, as though she were a young child. She nearly kisses a man, introduced as her Uncle Hassan, on the mouth, because she misjudges the direction of their air kisses.

"The men can be here because they're our father, our brothers," Randah says.

Flush with human contact, Hannah sits on the floor cushions between her aunt and maternal grandmother.

She tells her grandfather she has his letters in her purse. She wishes she'd brought her sketch pad so she could draw his face, so like her mom's.

"Do you want me to translate them?" he says.

She wants to say yes, but she also doesn't want to let the letters go.

"If I give them to you, you have to give them back."

"Promise," he says. He puts the letters in his pocket. "Come visit me next week and I'll return them to you." His English is better, less accented than she expected. It sounds almost British.

Randah's Sudanese cook, Lateefah, has made rice and lamb stewed in milk, diced cucumbers and tomatoes, and a kind of salsa. Eaten with hands and spoons, dinner is served after eleven o'clock. After the guests leave, Randah will not let Hannah go.

Randah's formal sitting room is decorated with traditional touches that somehow have a modern vibe—like Randah has taken care to reclaim the most relevant parts of the past. Embroidered dresses have been framed and hung on the walls. Instead of Western sofas or Eastern cushions, there are custom-made divans on wood frames. The little carved-wood side tables are topped with glass. A silk rug in dark blues and reds covers the floor from wall to wall. It is the kind of rug Hannah would call Persian, like she would call the gulf on the Eastern coast of this country Persian, when people here call it Arabian.

Randah says she has not talked about her sister in years. She goes on and on. She says she spent the years missing her younger sister—not knowing where she was. There will never be enough words to fill in the canyon of time, Hannah thinks, but Randah tries. She sits with Hannah far into the night, legs folded beneath her. Randah smokes a shisha, sucking on it slowly between sentences, punctuating her stories with a sound like that of a child blowing bubbles in a pool. Fruity smoke wafts up toward the ceiling. Saeedah often gazed at the sea, Randah says, dreaming about faraway places: Cairo, Rabat, Madrid, New York.

"We always fought." Two years older than Hannah's mother, Randah lived in Cambridge, England, for five years in the seventies, while her husband studied for a doctoral degree he has never finished. When she speaks in English, Randah's lips grasp the vowels like delicate pieces of glass. She doesn't swallow her *l*'s and *r*'s like an American does.

"Our aunties said, 'Sisters fight, but you fight like enemies.' They lectured us about the importance of family. They said, 'Me and my brother against my cousin. Me and my cousin against a stranger.'" Auntie Randah leans forward at her waist, takes a hit of apple tobacco, and touches Hannah's knee with her free hand. "You know the saying?"

Of course Hannah doesn't. She sips her Vimto, which looked so ruby-red beautiful when she accepted the glass, but tastes like carbonated, sweetened penicillin.

"Well, those aunties spoke the truth, yes?"

Randah's words come out throaty, coated in smoke. The way she talks about family—the way everyone here does—is more foreign to Hannah than anything else. She has always had only Mama. To have dozens of people feels like a gift, a gift of love that she never expected. Because she is family, they love her.

At the same time, their love is a pressure, a standard she will have to live up to. She can't abandon it or pretend they never gave it to her. They are family. She has to return their love. They'll expect her to stay in Jidda, she can feel that, too, and she's never intended that as an outcome of this trip. She knows her mind won't change. Why does that make her feel like a traitor?

"I've always wondered why my sister disappeared with you."

She sucks on her tongue to stay silent, as she does—did—when fighting with her mother. But she and Randah are not fighting.

"Of course she wouldn't tell you," Randah says. "Of course you wouldn't know." The disappointment in her voice belies the certainty of her words.

Did she think Hannah might have the answer?

"I'm sorry, Auntie," Hannah says.

Shuttled by Randah's driver, Hannah gets back to the apartment after two in the morning, feeling satisfied, though quite a bit sheepish that the poor man had to stay up so late to drive her home. The stories Randah told her tonight were like sandstone bricks slowly stacking up, building for her a past she'd never known she had. It isn't a solid structure. But she sees the ruins of the life her mother left behind, rather than an empty expanse of nothing. She's grappling with some of the details, things that would be punch lines in America but seem to be normal here. How her parents are cousins. How her mother's father for a short period had two wives at once. Randah told her about these aspects of their family as though they were nothing to hide. How shocked should she be? Could she love two people at once? Could she be married to two people at once?

Should she see any kind of equivalency between her grandfather's polygamy and kissing Zee at the beach?

How much a part of this family does she want to be? It's a constant thrumming question, but it confronts her loudly now. Her father stands outside the apartment building, bareheaded, his thawb unbuttoned at the neck. His white undershirt peeks out. She has never seen him angry before.

He opens the door for her, and the courtesy makes her want to spit before he speaks.

"Where the hell have you been?"

"You know. Aunt Randah's. Why are you shouting?"

"I'm not shouting."

"Why are you swearing at me? You could have called me at her house."

"You can't go gallivanting around Jidda in the middle of the night. If you get in trouble, I'm the one who'll go to jail. That's the way it is here."

She leaves her father in the apartment's entryway, pretending she'll never see him again, and crawls into bed, a thin wall separating her from the rest of the family.

The next morning, her father is eating breakfast on the living room floor when she comes out of her room. He apologizes.

"You came here to see people, to see your family. But call next time."

"I should go back home," she says.

"This is your home."

She hears how hard he's trying to persuade her.

RESOLUTION 678

Summer hears from someone who hears from Zee: He doesn't understand why Hannah stood him up. He wants to see her again.

"He's got a girlfriend," Hannah tells Summer over the phone.

"I can take you to the American Consulate to meet him. At the canteen they have ham sandwiches, beer."

"You're not listening." Hannah tries to think of what she misses about America; it's not ham sandwiches or beer. She misses the change of seasons. Brittle leaves on the ground. It's a week before Thanksgiving. They might have snow there.

"I heard you," Summer says. "But it's casual."

"I guess."

"I'll find out when he wants to meet you!" Summer squeals, seeming as excited as if the date were hers.

Summer tells Hannah about rumors that a group of women—university professors and businesswomen—have been apprehended driving in Riyadh.

"They're blacklisted. They lost their jobs."

"Wow." Hannah shivers. She misses driving, gripping a steering wheel, walking up the steps to her own apartment.

Three days later, at 11:30 a.m. sharp, Nasser delivers Hannah to the front gate of the consulate, and Hannah's American passport gets her in. She passes through a series of narrow, hospital-green hallways to the small dining hall where Zee waits. He wears his desert fatigues and looks younger than she remembers.

He orders ham and cheese and a Budweiser. She orders Caesar salad and a Reuben. He wants to know how long she's lived in the United States, how long she's been in Saudi, when she's going back.

"I've always lived there," she says. "I took the semester off. I guess I have to go back in January."

"Ohio's not so far from Indiana." As though there is some chance they can be acquainted beyond this isolated instant in history, this strange convergence of coincidences that has brought them together.

"Don't you go wherever the military sends you?"

"Sort of. I guess my girlfriend wouldn't like this." He points back and forth between them. "And neither would your boyfriend."

It's a joke to reestablish the boundaries of their relationship, which belongs here, in this country, in the few spaces where commingling of the sexes is allowed.

"Been back to the tape shop?" Zee says, as though wanting to return to their almost meet-cute, their original point of entry into each other's lives.

"My father doesn't have a driver."

"The music here is so much cheaper than at home. But I miss beer. And pizza." He offers her a sip.

"They have pizza here." She pushes the bottle away.

Another awkward half hour of conversation and he escorts her to the gate. He kisses her goodbye, though the guard is staring straight at them. She tastes beer on his breath. Is it the beer or being American that makes him so bold, so cocky?

In the car, she puts her hand on her racing heart. Can Nasser hear it? In her purse she has a package: a manila envelope she found in a drawer at her father's apartment, inside of which she has stuffed the FYC tape and the twenty-page letter for Malik—full of impressions of her visit, but no confession about Zee. Last night, she took ten minutes to decide whether to sign it "Love, Hannah," or "Sincerely, Hannah," or "Best, Hannah." In the end, she wrote "XXX OOO Hannah."

Before filling the envelope, she emptied it of old black-and-white passport-size photos with fluted edges like stamps, showing her father in a ghutrah, his face bleached by the flash so that he had no nose. The envelope had an address written on it in Arabic in permanent marker. On top of that, she Scotch-taped a piece of white paper with Malik's address on it. *M. Thomas*, she wrote, to be on the safe side. *Wouldn't want anyone to know I'm corresponding with a boy.* She meant to give the envelope to Nasser with a few riyals for airmail postage, to mail while she was at the consulate, but she forgot.

"Can we go to the post office?" she says.

"Miss, I have to go back to pick up Madam." Nasser accelerates through a yellow light as they speed below a looming underpass.

"I'll take a taxi."

"Your father won't like that, Miss."

"I've done it before. Who's going to tell him?"

"I can't leave you with a taxi driver, Miss."

She gives up. At her father's apartment, Lamees and Mary are setting the floor for lunch, which they eat at two o'clock. Muneer is not able to leave the paper for lunch today, Lamees says.

Hannah isn't hungry. She pokes at her rice with her spoon.

"You don't eat?" Lamees says. "Have you decided to be on a diet?"

The family naps in the midafternoon, and so Hannah waits till they sleep. As she slips on her sandals, she feels someone brush her leg.

"Fadi, go back to sleep."

He hums and tries to hug her. She can't resist him. Holding hands, they walk to the corner store. Two men lean against the store's shelves of toilet paper and biscuits. They wear their shimaghs with no iqal, and they chew reedy sticks that smell like tree sap. Hannah waves her phone card, and when they respond in Arabic, she waves it again.

The men point to the two orange pay phones in the back of the store.

Hannah half keeps an eye on Fadi circumambulating the store as she dials. She has to punch in the intricate combination of digits three times before she gets through to her mother's answering machine. In her purse are the letters to her mother from her grandfather, along with his translations. They contain no key to the mystery of why her mother chose to disappear and not come back to Jidda. Instead, they are full of two decades of news about births and marriages and her grandfather's newspaper, members of the Saudi royal family he's interviewed, a meeting with Muhammad Ali.

She should be happy to have this family history, but instead she's livid that she has to read it after the fact rather than experience it.

"Where the hell are you?" Hannah says into the handset while the message plays. It beeps over her words. She pulls her scarf closer to her hairline. The men stare. Have they never seen a woman before?

"It's me. I wanted to let you know I'm in Jidda. Seeing the place you grew up."

Hannah hasn't seen or talked to her mother in three years, since she ran away to Toledo. She sets the handset into its cradle. Calling her mother seemed like something she should do until she did it. She regrets leaving her ghostly, metallic voice—a piece of herself—on the tape.

Fadi is going up and down the short aisles of the tiny store.

She calls W, leaves a short message about where she is, and apologizes for not calling in so long.

Dialing the United States is getting easier the more she does it. She calls her mother again. Why not?

"Mama. Sadie. If you're there, pick up. Pick up, Mama."

She hears herself gasp when the phone picks up, as though she were eavesdropping on her own conversation.

"What are you doing there?"

"I want to know why. Why we had to disappear."

"You don't understand. They wouldn't have let me stay here with you. They would have taken you from me."

"Who's 'they'? Dad?"

"Everyone. Why am I telling this to you? You don't know."

She doesn't want to hear what her mother is saying, her side of the story. There should have been a better way, and why should she have to grapple with the choices her mother made?

One of the men stands near her, hand hovering, not wanting to tap her but wanting her attention. He speaks in Arabic, and she shakes her head. The other man tidies a display of Smarties and Chiclets.

"Miss. Your son?"

The door jingles shut.

"Fuck."

She leaves the phone handset dangling and rushes outside. The street is as hushed as a sepia-tone photo. It smells of spit and sand and metal. Fadi is nowhere to be seen.

"He walks off a lot," she says to the closed door of the shop, trying to calm herself down. The door is pasted with ads for ice cream, candy, phone cards. To the empty street, she shouts: "Fadi! Come here! I'm not here to have my father kill me for losing you."

She walks around the block five times, sticking her head into the corner store as she passes. "Yes, Miss?" the men say. Two more and she gives up. Her father is going to crucify her.

But in the apartment, everyone is asleep, except Mary and Fadi, who watch cartoons. Hannah finds herself silently repeating *thank-godthankgodthankgod*, though she's not religious.

Her voice comes back. "Fadi, why'd you leave me?"

"You took him for a walk?" Mary says. "I think he needs more walks, a playground. He loves his big sister."

Fadi gets up and hugs Hannah.

Hannah is done with her mother for a while, but the hug is enough.

By Thanksgiving, though, she needs more. She needs Malik's voice. It's been nearly two months since she said goodbye to him at the airport. So much has happened. She hasn't seen Zee since the consulate, but her low-grade guilt flares when she thinks about Malik. It will make her feel better, she thinks, to wish him a happy holiday. At naptime, she makes sure Fadi is with Mary—he's fallen asleep in front of the TV while Mary irons—before slipping out on her own to the corner shop.

She doesn't expect a dozen sanitary workers in blue jumpsuits to be waiting their turns for the phones. When she queues up behind them, the man ahead of her turns his head, and she accidentally makes eye contact. He looks at his feet.

Another man makes kissy sounds at her. His behavior doesn't faze her, but the shopkeeper notices and makes a fuss. He gestures toward the door, and Hannah realizes he is telling her to leave.

"Phone tomorrow?" he says.

"No, I want to phone today."

"Tomorrow," he says.

She doesn't want to cause a scene, so she leaves.

On Friday, at naptime, the shop is empty. The shopkeeper, alone that day, pours tea into a small glass and offers it to her.

"Maybe later," she says, but he won't let her refuse. She sets the glass on the shelf nearest the phone, next to cylindrical packages of cookies.

She gets through to Malik on her first try. The sound of his voice makes her yearn for him. She pulls her abayah tight around her.

"It's so good to hear you," he says.

"You too."

"I've been worried about you."

"I told you I might not be able to call."

"I know."

"I've got a twenty-page letter. Everything I need to tell you is in there."

"Why don't you send it?"

"I will. I'll give it to my dad."

"I love you."

She knows it's terrible to leave him hanging, but she can't think of what to say. The shopkeeper has gone outside. She sees him smoking through the glass doors.

"I was thinking." She flicks her nail at the little metal door on the coin return. "I was thinking you should see other people while I'm gone." Later—in a year, in two years—she'll recognize herself as the villain in this story. She'll recognize that the nonchalance with which she was willing to let him go was atypical for her, a person afraid of losing everyone. Except her mother, who she sees as the original bad guy, the villain in every other story.

Hannah's breaking her own heart.

The silence between them is filled with phone-line feedback. The distance that separates them is too much to bear.

"That wasn't the deal," he says. His words are puffed up with a sudden hatred that she knows she deserves. She ducks, as though he could throw something at her from where he is.

"I know, but—being here. It's more than I expected. The letter explains everything."

"You waited two months. Don't send the letter," Malik says. "You said everything you need to say."

Outside, the afternoon sun stings her eyes.

Hannah's father works constantly, especially after the UN makes its ultimatum at the end of November: Saddam has until January 15 to withdraw.

"It's good timing," Hannah tells her father. "Since I'm leaving on the twentieth. Hopefully he'll surrender soon."

"He won't surrender," Muneer says. "What if they close the airports on the fifteenth? You should leave sooner."

She's surprised he would suggest she cut her visit short. And she doesn't want to, though often she's bored. She wants to be like normal people and stick to a plan.

In early December, Summer drags Hannah to a holiday bazaar at one of the international schools and tries to convince her to buy pot holders decorated with an embroidered Saudi husband and wife— his head covered in tiny red-and-white check, hers in black. Their faces are made out of pantyhose pulled tight over cotton batting, and their sewn-on mouths curve into little red smiles.

"No way," Hannah says, and worries she's offended the nice British expat housewife who crafted the thing.

"We should plan a New Year's party at the beach," Summer says. "I'll invite that Zee guy."

"I don't think I should see him anymore."

"I met some cool Kuwaiti guys I could call."

Americans and Brits stream by. Hannah and Summer are among a few Saudis at the bazaar—and Summer looks like an expat. It is a strange friendship between them. When they go to stores at the mall, the shopkeepers speak to Summer in English and to Hannah in Arabic.

Hannah likes that here, at a foreigners' event, in a foreigners' school, they are almost on another planet. She likes that people here speak to them both in English; and they can walk around with their scarves around their necks, their abayahs wide open over their jeans and T-shirts; and the courtyard smells like hamburgers, which two middle-aged, blond men grill at another booth.

Something comes over her—she doesn't know what she's thinking—and while Summer is buying two hamburgers and the craft-booth lady is selling a tea cozy to a tall Scandinavian-looking woman with a blond pixie cut, Hannah sticks her hand into the pot holder and hides it under her abayah. It isn't like a cassette. It won't fit in her pocket. When Summer hands her a paper plate of food, she doesn't know what to do with the pot holder. With her back to the craft table, she presents it to Summer.

"You bought it!"

"Changed my mind. Can I put it in your bag?"

"We should go to the gold souk. You'll find better souvenirs there."

Hannah loves the souk. The whitewashed, wooden-windowed buildings lean against each other. What would it be like to live in one of them? What was life like for her grandparents' grandparents? She and Summer eschew the many gold shops, instead visiting a tiny silver shop. Hannah checks out charm bracelets with little high-heeled shoes and miniature houses and roller skates, silver rings that look like growling jaguars, and amulets with God's name on them. The far wall displays the pieces Summer likes best: a pair of hammered-silver earrings with etchings of crescent moons that appear shakily hand-drawn, another pair that looks to both of them like silver ear-chandeliers. Strings of thick, knuckle-size beads of coral and turquoise; amber beads that look like sugar dates.

"It's so hard to find this traditional stuff," Summer says. "Everyone wants gaudy jewelry. Diamond bracelets from Italy."

When Hannah says she can't afford to buy anything, Summer haggles with the shopkeeper in Arabic over the price per gram of silver. Unlike most of the men in the souk, he wears a black T-shirt and blue jeans, not traditional clothing, and he responds in American English. "I can't go any less—I'll lose money."

Summer keeps haggling though, till Hannah tires of listening. She steps outside and sits at a fountain listening to the water tinkling. As two men walk by, she thinks she hears one of them say, "Habibti"—my love, darling, sweetie. She flips them the bird. They keep smiling.

Summer has left the shop, and she cusses the guys out. "I told them to respect themselves." She hands Hannah a small black plastic bag. Inside is a velvet box containing the chandelier earrings.

"I can't accept that," Hannah says. "You keep them."

"No, no, you have to have something to take back with you. Something better than a pot holder."

Hannah has the stolen tape and the stuff Aunt Randah gave her. But she doesn't want to argue in public.

"What if I stayed here?" She is thinking of Aunt Randah, her father, her brothers, her grandmothers.

"You should keep the earrings."

On their way to the parking garage, where Nasser waits for them, they buy chickpeas with vinegar and pickled turnips from a street vendor. The call to prayer sounds and shops' metal grates start to bang closed, one by one.

"Afternoon prayer." Summer sucks on a chickpea and taps her plastic spoon against her cheek as they head to the car. "If you think you're going to have an arranged marriage and hire a driver and teach art at a private school or something—I mean, I guess you could stay. Sounds like a nice tidy life. No bands, though. No movie theaters. No road trips."

"You're telling me not to stay."

"But can you find pickles like these in America?"

On New Year's Eve, the war is two weeks off. Hannah stays home and draws for the first time in weeks. She puts on her abayah and headscarf, borrows her father's Polaroid, and takes an instant photo of herself in the entryway mirror. With a charcoal pencil, she copies the photo. She gives herself dark circles under the eyes. A toothless smile, like in the photograph. By midnight, her father and Lamees have been in bed for several hours. Hannah uses the phone in the front room to call Malik.

"Happy new year," she whispers.

"It's four in the afternoon. And I thought we broke up."

"I changed my mind. Please tell me you didn't listen to me and see other people."

"I'm worried about you," he says. "I'm worried about this war."

"My dad says it'll be over fast."

When she falls asleep, Malik is in her dreams.

The war starts on a Thursday at 2:00 a.m. Hannah finds out from her father at breakfast. He's been working nearly nonstop since the deadline passed on Tuesday.

The cheese and olives Mary prepared smell too strong to eat. Hannah keeps thinking how a lot of the US soldiers who came to fight are her age. Zee has probably been transported to the Eastern Province, maybe Kuwait.

"When the airport reopens, you're going home," her father says before heading back to the newspaper offices. He dips his bread into small bowls of honey and cream. "I want you to be safe."

She's ready to go, she realizes. She's not the same person she was when she arrived. She'll leave her family behind, but take them with her, like a pot holder or a pair of earrings.

CNN has replaced Saudi television. Hannah, Lamees, and Mary watch most of the day. At Dhuhr and 'Asur prayer times, the broadcast shifts to readings of the Qur'an, and Lamees leaves the room to say her prayers while Hannah and Mary watch the boys.

On TV, they show US soldiers writing "love letters" on bombs. At home, Malik is writing Hannah a breakup letter as though she hadn't already broken up with him, but of course she doesn't know that yet.

The boys go stir-crazy until Lamees turns the TV off and tells Mary to take them to the roof to run around.

When Hannah's father comes home, near Maghrib time, he's already taken his shimagh and iqal off and hung them in the crook of his elbow. He heads straight to the bathroom to wash up.

Hannah doesn't know how to wash for prayer, and she doesn't know how to pray. She puts on one of Lamees's long prayer scarves, a sharshaf, as big as a bedsheet. Lamees lays out prayer rugs, one vertical in front and a second horizontally, behind the first. Hannah stands beside her stepmother as her father leads them in prayer.

"*Allahu akbar*," he starts, and she raises her hands and lowers them to her chest, like Lamees.

Hannah doesn't understand the words her father recites out loud, and she struggles to mimic Lamees's and her father's movements. But she can pray with them. She needs to pray.

GONE

With Operation Desert Storm launched and the country officially-officially at war, they settle into a new routine. Fouad's school closes, and so the three boys are home. It's like being home because of a blizzard—except it's because of a war, and no one knows exactly when it will end, though Summer has heard that it won't last long. Flights start up again, but flights are limited; it's not clear when Hannah will be able to leave. She feels guilty at the idea of leaving her dad and his family behind to deal with the war without her, but she also wishes for certainty, for the Arabica coffee shop on Coventry Road, for a life drawing session, a French avant-garde movie at the Cleveland Cinematheque, a blizzard.

When Hannah gets tired of watching censored CNN in her father's apartment, she goes to Randah's or Summer's to watch more CNN and drink tea. They have drivers who can pick her up. The streets are empty, as they have been the last few weeks. People are staying home. Most nights, her father's not home till well after midnight. She and Lamees and the boys eat dinner without him: scrambled eggs with tomato, olives, feta cheese, and pita left over from lunch. No ful mudammas or muttabbaq, though, because these are street foods and they have no man to go out to buy them. No fresh bread from the bakery, either. Hannah tries to convince Lamees that she and Mary could walk to the commercial strip mall down the road and pick up food for their meals, but Lamees says, "No, no, no." Hannah wakes up to the sound of her father returning home in the middle of the night, and she turns over and goes back to sleep. In the morning, he's gone before breakfast, and he doesn't come home midday for lunch, as he did before the war.

Two weeks after the start of the war, he doesn't come home.

Hannah, Lamees, and Mary go to bed at midnight, as usual. Hannah expects to be woken by the lock clicking slowly as he lets himself in, by his footsteps down the hallway, by the faucet running as he washes for prayer in the bathroom. Instead, she sleeps soundly enough to have dreams. There is no click, no thump, no drip of water. She sleeps until morning. She wakes up expecting another day like the string of fourteen days before it.

But today, Mary is frantic.

"Your father, ma'am. He's not here."

"He leaves so early."

"No, ma'am. He was not here last night."

"Where's Lamees?"

"She's gone to talk to your grandfather Fareed."

Mary says Lamees knew something was wrong when Muneer was not home for dawn prayer. Lamees called the paper. She called Muneer's brothers. But for some reason, she did not wake Hannah up.

"What can I do?" Hannah says. "I'm sure he's OK."

She worries about car crashes—the driving in Jidda is horrendous, worse than California driving—she worries about heart attacks. Her chest constricts. How unfair it would be to lose her father right after she found him.

Mary tells Hannah she can watch the three boys alone. Within half an hour, Summer and Nasser arrive to pick Hannah up, and they rush to her grandfather Fareed's, an old-fashioned whitewashed villa in the Al Hamra district with wooden windows.

"Old money, Saudi style," Summer says.

Summer waits outside in the car. Inside, Lamees sits with Hannah's grandmother and grandfather in a room with low cushions around its perimeter, like many other salons in the city. They have cups of tea in front of them and the room smells like rose water. In a crisis, there is tea.

Lamees has not removed her abayah or tarhah but she has uncovered her face, something Hannah never expected her to do with a man present.

Hannah's grandmother Faizah says something in Arabic, something meant to be soothing.

Grandfather Fareed says, "I called people I know. They told me your father is in Riyadh. It's the columns he's been writing. They don't want anyone raising problems in the middle of the liberation."

"What the fuck," Hannah says. She claps her hand over her mouth to keep the obscenities inside.

"I'll jump on a flight," he says. "I'll call Bandar, too. You shouldn't talk about it to anyone."

"He's in jail? In prison? That's what you're saying?"

"Your father's a good man. They'll let him go soon, inshallah. He did something risky."

Hannah's grandmother Faizah touches her arm, tries to lead her toward the salon.

Her grandfather tells her to stay for tea, for dinner. He has to go back to the paper. The idea of sipping tea when her father is God knows where makes her so angry she's shaking, the way her leg shook once when she drove through a red light and missed an accident by a hair. She can't stop the tremors. Through the fog of her anxiety, she is able to digest that her grandparents are consumed with worry, too. Her grandmother fiddles obsessively with beautiful blue prayer beads; her thumb keeps moving the bead along the string. Hannah's grandfather twists his iqal back and forth. Their faces, too, are twisted with concern.

"Say a prayer," her grandfather says. It is what people here say when they want someone to calm down.

She barely knows how to pray. "I want him to be safe," she says. "I want him to come home. Is that a prayer?"

W

1987

Twelve years after we left W's house, I went back. You didn't expect that, did you?

Before my senior year started—you know this part—I left. Maybe you know why. Baba found me. It was like being visited by a ghost. My grief over his loss unburied itself and I didn't know what to do, but I knew I couldn't be under the same roof as you. Never again.

The part you don't know is that I took a Greyhound bus to Toledo and W picked me up. I'm sure the reason she recognized me was because I was the only Arab chick waiting in the station, or maybe because I looked like you.

Her hair was in the same short, grandma-ish style as it had been when we stayed with her. She'd come straight from work, in Peanuts scrubs and white sneakers.

She hugged me and kissed me on one cheek, held me at arm's length by my shoulders so she could look at me. I sensed people staring at us. A teenaged girl with pink hair, a young kid sitting on his mom's lap, a beardless old guy in the corner. I tried to stop caring about them by looking at her. Her eyes were as sardonic as ever—a word I didn't know when I was five, but I always knew she had no bullshit about her.

"What do I call you, honey?" she said.

I guess, when I'd phoned her to tell her I was coming, I hadn't called myself by name. I'd said I was the daughter of a friend of hers, and we'd stayed with her a long time ago. She'd told me of course I could stay with her, and she'd given me her address. She hadn't asked why I needed a place to go.

It wasn't shelter I wanted. It wasn't answers, either. Though I was going to ask her if she knew why you stole me.

"I'm Hannah," I told her that day she picked me up.

What I was looking for was something I could barely name. I hadn't expected to feel the way I did when I saw the smile rise in her face at the sound of my voice. She'd never heard me called Hannah before, but she recognized my voice.

I was home, for once. I was in a place where I belonged.

Toledo itself was unfamiliar. You and I had driven in and out, and the rest of the time we were holed up at W's. But her house . . . She hadn't moved, and seeing the stoop and the oak tree standing sentinel brought a flood of relief, because W was real and her house was real. You'd pretended plenty of times over the years that W didn't exist, like we'd never stayed with her. You didn't want me to be connected to anything we'd left behind.

I'd remembered anyway, but seeing for myself where we'd been was vindication, proof of what I already knew: how much you'd lied. How you'd tried to erase my memories but hadn't fully succeeded. I don't know why, but more than meeting my father, going back to W's taught me this: if I could hang onto memories of W, if I could find her again, I could escape you and your version of reality.

The inside of the house was not exactly as I'd remembered it. She'd painted the living room dove gray; pulled out the blue shag and refinished the wood floors; replaced some of the old, secondhand furniture

with trim Scandinavian pieces; and sold the barber's chair or donated
it to Goodwill. In its place in the basement was a treadmill facing a
brand-new television. But the bay window was full of greenery. And
the house was full of ghosts. Like, I could sense the presence of the barber's
chair whenever I went down to the basement to wash my clothes or jog
on the treadmill. I could feel myself passing through the specters of us—us
on the day we arrived, us on the day of the haircuts, us on the day we left.
Frozen as if in amber.

The memories are painful. Writing this is painful. But the memories
and the pain are mine. The story is mine.

I spent my senior year at W's house. I slept in the room I'd slept in before.
The walls were repainted dark purple, and W asked if I wanted to hang
up posters, "like teenagers do."

I had a couple Matisse posters from the Cleveland Museum of Art.
I'd brought them with me in a poster tube. I put them up with sticky
putty and thumbtacked some of my own drawings to the wall. I didn't
care if those got holes.

I had a suitcase of clothes—not that old blue one; this was my own,
tweedy brown—and I never unpacked it. One day, I came home from
school and W had put everything in drawers. She stashed the suitcase in
the basement, next to the treadmill.

"I don't want you to think you can up and leave," she said.

"But the suitcase is downstairs. I don't have much stuff. I can pack
anytime, if I want to leave."

"Tell me you're not going to leave till you graduate high school."

"I'm not going to leave," I said. "I'm not my mother."

"I'm still mad at your mother, but you're not allowed to talk about
her like that."

I told her that was a deal breaker. If she wanted me to stay, she had to understand that if anyone should be mad at you, it was me. That she couldn't take that from me.

We were standing in the basement.

"OK, honey," she said.

With those words, she was the first person—not including Baba—to acknowledge everything you took from me.

The year went by fast. W made me go to the movies with her on Friday nights. She cried when I left for college and made me promise to call her weekly.

When I started thinking about going to Saudi junior year, she didn't like the idea. You had gone through so much trouble to keep me from there.

I told her while I stayed with her the summer before I went. It was days before the Iraqi invasion of Kuwait, so we didn't have war to worry about yet. She was watering her plants. Midday light flooded the living room. It was so bright I shaded my eyes.

"Maybe your mom didn't do the right thing, but she had her reasons. It's a hard place for women."

"How do you know?" I told her. "I have to see it for myself."

"Fine. Don't tell me when you go so I won't worry. Don't tell me till you come back." She'd spilled water on the hardwood floor but she didn't rush to wipe it up.

"That's silly. You'll know I'm there because I'm not calling you like I usually do."

"I'll pretend I don't know."

So, I went radio silence while I was in Saudi, except for one answering machine message. But when I came back to Ohio, she was the first person I called.

CONVERT

1998

SANCTUARY

Coventry Second Church of Christ sits on a leafy triangle of land, surrounded by brick and wood colonials but a place apart from them. It is not near Coventry Road, and Sadie often wonders why it bears that name. Did the congregation move? Is there a Coventry First Church of Christ? Who are the people kneeling in the building's stained-glass windows? What would it be like to stand on the other side of the glass and have sunlight cast those greens and blues and reds onto her body?

After nearly thirty years of living in America, Sadie knows next to nothing about Christians. They have their Christmas and their Easter. Some of them are Catholics and some of them are Protestants and a few of them are other things, but she doesn't know what makes these groups different. Long ago she accidentally memorized the words to "Rudolph the Red-Nosed Reindeer" when Hannah learned it in school. The same year—or was it?—she bought a fake three-foot-tall Christmas tree from Kmart because Hannah wanted a tree. The box fit in the trunk of Sadie's car. As easily as buying groceries, she could bring Christianity into her house.

Oddly, her parents had had a Christmas tree in their formal salon before she left them, handed down to them by American neighbors who were returning to the United States. Sadie's mother thought the tree was beautiful, and hadn't cared about the religious symbolism.

Her father, on the other hand, questioned the tree in his pragmatic way.

"We are different than Christians," he said.

Sadie hadn't asked how, besides not celebrating Jesus Christ's birth.

She can't remember, but perhaps her father's mild objection years before was the reason she refused to buy ornaments for Hannah. They decorated the tree with crafts Hannah made at school: a popcorn-and-cranberry garland, green and red paper chains, tissue-paper snowflakes. They made gifts by hand and opened them Christmas morning. She'd embroidered flowers on a T-shirt for Hannah. Hannah had taped tissues into a ball and used a black permanent marker to write "I love you" on it.

The tree is in Sadie's attic; she hasn't set it up in years. She has long given up her own faith, lost it so gradually that only now, contemplating the beauty of a church, does she realize it evaporated years ago.

She moved to this neighborhood a few months ago, her first move in more than a decade. When she walks past Coventry Second Church of Christ during her morning walks, or drives by on her way to work at Dillard's, she feels a tiny flash of warmth in her sternum.

Her new place is a tiny purple bungalow amid Tudors and colonials. When she moved in, the lilac tree near the screened-in back porch dripped with blooms that blended into the siding. She clipped a dozen branches and stuffed the flowers into vases, water glasses, mason jars. The bush looked no less lush than it had before she took out her gardening shears.

The house before this one was her then-boyfriend Jim's—he was the reason she'd settled down for so long after years and years of constant motion—and he let her garden one small section of border alongside his vast Shaker Heights lawn. She grew snapdragons and carnations in the summer, easy things. She never got any better as a gardener over the years. When she first started buying flats of flowers from the garden center, she chose based on the colors and the smells. Not all flowers smelled like perfume, she learned. Some gave off the fragrance of cinnamon, others the odor of a skunk or the basic scent of soap.

She kept gardening at Jim's because she liked separating the roots of a plant with a trowel before she set it in the soil, setting it free from the strictures of the pot. She liked rising from the ground with damp, muddy knees. She liked smacking her gloved hands together to let loose the dirt that had clung to her.

Jim recently sold the house and moved from Ohio to North Carolina, where his daughter and grandchild live. He asked her to move with him, but she didn't want to move anymore. She didn't want a long-distance relationship, either. So they broke things off. They'd never talked about marriage.

Drifting apart seems like a natural end to things, but she misses him.

To put him out of her mind, Sadie wants to create her own world in her smallish backyard, dig up the grass, eat flavorful zucchinis and tomatoes, grow glorious wildflowers, learn to cultivate intoxicatingly fragrant roses.

She's going to people her life with plants.

The former owners left a rusty old hoe with a splintery handle in the garage and a sage-green wheelbarrow resting upside down against the back fence. Sadie buys a spade and a fork-tongued weeder, an edger, a lawn mower, thick gardening gloves, and rubber clogs.

The next weekend, buckets of rain fall from the sky. She can't garden, but she wants to be outside. She wears her rubber clogs and looks through her unpacked moving boxes for an umbrella. When she can't find one, she pulls on a hoodie. The downpour has let up briefly. She steps out into drizzle. Lots of rain will make it easier to dig up the lawn, she tells herself. That's what the lady at the gardening center told her, anyway.

She strolls down the block with rain in her face. The stately red-brick church's lights are on and its bells are ringing. Cars pull into the parking lot and men in slacks and women in skirts awkwardly push their umbrellas out the car doors and angle themselves out. The rain starts to fall harder, and Sadie puts her hands in her pockets. She's underdressed and wet, but she walks inside and sits on one of the long wooden benches, toward the back of the big, high-ceilinged hall. She rubs her hands together and tries to catch the warmth of the room, like cozying up in front of a fire.

The hall fills up a little more than halfway, with most people sitting toward the front. Empty seats surround her. The white walls of the church open her mind, and the stained glass comforts her. Someone is reaching a hand out to someone else in every scene.

When the service begins, she watches the congregants. She stands when they stand, picks up the hymnbook from the little shelf on the seat in front of her when they do, and sings when they sing—quietly, so no one can hear.

Later, if anyone asks her about her first time at the church, she will not be able to tell them what hymns were sung, what sermon was given, who attended that day in the sanctuary.

She will tell them, instead, how she never knew before how alone she had been.

FORGIVENESS

For months, Sadie reads King James and goes to Bible study and drinks instant coffee and asks God for guidance and helps sort donations for the annual rummage sale. She thinks about the Virgin Mary, alone with a child.

The pastor, Stuart, is a young man with amber eyes and hair. Like almost everyone at the church and in the neighborhood, save a few black families, he is white. He plays the guitar. Somehow, he gets the idea that she's a Catholic considering converting, and she goes with it. She never lies, but she never reveals the truth. She works hard not to let slip that she's never heard of Saul or Paul or Mary Magdalene or the Ecclesiastes or Psalms.

In early October, she plants bulbs in her front yard. They are plants that don't yet exist, a dream of orange and yellow daylilies, Purple Dream irises, Lilac Wonder and Spring Green tulips. She plants purple and white hardy mums to brighten the fall. She rakes oak and maple leaves. Among the rummage-sale loot she finds an old Burpee catalog. She takes it home and reads it. In the spring, she'll plant petunias, purple sage, cherry tomatoes, summer squash, pumpkins, cucumbers, peppers, lettuce, parsley, basil. She wants to plant everything.

When she decides to go through with being baptized, she calls Hannah. Hannah has never been as good as Sadie was at hiding. For six or seven years, she hasn't wanted to talk to her mother or see her—she says so whenever Sadie finds her. But Hannah lets the phone company list her number. Her Seattle law office website features a photo of her, in a sleek bob and a navy-blue suit. Her husband, Hamza, a Syrian guy, leaves voice messages on Sadie's answering machine, gently telling her Hannah will call her soon, and though Hannah never does, Sadie believes Hamza would persuade her in an emergency. He tries to be kind. When he intercepts Sadie's phone calls, he speaks to her in Arabic. She answers in English. He says he's sorry they've never met.

Hannah's unwillingness to communicate is like a sty that won't heal, no cure for it but hope. Sadie wishes Hannah had never gone to Jidda; ever since, Hannah has taken Muneer's side.

Sadie wants her daughter back. The years that have passed since they lived together have not changed that.

A month before her baptism ceremony, which will take place at the start of the Christmas season before things become too hectic, Sadie leaves a well-practiced message on Hannah's voicemail. She doesn't know how Hannah and Hamza will take the news that she's converting. So she says she's receiving an award at work. She would like them to be there.

A day later, Hamza calls her home phone while she's at Dillard's. She plays the answering machine message over and over: *Thank you for inviting us, Sadie. We'll be there.*

When she thinks ahead to the baptism, Sadie feels a sense of calm, like floating in a swimming pool with her eyes closed. When she thinks about Hannah, her stomach heaves. She tries to avoid picturing what their meeting will be like. But she needs to take control. She switches shifts with her coworker Aida and makes an elaborate plan to go to the airport gate to meet Hannah and Hamza.

If she welcomes them with the baptism invitation in hand and explains her white lie without hesitation, they're sure to forgive her.

She prays on the matter.

Hamza doesn't respond to her requests for their flight number. There are few flights from Seattle on the Friday they are flying in. Sadie drives to Hopkins at seven in the morning, gets the airlines' schedule booklets from the departure desks, and makes her way to the gates, one after the other.

The airport is quiet and nearly empty. Thanksgiving has barely passed, and the airport is already decorated for Christmas. The Christmas tree in the corner of the security hall rises up to the ceiling, strung with lights and silver and gold tinsel. Underneath are large wrapped boxes. *This tree belongs to me*, she thinks. *This place belongs to me, and I belong here.*

As the day goes by, the hallways fill with people rolling their suitcases and tugging their children. Christmas Muzak plays. She hopes for Rudolph; when she hears the familiar tune, she sings along under her breath. The rest of the day the song's in her head through the maddening waits for the planes to disembark. Her eyes bounce from person to person, straining not to miss Hannah behind someone taller. She eats a Cinnabon for late breakfast and Burger King fries for lunch. She can't imagine Hamza is religious—Hannah was not raised that way, and like marries like. She hopes he will convince Hannah to accept Sadie's conversion. She practices the words she will say to her daughter: "I am repenting for what I've done wrong. I will be wiped clean. Will you forgive me?"

She spots them at four o'clock, disembarking a flight that connected in Denver. She has resorted to standing on the black faux leather chair to see over the tall crowd of people greeting their families. These hours of waiting, she has seen the faces of joy as passengers recognize their loved ones and convinced herself she will receive such a look from her daughter and son-in-law: smiles that bathe her in love.

Instead, Hannah reprimands her.

"Mom. We'll see you tomorrow at the thing. You could have sent us the address."

She wears a loose black knit dress over black tights. Her long hair is in pigtails, like a child.

She's pregnant, Sadie thinks. She feels a rising anger that they didn't tell her before they came.

Hamza looks like he wants to take Hannah's words back, but he's helpless. His wavy hair is slicked with gel and his goatee gives him a distinguished, professorial look. Sadie likes the kindness in his eyes.

She sees the bundle in Hamza's arms.

"Oh my God," she says. *Not pregnant anymore.*

Hannah points to Sadie's neck. "What's that?" she says.

Sadie forgot the slender gold cross she has started wearing. She touches it and nods her head toward Hamza. "What's that?"

"It's our baby, Mom."

"Let's head to baggage claim, yes, ladies?" Hamza says. "And maybe a stop on the way to change Foofoo." He pats the baby's bottom with one hand.

Sadie feels the words she wanted to say—to explain why she'd invited Hannah and Hamza here—slipping away.

"Foofoo?" she says.

"His name is Fareed," Hannah says.

Sadie searches for a message in Hannah's voice. What does it mean that she has named her first child after Sadie's father?

"Do you want me to help change him?" Sadie asks.

"Hamza can do it."

Hamza clutches the baby, as though Fareed can save him from his wife and mother-in-law, and disappears into the men's room. Sadie feels sorry for him.

A cart beeps at Sadie and Hannah. The white-haired man in the front passenger seat holds his cane stiff against his knee, and the woman behind him clutches her pocketbook upright on her lap. The uniformed driver lays on the horn again. Hannah and Sadie step wordlessly out of the way and hang close to the wall.

Hannah takes off her sweater and wraps it around her waist. "Where is this ceremony happening?"

"At church."

"I'm sorry? Why is it at church?"

"I'm being baptized." Sadie whispers so no one will hear but Hannah. Hannah leans closer; the anger coloring her cheeks and brightening her eyes is contagious. Sadie feels the fever. "I didn't think you'd come if I told you the real reason."

"Have we become Christian?" Hannah says.

"You are whatever you are. This is me." Sadie has been carrying her wool coat and sweater over one arm but the weight of them distracts her. She lets them fall to the floor.

"I can't deal with you, Mom," Hannah says as Hamza emerges from the bathroom. He hands Fareed to Hannah and her face immediately calms, though the baby is wailing. She pats his back and he calms, too.

"It's disgusting in there. No changing table, of course."

"She's converting," Hannah says.

Hamza looks from mother to daughter.

"It's always lies between us," Hannah says. "She told us one thing, award ceremony, whatever, but she's being baptized. In church."

"That's wonderful. I guess."

"You have a baby," Sadie says.

"We didn't lie about that. Here he is. You can see him with your own eyes."

"Thank you. May I hold him?"

"Of course," Hamza says, but Hannah doesn't offer baby Fareed to her mother. She holds him tighter.

"Can we please get the luggage?" she says.

It is decided that Sadie will drive home and Hannah, Hamza, and the baby will take a cab to their hotel. They are a family, and she doesn't fit into the portrait. She writes the church address on a slip of paper and gives it to Hamza as she says goodbye to them. Hannah and the baby slide into the back of the taxi, and Hamza opens the front door for himself.

Sadie's hungry and tired and drained. "Hannah is so angry with me. Always," she tells Hamza. "I can't change it."

"Maybe you need time." He kisses her cheek. "We'll see you tomorrow."

His words don't reassure her. He's known Hannah a few years. Sadie's known her her whole life.

In the morning, Sadie dresses in the pink pantsuit she bought with her Dillard's employee discount, carefully applies the new pink lipstick and lip liner she chose at the makeup counter. When she walks into the church, people smile and ask if she's nervous.

She lifts the corners of her mouth into as stiff a grin as she can so she won't have to lie and say no.

Sitting in the pews waiting for the ceremony to start, she keeps looking back to the entrance. But Hannah never arrives.

Me and God from now on, Sadie thinks.

DETAINED

2003

MEMOIR

The first details Muneer set down, he tells Hannah, were the contents of the Riyadh prison cell he lived in for the six weeks before the liberation of Kuwait on February 28, 1991: The bunkbed pushed against the far wall. The plastic woven prayer mat, spread diagonally facing the qiblah. The cell's pale green walls were bare, except for a wall hanging of Ayat al-Kursi embroidered in gold thread on black velvet. Muneer wondered if the jailer who hung the ayah there thought about its words: *To Him is everything in the heavens and in Earth ... He knows what is between their hands and what is behind them.*

The men who apprehended him had met him outside the newsroom, on a dark Jidda street smelling of wastewater and, when the breeze blew a certain way, night blossoms. *Someone should investigate why the municipality irrigates parks with sewage*, he remembers thinking. *American parks never have such an odious odor.*

Two days had passed since the middle-of-the-night start of the war—timed for American prime-time television. A day had passed since Muneer wrote an editorial column condemning the American invasion of Iraq. Saddam Hussein should not have invaded Kuwait, of course. He had not yet started dumping crude oil in the Gulf—that would happen while Muneer was in jail—but he should not have done that or a thousand other terrible things he'd inflicted on Iraq, on Kuwait, on Saudi.

But Muneer did not believe this war waged by the American president was the answer for the Saudi nation.

The government disagreed with him. He knew he'd taken a risk. He'd hoped, he'd prayed to God they would let him be and understand he wrote his words because he loved his nation. That's how he ended the column: by saying his love for country, flag, and king was deep, that nothing could change it.

The men—there were three, maybe four of them, he couldn't remember exactly—had Najdi accents.

"What's your news?" one of them said, smirking at his own joke. Muneer knew immediately why they had come.

He assured them he wouldn't resist. They didn't need to blindfold him or bind his wrists. He took responsibility for the things he'd written.

At least this wasn't Iraq. He didn't fear violence. He worried no one would tell his family he'd been taken to prison.

They didn't find out for days; Bandar didn't show up for a week. When the guards brought Muneer out to meet him, Muneer was glad for the first time that his father was not alive to see him in prison.

Muneer wanted to hear about Lamees, the boys and Hannah, his mother, and Operation Desert Storm—in that order. Bandar had brought letters from them, but the police confiscated the pages. He brought word, too, that Hannah's mother's father, Fareed, was pulling strings, trying to decipher what could be done to rescue Muneer.

Did Hannah's father resent being helped by the father of the woman who stole his daughter from him?

For more than a decade, ideas for a book about his experience have swirled in Muneer's head like white glitter in a snow globe he once bought in the San Francisco airport while attending a journalism conference. Shake the globe and the Golden Gate Bridge was engulfed in a blizzard like it never saw in real life.

It's this funny, interesting way of putting things that Hannah thinks will make for a good memoir. But despite the blizzard in his brain, until a few months ago he hadn't written a word of his memories down. Hannah has spent years trying to convince him, but he says no one else would want him to talk about this injustice. He doesn't regret speaking out against the war, but he's never been emboldened to cross the line again. Not even after 9/11, when it became clear that most of the hijackers were Saudi. Behind closed doors, Saudis talked about what that meant. But in public? In the pages of a newspaper or online? Never.

Certain stories are best left untold, he has said to Hannah many times. If Hannah doesn't understand, it's because she's American. She shrugs the accusation off. There are a lot of things she doesn't tell people, and it's not her fault she was born there. But the lawyer in her wants him to tell this story of her father being wronged by his own government.

"How could they imprison you without a trial?" she'd said once when he called to wish her a happy birthday. She brought up the book regularly. "What law were you breaking? Some unwritten rule about not rocking the boat?"

He insisted he didn't have the time to write about his days in prison. He didn't want to argue about it.

He changed his mind last year after going to a journalism conference in Cairo, where he met Bassam, an up-and-coming

Lebanese American agent who asked if he'd ever thought of writing a book. With the hubbub of the conference swirling around them, he was emboldened to say yes and, in the dark, far corner of a hotel restaurant, to spill his secret to this stranger. Confessions, Muneer insisted, are often easiest to make to people who don't know us, who have no ingrained picture of us to be muddied and mussed by revelations we've kept to ourselves for so long they seem impossible to accept, dangerous to believe.

"I suppose so," Hannah says. She's a little miffed he listened to the agent and not to her.

On a spring evening, Hannah and Muneer are eating dinner, the two of them, in a fancy seafood restaurant in downtown Seattle, blocks from her office. He insists on treating her, and she knows better than to argue.

"I'm not surprised this agent guy wants your book," she says. "Everyone everywhere in the world wants to know the hidden details of life in Saudi."

"Hidden from whom?" He sips ice water. "We know who we are."

Hannah has agreed to help him write the story of what he lived through in those dark days of 1991.

"Of course I'll help," she says. "I've been wanting you to write this for ages."

He says he does not need new trouble, so he has insisted the book be published under a pseudonym. His editor in London doesn't know his real name.

Hannah asks if he has journals he wrote while he was detained. She wants to know why it happened.

"The government was investing a lot in the war, in convincing us it was the single path possible. They didn't like the columns

I published questioning American motives. They needed silence until the war was won."

"And you wouldn't stop?"

"I would have stopped if they asked me. They didn't ask."

"Shouldn't a journalist believe in the absolute right to a free press?"

"Your press is buying the Bushes' new war hook, line, and sinker—like they swallowed the first Gulf War," he says. "I met them, the American journalists who came to cover that war. They had never been to our country before—"

"Because the Saudi government wouldn't let them."

"And they thought they knew our 'Arab minds.' We were not trustworthy. We haggled in the bazaars, we didn't have a word for *negotiate*."

"The Iraqis are who they were talking about."

"The Arabs. Anyway, the press is treating this new war the same way. They would've made up an excuse for it if the government didn't already have one."

She picks a sliver of jicama out of her salad and chews on it. Sometimes, she wants to go back where she came from, like the racists demand. But she's tried that already. Sometimes, it seems like there's nowhere in the world to be.

"Ours is a good country, with good people. I left the prison cell and went straight back to journalism. The secret police not-so-secretly shut down *Akhbar al-'Urus*, but no one stopped me from starting another paper. Now, after 9/11, I am saying many things about our country, good and bad, that the world should know."

"You're putting that in your book?"

"We're better off today than we were in the past. We have to stay on the road of modernization our rulers have put us on. But our society wants to forget the past. That's the root of our problems. We have to know our history."

"Bad people are the root of everyone's problems."

"That's simplistic."

"OK, Baba." This project might be more difficult than she thought. She had hoped for a way to bond with her father, to spend time with him, carve time out of her busy life. But they would not agree on everything he wanted to say. She couldn't always put herself in his shoes, but she would have to learn to be his conduit.

Tonight, Hannah's father wants to tell her something else, not related to the book. They order coffee—fully caffeinated for both of them, though it's after seven o'clock—and he takes a letter out of the breast pocket of his tan suit. It arrived the day before his planned flight to visit her about the book project, he says.

She holds the letter in two hands, as though reading a newspaper. The note appears to be from an American law firm, and she's unprepared for the punch it delivers.

We are writing to inform you that your son, Fouad Muneer, has been detained illegally by the United States government. We learned of his detention from another illegal detainee, an Iraqi client of ours who has attended Muslim Student Association meetings with Mr. Muneer at the Sullivan School of Business and has not been told his own reason for being detained. We fear the same is likely true for your son.

Mr. Muneer is being held at the federal facility in Miami, Florida. We would be happy to assist with his legal counsel. Please contact us at the number included on this letterhead.

"You buried the fucking lede, Dad. My brother's in jail?"

"Don't swear, habibti."

That word: My love. My dear. It still has the power to slay her, to surprise her. It's the dream she worries she'll one day wake up from: her father is alive, and he loves her.

GONE SOUTH

Hannah never finds out for sure if her father has worked on Hamza behind the scenes, but in the end Hamza convinces her to take on Fouad's case. Her firm's partners agree to let her do it pro bono.

She's seen Fouad a few times since she first met him in Jidda when he was six. A couple of summers later, her dad brought the kids and Lamees to visit her. When Fouad started college, she meant to go see him in Florida. She regrets she hadn't gone down before.

Foofoo wants to meet his "Young Uncle," as Hamza and Hannah start calling him.

"Is he five like me?" Foofoo asks.

"No, he's nineteen."

"That's not young."

For the past year and a half, since the United States invaded Afghanistan, Hamza has been saying Iraq would be next. With the war there started, Hannah can't sleep more than a few continuous hours. She wakes up sweating from dreams in which she dives into the Red Sea with her clothes on.

"That dream has nothing to do with war," Hamza says.

But it does, because the last war was happening when she saw the Red Sea.

"Everything has to do with the war," she says. "My brother in custody has to do with the war. It's a war on us."

A war on us even though she is not religious. They are not religious. Which sounds like a cliché, something many of her Christian and Jewish friends say whenever anything vaguely God-related comes up. But the problem runs deeper for her, taps into how weird her childhood was. Lack of religion was part of the disguise her mother created for the two of them.

Hamza's got the opposite reason for not caring much for faith. He says he was suffocated by it growing up. After 9/11, he shaved his goatee and told her to call him Ham at the grocery store, the movie theater, the pool. "That'll throw the Islamophobes off," he said at the time.

Because Hannah's a sleep-deprived mess, Hamza takes over planning her life. He buys tickets for her and Muneer to fly from Seattle to Miami.

In the airport, as expected, her father is pulled aside.

She waits while the TSA folks spend fifteen minutes patting him down and questioning him in a separate room. When he comes back she shoots him a question with her eyes.

"I'm taking my daughter to Miami on vacation," he says. "That's exactly what I told them."

Thank God. He knew better than to say what they were up to.

When they arrive, she's struck by how Miami light is so similar to Jidda light. Every scene is a paradise Hannah would like to paint. She'd create the bluest sky and most turquoise sea, the most graceful palm trunks and greenest fronds, the clearest light and the most distinct shadows, suggesting coolness and respite.

Muneer is calm through renting a car and driving to the detention center. As they approach the gatehouse, he loses it.

"*Bismillah, bismillah. Allahu akbar.*" And other words she can't make out.

Hannah feels shitty for saying it, but he can't talk that way here. "Dad," she says sternly, hoping he will notice she is not calling him Baba. "You cannot speak Arabic here. You especially can't say any religious stuff. OK?"

He cups his hands and mutters something under his breath, finishing with "*Ameen.*" Amen.

"I'm done," he says. "No more religious stuff."

At the gatehouse, the guards' dark sunglasses cut their faces in two. They check IDs and point to a section of the parking lot.

Hannah backs into a space, pulls up hard on the parking brake, and leaves the engine running.

"Stay here. Keep the AC on."

Inside, the guards tell her the facility holds no one by the name of Fouad Muneer or Fouad Muneer Abdullah or Fouad Abdullah or Fouad Al Shaykh or Fouad Muneer Al Shaykh.

"Are you sure?" she says.

On the way back to the car, she's enveloped in humid heat and the sunlight no longer impresses her with its beauty. It attacks her, and a headache flares behind her temples.

"They're effing lying to me," she says. "He's in there but they won't say so."

When they go inside together, she shows the guards the letter.

"We've got a couple Iraqi guys," they say.

Through the several hours that Hannah and her father wait, the minutes are punctuated by the *hummm-kachunk* of the vending machine in the waiting room. Hannah wonders if coming to this place reminds Muneer of his own detention in a different country a dozen years ago. He has fully recovered his composure and kept himself busy reading a *Miami Herald* that someone left behind on a chair.

As lunchtime rolls around, the room smells like Cup-a-Soup and microwaved pizza, probably coming from the guards' lunchroom. Hannah buys two bags of Cheetos.

"I would rather have that other kind—Doritos," Muneer says.

He eats a whole bag of Cheetos. After finishing, he holds his orange-crusted fingers up to the ceiling, almost in the position of supplication.

"It's time for prayer," he says to her quietly.

"Keep a low profile," she says. "Wait till we're at the hotel."

Despite her warning, he disappears to the bathroom and comes back with water-slicked hair. If some guard had seen him washing his feet in the sink, she doesn't know what would've happened. He asks for the car keys.

"I will sit in the car," he says. "There are ways for travelers to—do it."

"Can you make it look like you're, I don't know, on the phone?" she says. "And turn on the air conditioner or you'll roast."

He nods. While he's gone, she talks to the guards again.

They swear Fouad's not here. Perhaps, they suggest, he's at another detention center.

In the parking lot, she calls the other lawyers on her cell.

"He's there," they say on speakerphone. "Our client told us he's there."

Her father is creakily letting himself out of the car. He seems to have weakened in this short passage of time, but he waves her away when she offers him a hand.

The guards snicker when they see her.

"This man is waiting to see his son," she says. "Do you have kids?"

One of the guards looks sheepish. Hannah tries to imagine his life. Maybe he coaches his kids' sports teams. Maybe he's a former military guy. Maybe he's the child of immigrants.

"Four o'clock," he says.

It's two o'clock.

Hannah and Muneer share sections of the paper. She reads sports, he reads style. She can't bear to read about the war.

Baba pulls out a notebook. Over his shoulder, she sees he's making notes in English for his memoir. Or maybe not. He writes:

This room. This waiting for my son, which is like waiting for my heart to be replaced in my chest.

She told him to cool it with the Arabic, but she wishes he were writing in Arabic so she wouldn't understand.

She reads a thick stack of papers for a case she is handling at work. Every few minutes, she checks her silenced phone in case someone is trying to reach her.

Four o'clock rolls around, and no one comes out to tell them why they can't see Fouad or why he's being held. Phone already in hand, Hannah tells her father she's going outside to call the lawyers again.

"Maybe they can tell me something about how this place works."

"Don't leave me," he says.

"Come with me."

"They'll think we left."

So they sit.

At five o'clock, a guard enters the room and Muneer stands immediately, ready to see his son.

"Time to go," the guard says. "We're closing up."

Hannah stands up, too, but she is invisible to them. Her father and the guard size each other up. They are the same height, but one is thirty years younger, white, muscled, and in the place where he belongs. The other does not sense the differences between them. Later, Muneer tells Hannah that the day's waiting suddenly overcame him and reminded him how hateful it felt to be held against his will. He didn't tell her how those few hours of waiting felt as long and hard as waiting for her return. A day doesn't compare in the slightest to fifteen years, of course, but losing a child for any amount of time is torture.

She sees a middle-aged man forgetting he is middle aged and foreign and not in charge, arguing and shouting, stupidly reaching for the guard's throat—despite the man's uniform and the gun in his holster, his broad shoulders, his crew cut, his fiercely square jaw. Before Muneer can touch the man, Hannah shoves herself between them, but the guard's arms are long and muscular, and he grabs Hannah's father by the scruff of the neck.

"He wants to see his son," she yells, and her father is saying, "I'll go, I'll go! Let me go!"

"What the fuck are you doing?" says the guard. "Do you want me to lock you up with your terrorist son?"

"Whoa," says Hannah. "You've got no proof of that. We've been told of no charges." This is her brother the guard is talking about, but she's going to keep it professional. She doesn't want him to know Fouad is her brother, her baby brother who loves DC comics, Batman especially, and used to ask her to send issues back with their father whenever Muneer visited her.

"Get this old guy out of here. He's not going to see his Al-Qaeda son today."

Muneer mutters in Arabic, "Goddamn him to hell and make his teeth fall out."

"What's he saying?" Behind the guard, more men shaped like bears hover and growl.

Hannah tugs her father by the sleeve. "Don't do that. Don't talk in Arabic. You're going to make things worse."

The guards escort them out. One of them tells Hannah, "Don't bring him back. His son is not here."

"Someone should tell him where his son is," she says. "You can't detain someone without reason."

"Only scum would defend a terrorist."

She should stay calm for her father, but her heart slams against her chest, trying to escape. He sinks to his knees, panting, unable to stand any longer. Hannah slips her arms under his armpits and pulls. Swiftly, she grabs him by the waist and says, "Lean on me."

None of the guards moves to assist. Hannah screams, "One of you help me carry him to the car, whether you like it or not. If you've given him a heart attack, I will sue your asses."

"Be calm, be calm," Baba says. "I can walk to the car."

They've missed a downpour. The sidewalks and pavement are darkened by wetness. Steam rises from the hot surfaces. It touches their faces, and she feels as though they're walking through a gauze curtain. The cars look fresh and clean. Hannah breathes the moist air.

Sitting in the driver's seat, she brings her hands to her face. Soon her shoulders shake and she sobs as though she has lost someone she loves. Her face is a wall of tears, her mouth a cave of saliva.

Baba puts his hand over hers on the steering wheel. "Are you OK?"

"We can't leave him there," she says.

She has been calm and stoic. She has been pragmatic. Her dad must not speak Arabic. They must not appear angry. But Fouad's situation hits her hard. She is thinking about how she never knew what she was missing the years she was gone. She has family again, she knows. She feels how scared Fouad must be.

"We'll get him out," Muneer says. "God willing. They can't keep him forever."

She's too distraught to drive, so they switch places. She lowers her window and puts her arm on the sill, her head in the crook of her elbow. The breeze on her face lulls her.

At the hotel Muneer calls Lamees. He is ashamed of what happened—attacking a guard—and yet not ashamed. This is what you do to protect your family. You act and pray to God for forgiveness. You use vitamin Waw—for *wastah*, connections. Hannah will not understand, but wastah works in America, too. On his instruction, Lamees calls Uncle Fareed, who calls a guy who knows a guy who knows a prince who knows a US official. By the next day, everything is arranged.

In the morning, over coffee and muffins at the hotel Starbucks, he tells Hannah they can go back to the detention center to pick Fouad up, and he won't need her help with the book anymore.

She asks if he's sure. She wants to be involved, she says.

"I'm tired," he says. "Perhaps I will write it later."

Hamza sees the connection before Hannah does.

"He doesn't want to rattle cages," he tells her over the phone, while she and her father and Fouad are waiting for their flights at the Miami airport. Fouad will go back to Jidda. His education in America is over. He won't talk to anyone about what happened in the detention center. He swears wallahi he's never hung out with terrorists or zealots. He wants to go home.

"Whose cages?" she says.

"The people who shut him up last time, who put him in prison. Those are the same people who got his son out."

She's not naïve. She should have seen it.

DREAMS

2018

LAST WISH

Hannah prophesies her grandfather's death.

She's always had memories of dreams here and there, like anyone else, but since her forty-eighth birthday two months ago, her dreams have been more vivid. She wakes up with memories of symbolic sheaves of wheat and fat sheep and never-ending stairways and the family in Jidda burying her mother.

Unlike the Prophet Yusuf, she has no one to explain the symbols to her.

For several weeks before the news of her grandfather's illness arrives, she dreams of emaciated animals—dogs, cats, goats, chickens, a lion, a hyena, a zebra. She dreams of wilting fruit trees and straw-brown lawns. At first, she attributes these visions of near-death to the onset of her eleventh New England autumn, the primary intensity of the trees bursting against the deep blue sky, that last gasp before winter. She's no wimp about winter; she grew up with the northern Ohio lake effect, frozen eyelashes, snow boots, snow pants, and snow mittens clipped to her down coat. The time she spent in temperate and tropical places strengthened her fundamental resilience.

Still, fall depresses her. It conjures death. Hamza makes fun of her for saying that, but she knows she's not wrong.

She wakes up on a fall Tuesday morning and digs her sketchbook, which she hasn't touched in years, out of her nightstand drawer. It's the same fat book she took on her first trip to Jidda, set aside when she ditched art school for pre-law. Last night she dreamed she was drawing in it—was it a dream of the past, or the future? She isn't sure. The sketchbook has been hiding under random photos of Fareed as a baby, as a toddler, in first grade; under a half-knitted scarf and smooth wooden knitting needles; boxes of not-her-taste jewelry from aunts and cousins; forsaken cell phones; and an iPod Shuffle.

She sketches, in pencil, trees outside the window and snippets of her dreams, trying to capture in-betweenness: the space between seasons, between waking and sleeping, between life and death.

A few hours later, Aunt Randah sends a WhatsApp message saying Hannah's grandfather is in the hospital and she should visit him one last time. No one knows exactly how old he is, because there were no birth certificates when he was young, when her parents were young. And no one but God knows when a man's time will come, Randah writes. But he's old, and these are possibly his last days.

In between classes at the ESOL school where she teaches, Hannah reads the message. She's alone in the windowless cliché of a teachers' break room, which smells of burnt coffee and reheated spaghetti and chicken.

She does the math in her head to calculate what time it is in Jidda. It's a decent hour, and probably not prayer time. It seems simpler to call Randah than to write back.

There's no debate over whether Hannah will go see her grandfather in the hospital. Randah takes it as a given. Hannah and her grandfather Fareed have grown close in the years since her reunion with her family. A dozen times or so he's come to visit or asked her to meet him wherever he was speaking or attending, when he was younger and more able to travel. She flew to Chicago, New York, and LA to see him. It's been a few years. She liked the light banter they had the times they met for coffee. He brought her clothes and jewelry from her aunts and uncles—sweaters, oddly enough, and rhinestoned things and good, soft gold earrings, and pretty embroidered abayah and tarhah sets in the latest colors (it's not all black anymore). Over the years, he's emailed her articles he wanted her to see, about youth in Saudi, about changes that are coming ("economic diversification") and changes that seemed like they were not, but finally did (women driving). He has a rascally seriousness she wishes he could gift to her, instead of the jewelry and clothing. Sometimes, she almost forgets he is her mother's father. He's more like her dad in many ways. Curious. Opinionated. A truth teller.

Her grandfather has never said whether he sees her mother in her. He never asks about her mother.

And though she named her son after her grandfather, Hannah hasn't told her father about the times she's seen her grandfather Fareed, since the first time she mentioned him in passing. Her father paused so long on the phone she thought the line had dropped.

"That part of the family," he said. "I am not on good terms." She would expect him to be grateful that her grandfather had helped get Fouad out of detention, helped her father get out of Saudi jail. But her father is embarrassed of these favors he can't repay.

She has never wanted to ask her grandfather if her mother spoke to him when they were hiding. She does not want to have to blame him. She will go visit him one last time, though it will be impossible to do that without telling her father she's coming to Jidda.

Randah is intent on complicating her life further with a request that pulls Hannah's heart up into her throat. She chokes a little when she hears it: "Can you convince your mother to come?"

Hannah swallows her heart into the pit of her stomach. "I don't know where she is."

It's a way of not saying: *If I thought I could persuade her, I wouldn't want to.*

Randah has a way of guilting her, though. "Please, habibti. It's your grandfather's last wish."

At home, Hannah pulls the calendar down from the bulletin board in the kitchen to try to find a weeklong break in her schedule. Hamza is browning ground beef for tacos. She wishes Fareed were here to grate the cheese, but he won't be home from University of Washington till the holidays.

"The family must be distraught to be losing their patriarch," Hamza says.

In this kitchen smelling of hamburger and onions, cilantro and Colby-Jack, she feels trapped by Taco Tuesday, the Americanness of her existence.

RELICS

When they moved to Cambridge ten years ago, so Hamza could code for a genetics startup, Hannah told herself one of the benefits would be living closer to W. A long drive or a quick flight, and they are in Toledo. They see W at least once a year, at Thanksgiving or Christmas or spring break. She visits them or they visit her. She's edging up on seventy, and her accent is as hard-edged and as distant from Hannah's mother's accent as ever.

Hannah hadn't, at the time, thought about how Cleveland lay en route to Toledo, how her mother, as far as she knew, was a mile marker on the way to W. She's never run into her accidentally at Hopkins Airport—the last place they met—but the possibility is a burden. Whenever she thinks of W, her brain has to pass through Sadie on the way there.

Telling Randah she doesn't know Sadie's whereabouts wasn't a lie. Hannah doesn't know her mother's home address or her place of business. She doesn't know if Sadie is dating anyone, or married, or what church—church!—she attends.

But she has a phone number that's probably good. She changed her own number years ago so her mother couldn't reach her, figured out how to keep it private so her mother couldn't find her again, like she always seemed to. But on purpose, in case she ever needed it, Hannah saved her mother's number. Not at Hamza's encouragement; on her own she'd done it. Written it down on a piece of paper because she didn't trust her SIM card. In the end, the SIM card worked. It worked so well, her mother's name is in her contacts twice.

She texts the number. If her father were dying, she would want someone to tell her.

"Your father is in the hospital. I'm going next week. Randah wants me to ask you to come."

Immediately, regret hits her like a hangover. She should have told Hamza to do it, or given the number to Randah. Why hadn't she? Why hadn't she thought of that years ago?

It's a relief and an annoyance that she gets crickets from her mother in return for her message.

"At least she knows," Hamza says over tater tots and pizza on Takeout Friday. "No one expects her to go. Her Saudi passport is probably decades expired."

When Fareed was younger, she rarely talked about her mother in front of him because he worried about everything—his grades, whether his parents would come home or end up in a fiery car crash, whether things cost too much, whether he was coming down with chicken pox (it was acne). So much worry was strange, she thinks, for a kid who grew up with stability she never had. She's never told him about her childhood. She never explained why they didn't see her mom. His Syrian grandparents were doting and visited often. There was no reason to tell him the truth about Sadie.

She wonders if she should tell him now.

Her phone begins to buzz. It's her mom.

"Thank you for the message."

She can't do this alone. She puts the phone on speaker so Hamza can hear.

"What's up, Mom?"

"When are you leaving for Jidda?"

"Monday."

"I think I should go," her mother says. "I think that's probably what I should do. I don't know. . . How is my father?"

"He's in intensive care. I couldn't book an earlier flight."

The teakettle whistles. Hamza removes it from the stove and pours water into a teapot with mint and two Lipton's tea bags.

She tries to put herself in her grandfather's place. If she were on her deathbed, who would she want there?

"I don't know if I can get a ticket," Hannah's mother says. "I have to go to Washington first, to the consulate, for a temporary passport."

Hannah had hoped her mother would easily say no. She'd asked to please Randah.

Her mother's response sets her ears buzzing. Why, after more than forty years, does her mother want to go home? It's a betrayal. If Sadie goes back, why did Hannah go through everything she went through as a child?

"Do you want me to come?" Sadie says.

Hamza pours tea into glasses.

"OK, Mama, come." She doesn't mean it, but she doesn't want to be the person she is, the person who wants to say no, who wants to keep Sadie from seeing her own father.

PASSPORT

Hannah waits to meet her mother outside a café in Foggy Bottom, blocks from the Washington, DC, consulate, where her mother has gone to renew her Saudi passport. She and Hannah are US citizens, but they never gave up their Saudi citizenship.

Hannah is of two minds about waiting outside the café. Her skin is warmed by the late autumn sun, her bones are chilled by a brisk breeze. She'd rather wait outside though, not be trapped indoors for their first interaction. Washington is ten degrees warmer, at least, than Cambridge, and she's dressed too warmly. She removes her jacket and hangs it over one elbow.

She has been mentally preparing for this reunion ever since they got off the phone, and the result is a raging headache, constant acid reflux though she eats very little, and ragged nails bitten in private.

Sadie is with a man, a tall redhead. Hannah had worried she might not recognize her own mother. But age hasn't changed Sadie that much. Gray hair doesn't change who you are.

"Good to finally meet you," the man says.

Finally, as though they are a normal family. Hannah wonders what he knows. Her mother leans in to kiss her, and Hannah steps back.

"Were you able to get the passport?"

"They told her to come back tomorrow," the man says. His name is Glenn.

"I'm leaving tonight," Hannah says. She can recognize the tourists passing by their look of glazed wonderment. You can see things from far away in this city. The Washington Monument. The Capitol. Virginia.

There's time to kill before Hannah leaves. They buy cups of coffee and walk to the Potomac, up along the trail to Georgetown, up a hill to the chichi shops. They're not talking much. The wind has died down and Hannah starts to feel hot in her wool sweater. Sadie mentions church and Hannah realizes she had forgotten the last time she saw her mother, in the airport, how Hannah convinced Hamza they shouldn't go to the baptism. They turned around and got on the next flight. It had to be true love for him to listen when she asked for crazy things like that.

Hannah's a more experienced mother now. But she doesn't understand her own mother better.

Sadie goes searching for a bathroom, and instead of following her into the mall, Glenn and Hannah stand at Wisconsin and M, people watching. It's mostly tourists here, a few students and businesspeople.

"Can you tell where people are from by looking at them?" she asks Glenn.

"Wisconsin," he says, laughing, pointing at a middle-aged man and woman in University of Wisconsin sweatshirts.

"Too easy."

"Iran," he says, nodding at a group of well-dressed twenty-somethings speaking in a language other than English.

She catches a few words of Arabic. "No, pretty sure they're Gulfies," she says.

"Ah, you know the nuances better than I do."

"She never told people where we were from, before. It's something that she told you."

"I wish I could go with her to see her father. But she says no, it would be too hard to get a visa, and too hard to introduce me when she hasn't seen people for so long."

It's weird to hear this confession. He's in his fifties or sixties, probably. She is not used to people older than she is, her parents' age, speaking with longing.

Sadie comes back, holding a new cup of coffee. She's smiling, happy to see them talking.

"We're guessing where people are from," Hannah says. "No one could ever guess where *we* were from."

Sadie's face snaps into the serious expression Hannah remembers from her childhood. How she rarely smiled—because she was afraid of getting caught? Hannah doesn't care why things were the way they were, though. What matters to her is years of not knowing who she was.

Sadie doesn't want to talk about it. Hannah can tell by the way she flips her hair back, indignant that her daughter would bring up such long-ago history.

It's not anything in particular her mother does that afternoon, or says. But Hannah knows, after years of therapy, that she is not to blame for her mother's mistakes. That's what she wishes she could explain. How she was affected by the choices Sadie made decades ago, the years of brainwashing, the wrong memories. She remembers grieving for a dead father. She did that. It's a true memory. But he was not dead. It was grief she didn't have to experience.

"She shouldn't come," Hannah says, keeping her eyes on Glenn. "If she goes, I'll have to explain to my dad that she's there. I don't want to lie to him. I won't. I'll have to tell him I saw her. If she doesn't go, he won't ask, and I won't have to lie. I'm done lying. I don't know what she's told you about my childhood."

Is it her place to tell him? She doesn't have to contemplate the question, though, because he knows.

"I'm sure she had a good reason. I'm sure she felt she had no other choice. You were safe with her."

With someone else, she might have let it slide. But he belongs to her mother, and she doesn't want Sadie to think she is forgiven.

"No. There's no good reason. You don't understand. I can never trust anyone because of her." She knows she sounds overwrought.

Glenn's listening though. "Maybe your mother needs to hear that from you."

"She knows. I don't want to talk about it."

Her mother has stepped away, which seems like a mature, maybe even *Christian*, thing to do. Maybe Glenn has been a good influence. He's a nice guy, funny. He holds doors, Hannah's noticed, for men and women. He holds her mother's hand. He's so nice it makes her rethink her views on Sadie. Why would he like Sadie—love her—if there weren't something redeeming about her?

"Tell her not to come. Convince her. I don't care what reason you use. You can tell her I don't want her to come."

"You reached out to her."

He's angry on her mother's behalf, she can tell. He rolls his eyes, like a twelve-year-old who doesn't get his way, and reaches into his back pocket for his wallet. She's about to protest—why on earth would he think it's appropriate for him to give her money?

What he takes out is not a bill. It's a faded wallet photo of a little girl with missing front teeth. And another photo, folded gracelessly because it's too big for a wallet. A family portrait of a thirtyish woman who looks like the girl, with a handsome man and two towheaded boys.

"That's Jill, my daughter."

He puts the photo in Hannah's hand. She refuses to hold it, and it lands on the sidewalk. She's not that petty, she tells herself, and she picks it up, smooths it out, pretends dropping it was a mistake.

"Beautiful family," she says.

Sadie returns, fingers on her cross. "Oh, it's Jill," she says.

Hannah feels a stab of jealousy.

She wants to be alone. She's walked down to the canal before, and she likes how hidden it feels, like you're going back to a time when no one you know was alive. But Glenn and her mom want her to walk to Key Bridge with them so they can set foot, "for a minute," Glenn says, in Virginia. He was born there, moved to Ohio when he was a baby.

There's a hotel at the end of the bridge. She can catch a taxi there.

They walk past the boutiques and restaurants of M Street, the Dean & DeLuca, a Middle Eastern restaurant, a burrito place.

"Don't come, Mom," Hannah says. "What if your dad dies and your brothers won't let you leave? What if they find out about your cross?"

"Why would they keep me there? I'm old. It's not like I'm young and they'd want to marry me off, or something." She laughs and glances at Glenn. "I'll leave my cross here."

"Nothing to lose," Glenn says. He hesitates. "Unless you consider me."

"I want to go," Sadie says. But Hannah can tell she's sown a seed of discord between them. And later, when her mother calls to say she's changed her mind, and will Hannah pay her respects, Hannah is not surprised.

RETURN

At the Jidda airport, her father is waiting. He asks about her grand-father, about Fareed and Hamza. He hands her two hundred riyals "in case." The darkness they drive through, before they reach the city, feels different yet familiar. She has not been back since before Fareed was born. Every time she returns, it's to a place she remembers, like a favorite tourist destination. With family baggage.

Her father drops her at the hospital, where the Saudi and Filipino front desk workers speak English. They send her upstairs, to a suite of sorts. Her grandfather has been downgraded from intensive care—though the brief interlude of healing will not last. In a small sitting room attached to her grandfather's hospital room, members of her mother's family are taking tea. Without asking if Hannah wants any mint, Randah stirs sugar, hot water, and mint in a finjan. She knows how many spoonfuls of sugar her niece prefers. The crystals and leaves swirl in the tiny glass. Hannah doesn't want the hot liquid, but saying no would be rude, so she accepts the mint tea and sips. A young man in a crisp white thawb and well-ironed shimagh comes in with steaming bags of muttabbaq, ful, and tamees. Most likely he's a cousin who was little the last time she saw him. Teenage girl cousins in tarhahs, tittering around her, look like colorful birds.

"How was your flight?" one asks in English, the consonants emphasized. Hannah's heart flutters at how the words sound heftier, more earnest, when spoken this way.

"Good, alhamdullilah," she says, and wonders how flimsy her Arabic sounds to them.

Randah lets Hannah's grandfather know she's there, and gestures for her to come into the room.

"You came," he says in English. Her grandmother Faizah, who speaks only Arabic, sits at his bedside and smiles.

Grandfather Fareed's face is puffy, his hair whiter than Hannah remembers—and sparer. His teeth are hanging on for dear life in his gums. She holds his soft hand.

"I have a picture of my son Fareed for you."

He brings his hand to his heart. "Very handsome."

They sit quietly for a while.

"In a few weeks, women will be allowed to drive here. June 24. My daughters and granddaughters are getting their licenses. Alhamdulillah, it will be a great day for them."

"Yes, it's wonderful news." How different would her past visits have been if she had been able to drive?

"Those women and men activists, the ones arrested for colluding with enemies—too many Saudi papers called them traitors. Innocent until proven guilty, I say."

"I don't follow the news much. That's terrible."

"We don't want the unrest of other countries. Remember the Arab Spring? But small social changes—we need those. What does your father say?"

"I didn't ask him that."

Randah called her to eat before they put the food away. But she was hungry for this, sitting with her grandfather, not for street food.

She watched saline drip from the bag. He fidgeted against the raised back of the bed.

"Where's your mother? Randah said she was coming. Did she fly with you?"

She can't tell him the truth: that she, Hannah, denied him the possibility of seeing his daughter.

"Do you remember what she looks like anymore?"

"Of course I do."

"I don't have a photo."

"I don't need a photo."

He seemed wide awake when she came in, but now he seems a bit groggy. It would make her feel better about her dishonesty to know the answers to some of her questions.

"When I was a child, did you know? Where she was? Where we were?"

"I didn't know. We had—what do you call it? A private investigator. I wanted to know where she was, but I couldn't bear to make her come home. Her mother would have wanted me to. Randah knew. Randah got the reports. She never told me. I paid for the PI. Your grandmother thought you should be here, with your father, but I couldn't cause you to be taken from your mother."

They could have brought her home. Maybe her isolation from her family could have been briefer, a blip she would barely remember.

Or maybe nothing would have changed the fact that her mother had stolen her.

Several family members have left the sitting room—she feels bad she doesn't know their names, but how can she be expected to keep track of so many? Randah and Riham are packing the food back into its bags and tying the plastic into tight, nearly impenetrable knots. A plate of food they made for her sits on the coffee table.

She eats so she won't have to talk.

When she finishes, the words gush out. "Randah, you knew where we were."

"We found her, and she begged me not to bring her back."

"Found her where?"

"When you were in California, before she moved you back to Ohio. I don't understand why she did that."

She will have to keep this secret. She won't tell her father. She won't feel bad that she convinced her mother not to come.

When her father comes for her, it's late. They head to his villa. For at least ten years he's lived north of town, in an area that was probably empty desert the first time she visited. Fouad and Hatim live in the same neighborhood, with their own families. The sea is ten miles away.

Her father's villa has a big, tiled yard with flowering bushes that overpower her with their scent. Lamees is inside, laying out Broasted chicken takeout. Hannah feels most guilty about not having seen Fadi in so long. He's a grown man. He lets her hug him and sits next to her at the sufrah, eating fries. His mother pretends to add salt, and he puts one in his mouth.

After dinner, she shows Fadi her sketchbook, the drawings he made nearly thirty years ago. She puts a pencil in his hand and they draw together, a self-portrait of the two of them.

Outside, on a small patio attached to the family room, her father smokes shisha. When Lamees takes Fadi to bed, Hannah joins her father. He hands her the nozzle and she sucks the hot smoke deep inside. He's wearing a white T-shirt and a plaid foutah wrapped around his waist. His skullcap blends into his white hair. He looks relaxed. He's going to retire from journalism soon.

"I'm going to leave it to the bloggers," he says.

She hands the shisha back. He leans elbow against knee with the nozzle in his mouth. He seems calm, at peace. It's late and the full moon is high in the sky. At least, that's how she will remember it later. A bright light, quiet talk with her father, the voices of children playing in adjacent yards at an hour when American children would have been fast asleep for hours.

"I miss my boys," she says. "Fareed and Hamza."

"Of course you do. Inshallah, you'll be reunited with them soon."

Inshallah—God willing. It sounds like a fudge to her, something that should make her worry. Maybe you'll see them, maybe you won't. Who knows? God decides.

But for her father, inshallah expresses the most certainty a person can have. Because God is good. And with God's will, *you will be with the people you love.*

READER'S GUIDE

1. The novel opens with Hanadi having a dream about Saeedah's funeral. Why do you think the author begins the story with this imagined loss?

2. What do you think of the rotating points-of-view in the novel? How would this story be different if it were told entirely from Saeedah's perspective? Or Muneer's?

3. Describe the various portrayals of marriage in the novel. What are some similarities or differences you see across generations?

4. The plot hinges on Saeedah's decision to take Hanadi without Muneer's knowledge. What does Saeedah willingly give up by staying in the United States and disappearing, and what does she lose despite herself?

5. When she first arrives in Jidda, Hanadi thinks that "she could tell, being here for less than half an hour, that she was a different person than she might have been if she'd grown up here, with her family intact.... What other lost elements of herself would she find here?" Do you believe that your birthplace shaped your identity? Have you ever found "lost elements" of yourself in an unexpected place?

6. While exploring Jidda, Hanadi recognizes that "this place—this bride of the Red Sea, as her father calls the city—is the origin of her mother's phonemes." What do you think Quotah is saying about intimacy and alienation in parent-child relationships?

7. Which character makes the most egregious decision in this novel? Does your answer to this question change depending on where you are in the story?

8. Over the course of the novel, more than forty years pass. What character changes the most in that time, in your opinion?

9. What role does secrecy, both voluntary and involuntary, play in this novel?

10. What do you think of Hanadi's dreams and prophecies throughout the novel? Have you ever had a dream that seemed to predict later events?

11. How do the various sections—the chronological history and Hanadi's flashbacks—affect your reading of the book? Why do you think the author chose to structure the novel in this way?

ACKNOWLEDGMENTS

Family first: Thank you to Andrew Chen who always knew I could do it. My parents and brothers who were there in the beginning and who taught me faith. My grandmother, who is all over this book even though she couldn't read. My kids, for whom I try to be better every day.

Thank you to Sarah DeWeerdt for being my reader from way back. Sarah Schmelling, Sara Gama, Majda Gama, and Janelle Rucker kindly read an early version. Danzy Senna and Justin Torres' workshop at Bread Loaf Writers' Conference gave feedback on an even earlier chapter.

Thanks to the Maryland State Arts Council and the Arts and Humanities Council of Montgomery County.

Like most writers, I juggle novel writing with a day job. While working on *Bride of the Sea*, I was blessed to have two bosses—Jennifer Rich and John Siniff—who wholeheartedly supported my creativity and my need for time.

Thank you to Steven Chudney for being my tireless advocate. And to Laura Chasen for pushing me.

Finally, thank you to Masie Cochran for seeing straight through to the heart of my novel, and to the other members of the Tin House crew—Craig Popelars, Elizabeth DeMeo, Alyssa Ogi, Diane Chonette, Nanci McCloskey, Molly Templeton, and Yashwina Canter—whose enthusiastic work made my book dreams come true in the midst of a pandemic.

PHOTO: © ANDREW CHEN

EMAN QUOTAH grew up in Jidda, Saudi Arabia, and Cleveland, Ohio. Her writing has appeared in *The Washington Post*, *USA Today*, The Toast, The Establishment, Book Riot, and other publications. She lives with her family near Washington, DC.

CPSIA information can be obtained
at www.ICGtesting.com
Printed in the USA
LVHW031929020221
678151LV00006B/1311

9 781951 142452